Silence in the Desert

David Longridge

Front cover: St. Catherine Monastery ('KaiAbuSir'
<https://commons.wikimedia.org/wiki/File:St._Catherine_Monastery_-_
Surrounding_Mountains_-_panoramio.jpg>)

Matador
9 Priory Business Park,
Wistow Road, Kibworth Beauchamp,
Leicestershire. LE8 0RX
Tel: 0116 279 2299
Email: books@troubador.co.uk
Web: www.troubador.co.uk/matador
Twitter: @matadorbooks

ISBN: 978 1788034 500

British Library Cataloguing in Publication Data.
A catalogue record for this book is available from the British Library.

Typeset by Mach 3 Solutions Ltd (www.mach3solutions.co.uk)
Cover designed by Paul Hewitt, Battlefield Design (www.battlefield-design.co.uk)
Printed by TJ International Ltd, Padstow

Matador is an imprint of Troubador Publishing Ltd

MIX
Paper from
responsible sources
FSC
www.fsc.org   FSC® C013056

To Charlie and Edward

1

The English West Country, May 1941

His eyes flick up to the convex mirror above the canopy. He knows this student is the clinging sort. Nothing wrong with that, after all it's a tail-chasing exercise. Man after his own heart. He hasn't thrown him off yet. Tight turns, loops and dives, he's still there. The programmed exercise in follow-the-leader is finished. Still fifteen minutes before they're due to return to base. He'll test the other's nerve a bit more. That must be the Abbey tower about five miles ahead, stark against the boring countryside, what a landmark. Just in front of it, the mass of high trees coming into view, two clumps of them on either side of the patch of green. Something special's called for. He'll zoom in really low, circle around for a few minutes and then, when the student pilot's least expecting it, cut inside the circle, fly straight across the open area and go into an almost vertical climb on full boost.

The tower's coming up fast. Now for it. Back a bit with the throttle control lever, foot down on the left rudder plate and into a full 360-degree turn around the area. The student's right there, still on his tail. Round again, must go as low as humanly possible. Several matches being played down there. Round a third time, but now to cut in across the cricket grounds. Stay as low as you dare. Just above those large clumps of firs. Make it really tough for him. Now, without warning, above the central cricket pavilion, back with the control stick. Pull on the boost control lever. That sudden whine as the supercharger cuts in, the Merlin howling back at him. The fuselage rockets towards the vertical.

He looks down, sees the white figures on the pitches across the mown grass. Lots of spectators too, mainly other boys sitting along the grass bank either side of the pavilion. This will give them something to write home about. The whole school must be there, several hundred of them. They're looking up.

He flinches. What's that flash? Now an explosion, the plane's frame judders in the shockwave. He cuts off boost and side-slips to port, out of the climb and towards the spot where he can see flames and smoke. Smack in the middle of the upper and lower cricket fields. There are bodies on the ground, splayed out along the bank and on the lower pitch, not moving. Others are running. Sharp cracks as ammunition belts go off in the intense heat from the fuel burning on the ground. Two figures in black habits are rushing into the inferno. He glances in the mirror, immediately fearful. No sign of the student pilot.

He knows. Terror grips him in the chest. Realization, then horror, rush through his mind, his body. The student didn't make it over the first tree-line, and has ploughed into the long bank between the cricket pitches. He starts to shake. It must be carnage down there. He's responsible for that student, now in there among them. The pilot must have hit the top of a tree as he concentrated on the Hurricane in front, on his instructor. 'Never take your eye off my tail.' Those were his words to the student as they walked to their respective aircraft less than an hour ago. Must be all the boy thought of as the two Sea Hurricanes climbed away from Yeovilton to start their exercise.

Can't help them from up here, he thought. Must get a message to Yeovilton. They have to organize help. Oh, God, have to get back, face the consequences. Straight to the CO, even before preparing a report. A straightforward crash and loss of pilot is a tragedy and means an immediate inquiry. But this, how many are dead down there, the injured, the burns? Schoolboys, what will it lead to, what will they do to me?

The House of Lords, June 1941

It came suddenly during a few days' leave, the telephone message. Was Bill Lomberg aware of what just happened at his old school? Nine boys killed by a Sea Hurricane on a training flight. The student pilot killed also. The request to assist in the case of the Fleet Air Arm flying instructor accused of causing the accident. It came from the person who was to act as counsel to the defendant in the pending court martial. Would he, in the meantime, attend in the public gallery of the House of Lords on 10 June when questions were to be raised on the circumstances of the crash?

So Bill sat there in the gallery of the Lords, a lone spectator in RAF uniform of a flying officer save for Counsel to the Defendant, seated beside him. He looked down intently at the noble Lord who was speaking.

The noble Lord asked whether it was proposed to hold any sort of inquiry, and if such inquiry would be public. An inquest had been held but that was to establish the cause of death. It could not be directed to establishing the cause of the accident, and the facts leading up to this disaster had not yet been made known authoritatively to the public. He recalled a remarkable cross-examination in the *Titanic* inquiry.

People were not perturbed by the facts which they learnt during the inquiry; they were reassured by feeling that the matter had been probed and that steps would be taken, in future, to prevent an occurrence of such a disaster. An inquiry of this kind is not a hunt for a scapegoat, it is only an endeavour to find out what was wrong and to make sure the necessary precautions will be taken in the future.

Bill looked sideways, muttering 'Can't argue with that.'

Counsel nodded. 'As soon as this is finished, let's go to my chambers, and we can talk about the court martial.' The noble Lord was summing up.

I hope I have not spoken too strongly on this matter, but I know that cricket field. One cannot imagine a more typically English scene than those boys playing cricket on that Saturday afternoon, and to think of that cricket field being suddenly turned into shambles by this inexcusable action is something which I confess has filled me with very deep feelings of pain and indignation.

The Inns of Court, June 1941

'Come on into my lair, Flying Officer Lomberg,' said Counsel as he showed Bill into his comfortable office. He pointed towards leather armchairs in the corner by the window overlooking the church and lawns of Middle Temple. 'Let's be on first name terms, I'm Adrian.'

'I'm Bill.' He must be twice my age and half my height, thought Bill, watching the wizened face and keen eyes behind half-moon glasses. Too old for service in this war. Looks kindly enough on the outside, but I bet he's like steel underneath. Wouldn't fancy being cross-examined by him.

'So, the reply of the Parliamentary Secretary of the Admiralty didn't take us any further,' said Counsel. 'Just stressed that the

Admiralty viewed it as a terrible calamity. That he didn't want to go into the accident in detail for the simple reason that further proceedings were pending. There was to be a court martial, and it would be highly improper for him to say anything that might in any way affect the trial of the officer concerned. What I expected him to say.'

Bill nodded. 'Yes. I must say I wouldn't want to be in your client's shoes when he is marched into the court at Devonport.'

'That's why I'm asking you to help. You're an old boy of St Gregory's College, in the school only three years ago. You know the geography.'

'Yes,' said Bill. 'I've a pretty good idea how it must have happened.'

Counsel went on. 'You're an experienced Hurricane pilot. You and my client, Sub Lieutenant John Smith, must have Hurricanes and low flying in the blood.'

'You could say that. I've been at it for two years now, been lucky to survive,' said Bill.

'I don't have to tell you, Flying Officer, this country's in a gigantic struggle. One side trying to get the edge over the other. Risks must be taken, in training as well as in action. That's what it's about.' He paused, looking hard at Bill. 'I need you to explain that in your own words to the Board. The defendant is probably going to plead guilty. Therefore, it's in backing up the plea for leniency that your evidence as an expert witness will count.'

'I understand,' said Bill. 'I'll do what I can.' Bill wanted to help. Yet, he couldn't help imagining the carnage on the ground when the student pilot and his Hurricane ploughed into the mass of boys and masters watching the matches that day. The pain in the faces of the parents and families of the nine boys killed, and those badly injured. He reasoned to himself how accidents and their consequences were more likely in wartime. But did that make the flying instructor morally less culpable?

Devonport Court Martial, June 1941

Bill was already seated in the back of the courtroom, thinking of the several discussions with John, the defendant, who was ready for the worst. The Fleet Air Arm instructor knew he'd flouted the regulations on low flying, and the horrendous consequences that followed.

He took a liking to John as their talks progressed, and wanted to help the instructor pick himself up after the shattering events of six weeks ago. With Counsel, they'd drawn up the case for leniency, submitting it to the Court the previous day. The aim was to ensure the Board would take account of the mitigating circumstances in this case. As an old boy who knew the school inside out, and experienced Hurricane pilot, his deposition should lend weight to Counsel's argument for leniency in arriving at the sentence.

Bill knew that John, like himself, remained an ardent believer in the effectiveness of ultra-low flying in ground attack. He understood the instructor's frustration when, on arriving at Yeovilton only a week before the accident, he found no official low-flying area was established. Student pilots were either not being given low-flying training, or instructors were breaking the rules and hoping for the best. He understood how the instructor wanted his pupil to develop that extra edge in attacking enemy surface vessels. Destroying a U-boat on the surface removed a giant threat, both militarily and in terms of supplies the nation badly needed. All this he had written down in his deposition and signed. John's fate now rested with the Court.

The Chief Petty Officer marched John into the large oak-panelled court room, together with Counsel. They halted and saluted in front of the Bench. The Judge Advocate of the Fleet sat in the centre of the long table facing the defendant, with the four officers who made up the Board spread evenly on either side.

After waiting for everyone to settle down, the Judge Advocate opened the proceedings by addressing John directly.

'Sub Lieutenant. You have pleaded guilty to the charge "For acts prejudicial to good order and naval discipline: low and dangerous flying outside the practice area". The role of the Board is therefore to recommend sentence, to establish the punishment after taking all fact-based evidence into account.' The Judge Advocate paused.

Bill felt the pressure. It could be him in the other's position. Accepting a gross error of judgement was the cause of death of those young people, cut down on the lawns of his old school. Imagine the pain of the wounded, the grief of the parents. The consequences of the instructor's actions were too awful to be avoided in any way. John would live with the experience of that day all his life.

The Advocate General continued. 'The factors submitted by your Counsel will be taken account of in the Board's judgment. Counsel for the Defence stressed your exemplary service record since entering the Fleet Air Arm two years ago. That you passed from being an exemplary student pilot almost directly to becoming instructor. That you arrived at Yeovilton only the week preceding the accident. That front line Fleet Air Arm pilot training was, by necessity, creating young flyers who could live with risk. That inevitably some would be hot-blooded.'

The Judge Advocate turned to the officer previously appointed President of the Board. 'Captain, has the Board agreed upon the punishment appropriate to the charge for which the defendant has pleaded guilty?'

'Yes, sir, we have agreed unanimously how the defendant should be sentenced, having taken full account of the evidence laid before us, and after considering the defendant's plea for leniency.'

'Thank you, Captain,' said the Judge Advocate. 'And what is your finding?'

'We find that the defendant be "dismissed his ship" and "severely reprimanded".'

The eyes of the Judge Advocate gave away nothing of his own feelings as he turned back to face the defendant, asking 'Do you have anything to say, Sub Lieutenant?'

'Thank you, sir. I accept the sentence, and have no intention of appealing.'

Outside the court room a few moments later, the three of them came together. 'So what exactly does that mean?' John asked Counsel.

Counsel replied 'It means that your career record will forever after be marked "severely reprimanded". And that you are grounded until the Royal Navy decides what to do with you next.'

Bill looked at the young Fleet Air Arm instructor, admiring his composure. A combination of foolishness and the hand of fate led to this horror. The moral responsibility lay on him. How would he live with it? Bill had an idea, something that would challenge him to win back his esteem, and be recognized by others as doing just that.

2

Three years earlier. The English West Country, June 1938

The coolness of the walls and the sweet smell in the air were comforting in a strange way, as he reached the end of the long passage. Henri gripped the heavy iron handle, opening one of the large oak doors, making his way into the great edifice which towered above him. Turning right, and following his way in the semi-darkness round the back of the chancel, he arrived at the entrance to the vestry. Henri looked at the several hooded figures readying themselves, each tying a cincture or rope round the waist of their habits. Lifting over their heads the vestments that had lain in the wide drawers of the chests along the walls, they were adjusting the cowls from behind the neck. He went up to one of them and bowed to the monk. Picking up a tray of water and wine, he stepped in behind the priest as they walked out of the vestry, turning right down the nave towards one of the side chapels.

The ritual commenced, devoid of audience, devout in its execution, the sublime Latin phrases and responses flowing between them. As he knelt behind and to the right of the bowed figure, Henri felt for the bell which like everything else had its part to play. To him, all was second nature. Yet today was somehow different, the last time he would serve in this place which had been an essential part of his formation for the past five years. When all was done, as they walked back to the vestry and Henri began to think of his breakfast, the monk turned and over his shoulder said, 'Rochefort, let's have a talk in my study after supper this evening.'

and over his shoulder said, 'Rochefort, let's have a talk in my study after supper this evening.'

Henri made his way from the House refectory to Rooky's study, knocking on the door marked *Dom Brendan Rooker OSB, House Master*. He heard the gruff 'come in,' and entered. There was a decanter of sherry and several glasses on a small round table next to the chair in which Rooky, as Dom Brendan Rooker was known to the boys, sat comfortably, pipe clenched in his teeth. Opposite was a sofa which served various purposes including a support for unfortunates sentenced to a beating.

'Help yourself and pour me one,' the monk said, gesturing towards the decanter. As Henri handed him a full glass, Rooky said 'I hear you're destined for military college in your father's home country,' referring to the new life Henri would soon find himself in. As he filled his own glass, he felt strangely apprehensive, knowing the next day was to be the end of the summer term and his last at the school. He would be launching himself into an uncertain world, with talk in the papers of another war.

'Yes, sir,' he replied. 'It's been a tradition of our family that one of the sons of each generation should serve in the Legion and since I'm the only son this time around, that's where I'm going. I suppose that with an English mother I could head in a different direction, but I don't feel myself pulled into anything else.'

'It won't make a vast difference,' said Rooky. 'We're all going to have to fight, and you can choose a career later.'

Henri was surprised. 'How do you mean, we must all fight?' he said. 'Surely as a Benedictine monk and priest, you're not going to be called up?'

Rooky looked at him intently for a moment. 'Correct, but I'm on the Reserve list as an army chaplain. 'I was a Platoon Commander in the Irish Guards in the 1914 War, and then came here to study for the priesthood. Tell me, what's special about the French Foreign Legion?'

'Well,' said Henri. 'It was founded early in the last century to fight overseas for France and its allies, and was composed of mainly foreigners who were not welcome in their home country, revolutionaries and the like, and commanded by French officers. The Legion's depot is at Sidi Bel Abbès in Algeria, and that's still how it recruits.'

'There seems to be a degree of glamour attached to it,' said Rooky, 'What with Beau Geste and all that stuff.'

'I have to get through Saint-Cyr military college first, and pass out in the top group to be eligible for the Legion,' said Henri. 'I start there in September.'

There was a knock on the door. 'Ah,' said Rooky. 'I asked your two pals, Beckendorf and Lomberg to join us.' He raised his voice. 'Come in, gentlemen.' A short, tough-looking boy walked in, followed by a much taller broad-shouldered one. 'Help yourselves to sherry, and get comfortable. Being your last day here, I thought we might all have a chat about the future.'

'Jolly kind of you, sir' said Leo Beckendorf, his clipped way of speaking accentuated a slight German accent. 'It certainly is, sir,' added Bill Lomberg, who spoke in a very English way although he was South African.

'All three of you have had your ups and downs here,' said Rooky. 'But on the whole, I think you can be good advertisements for the school.' There was a silence while this mild praise sank in.

Rooky went on, glancing at Leo. 'My fear is that we're all going to be fighting one another shortly.'

The short tough one, Leo Beckendorf, looked down at the floor, then raised his head. The blond hair had not yet recovered from its last school haircut. 'I want to be a pilot,' he said. 'In the new Luftwaffe, but I don't see why there should be a war involving Britain, Germany and France,' he exclaimed, looking at his best school mates.

'We shall see,' said the monk. He switched his gaze to the tall broad-shouldered boy. 'And you, Bill Lomberg, I hear you've won an RAF scholarship to Cambridge, so you'll be flying as well. Just remember to keep up your rugby. You might play for the Springboks one day.'

'Certainly, sir,' responded Bill. 'I should get my pilot's licence while at university. If there's going to be a war, then when will it be, I wonder?'

'Sooner rather than later,' said Rooky. 'And I've a special concern of my own.' The three boys looked at him in some surprise.

'You know well that an essential part of the education at St Gregory's is to give you a good grounding in the Catholic faith. We discuss the moral law. I'd like you to think about that as you go out into life. In peacetime, so-called natural law is equivalent to the moral law. But in times of strife, the two can diverge. After all, the rules of life in a civilized country in peacetime follow closely moral principles. But there are times, not just in a war, when laws are suspended or altered so those in power can impose their ideology. Do you follow me?'

The others nodded, although there was some hesitation on their faces. Leo Beckendorf was the first to speak. 'We've learnt that all men are equal in the eyes of God, that they are his creatures and receive his Grace. I've thought now and again about the policies of the Nazi party in my country towards Jews. Is that in your view a suspension of the moral law?'

'My dear Leo,' said the monk. 'I can call you by your first name since from tomorrow I'll no longer be in charge of you. I don't want to criticize one race or country. But the Jews have been treated as inferior and devious by most countries over the ages, and the way they are now prevented from practising their professions and a normal life in Germany, just as some native peoples are so prevented in colonial countries, is contrary to the moral law.'

There was a pause, and Henri wondered what was coming next.

Rooky went on. 'You may wonder why this should concern the three of you. Well, in war, you may suddenly have to decide whether something you're being forced into is morally acceptable or not. I hope your time spent here will help you to decide.'

'I expect it will,' said Henri, although he was unsure how he would react if faced with such a dilemma.

'For me, there's an issue concerning the Church in this regard,' said Rooky, as he got up and went over to his desk, pulling a thin file out of a drawer. From it he extracted a few sheets of typed paper. 'The new Pope, when he was still a Monsignor in the Vatican, edited a notice to be smuggled secretly into Germany last year and read out in all Catholic churches in that country. I received this copy from a friend in Rome. It's written in German, and headed "Mit brennender Sorge".'

'Which means "with burning concern" I think,' remarked Bill, whose knowledge of the Afrikaans language made German easier.

'Spot on,' said Leo, who had been told of this papal encyclical by his parents, after they heard it read out in their local church just outside Berlin. 'Apparently, it made Hitler and his top people furious.'

'Yes,' said the monk. 'It addresses the interference of the Nazi government into the religious education in Catholic schools, and also made reference to the oppression of parts of society, without actually naming the Jews. My concern is whether when war breaks out, the Church will be seen to be standing up for the principles it set down for its followers in Germany.'

Henri interjected. 'I see how modern warfare will challenge moral principles, after all extreme measures may be taken against humanity, such as by bombing civilians and racial persecution.'

'Exactly right, Henri,' said the monk. 'The Church must be seen to stand firm against crimes against the moral law. Just as you have to be alert to actions which are morally unacceptable, so does the Church have to set an example. Now, have another glass of sherry all of you, and let's talk about something less serious, such as rugby, or girls.'

Henri lay in bed that final night at school, mulling over Rooky's talk with the three of them. His thoughts moved on to how demanding his training at Saint-Cyr would be, whether he would overcome the nerves he suffered when faced with something tough or unpleasant. Then his mind went back to his earliest memories, the garden and house in Bordeaux, and his twin sister Françoise, how their mother spoke to them in English much of the time, and how they read English children's books as well as French. The way they looked forward to the trips to their grandparents in England. Lucky that France and England are allies, he thought. What would happen to Leo, should there be a war with Germany?

He thought about his parents, the wrench he felt each time he went away to school in England. All right for Françoise who stayed in Bordeaux, at the *lycée* for girls. As twins, the two were close and in their teens would sail for hours together in the family boat, taking their lunch and landing anywhere they fancied along the banks of the Garonne estuary. Now, suddenly, their school days behind them, Henri wondered how he and Françoise would cope with the dangers a war would impose on them.

3

Norway, April 1940

Henri felt nervous and scared, suddenly awake after a fitful sleep, conscious of the background drumming from the engine room and the invasive smell of hot oil. Only recently promoted from Aspirant to Sous-Lieutenant, what was he doing now in the bunk of a troopship heading for the north coast of Norway? Why was it ice and snow he'd have to face, after being trained with his fellow legionnaires for the Algerian desert and the mountains of Morocco? How would he react the first time under live fire from a determined enemy?

His mind flashed back to Saint-Cyr military college, remembering how lucky he was to pass out high enough to qualify for a commission in the French Foreign Legion, based at the Legion's HQ at Sidi Bel Abbès in Algeria. The gruelling desert and mountain training he somehow survived. Then suddenly it happened. France was at war. His posting came through to join a new Legion half-brigade, 13ème Demi-brigade de Légion étrangère or 13 DBLE. Large numbers of Spanish Republicans were among the legionnaires assigned to 13 DBLE. Refugees who crossed the border into France at the end of the Spanish Civil War, already trained and experienced fighters who detested the Nazis for the support they gave Franco.

The endless train journeys up France and Britain until the unit arrived in Glasgow. Orders to embark on *Monarch of Britain* which was serving as a troopship. With them were Chasseurs Alpins, French alpine troops, and Polish refugee soldiers. Alongside this force, the British 24th Guards Brigade.

Lying there in his bunk, as the *Monarch of Britain* steamed east after clearing Scotland, Henri wondered how long it would be before the siren went off, and they would be on their feet, grabbing at the kit so meticulously prepared a few hours earlier. Each man would be having his own thoughts. Few of the young officers, French and British, could claim any battlefield experience. Except, of course, Captain Gordon-Watson, he'd got to know before they sailed, in his role as de facto French liaison officer with 24th Guards Brigade. That was thanks to Henri's English being far superior to anyone else's in the French contingent. Michael Gordon-Watson, intelligence officer of the 1st Battalion, Irish Guards, was a veteran of the Abyssinian campaign a few months earlier and wore the ribbon of the MC on his battledress tunic.

'It's Narvik that everyone's excited about,' Gordon-Watson told him back in Glasgow. 'That's where we're going, to the far north of the country.'

'Why right up there?' said Henri.

'Iron ore,' said the Guards Officer. 'Essential to German industry, it's transported by rail from Sweden across the top of Norway. Narvik's an ice-free port with year-round access for German freighters.'

He and Henri were having a drink in the officers' mess at Greenock, the day before embarkation. Suddenly, a familiar figure approached them, in battledress of an army chaplain rather than the black monastic habit of a Benedictine monk.

'So, de Rochefort,' said Father Rooker, or Rooky as everyone knew him, 'you made it to Foreign Legion officer, my congratulations.'

Henri jumped to his feet in surprise. 'Father Rooker. That's amazing. I remember you saying on my last day at school, you would be a padre in the Irish Guards if there was a war.'

Rooky beamed at both of them, drawing his tall thin figure up to full height. 'Extraordinary to meet again in Glasgow, of all places. After Algeria, you must be missing the silence in the desert, Henri. How's your family, I think you've a twin sister?'

'Yes, Françoise finished school last year. She's mad about a naval cadet on a French battleship.'

The padre rubbed his chin, thinking back to that last day of term a couple of years ago. 'I wonder what's happened to those two great chums of yours, Leo Beckendorf and Bill Lomberg. I seem to remember there was some friendly rivalry between them, one set on going into the Luftwaffe and the other the RAF.'

'I believe they kept in touch until war broke out,' said Henri.

Michael Gordon-Watson was looking on in some surprise, and broke into the conversation. 'So, Henri, you must have been educated by Rooky and his fellow monks at that other establishment to where I was.' The three of them had a good laugh, and went in to dine together.

＊＊＊

As the venerable liner ploughed on, Henri repeated to himself the essentials of the on-board briefing the day before. Given by General Béthouart who commanded the French contingent, and RN Liaison Officer Lieutenant Dan Duff. Duff's job included command of the landing craft and Norwegian fishing boats which would land the legionnaires. Everyone paid serious attention until Béthouart turned to Duff and told him that priority must be given to the cargo of barrels. They each contained 50 litres of wine.

A piercing siren brought Henri to his senses, and in no time he was on deck in full battle kit. The icy wind from the Arctic whipped the waves into a creamy froth and tore at his face. He made out on the horizon the outline of Nerjangs Fjord, white hills on either side, with mountains beyond. Almost a snow-covered version of how he remembered Algeria.

The French were to land at Bjerkvik, about twelve kilometres north of Narvik. As they drew closer, he could make out warehouses on the shoreline, some on fire, and brightly painted wooden houses beyond. Naval gunnery was pounding targets onshore, preparatory to their landing. Dan Duff, who had still been awaiting his gunnery exams when assigned to the mission, handled the bombardment of the French landing zone from the destroyer HMS *Fame*, just ahead of them. He knew that Duff was again astonished by the French General when Béthouart said the legionnaires would advance through the gunnery target area during the bombardment.

Two blasts from a whistle, the moment for Henri's platoon to transfer to one of the craft provided by the Royal Navy for the amphibious assault on Bjerkvik. He saw 13 DBLE's commander, Lt. Col. Magrin-Vernerey, at the top of the rope ladders. The Polish and British, from the accompanying troop-ships, were already ashore and awaiting the order to advance on Bjerkvik. The order never came. Instead, the French assault fleet, led by the battleship HMS *Resolution* sailed past them, up the fjord with the Legion's 13 DBLE on-board.

So for Henri this was real action. Landing onto a jetty alongside, they ran forward towards the port buildings as machine gun fire opened up on them. Cover was taken wherever they could find it. Then a crashing blast of dust and debris as a mortar bomb blew apart the truck being unloaded close by. Henri turned his head sideways to check for casualties in his platoon. There was Juan Morel, one of Henri's corporals looking across at him and grinning, no doubt in an attempt to reassure the new young officer, saying something in unintelligible Catalan.

Sick with nervousness up to this point, Henri now felt somehow different. Steadier, more focused. Must be his training, he thought. He pointed to a warehouse building just off the port's sea front. It seemed to be the closest source of enemy fire. Calling for covering fire, he crawled forward in the snow to get a better view of where the machine gun and mortar fire was coming from. Taking another Spanish legionnaire with him, they worked their way round and towards the rear of the warehouse.

Machine gun fire opened up again, coming from the front of the first floor. Then the thump of a mortar bomb being fired. Gradually they approached the building, keeping out of sight as best they could. Now at the foot of the rear wall. A hoist and steps led to the upper floors. There was a stench of fish, indicating the building was used for canning herring or perhaps cod. They climbed silently to first floor level, and crept round the structure of the hoist so they could see the machine gun and mortar teams on the other side. Each detached grenades from their webbing, withdrew the pins and rolled them side by side towards the front of the building, taking cover behind the casing of the hoist. The grenades exploded simultaneously.

Henri and the Legionnaire rushed across, firing short bursts from their Thompson guns. Two *Gebirgsjäger*, Austrian mountain troops, leant beside their machine gun against the front wall. One appeared dead. The other was shouting, one hand on a wound spouting blood from his groin and the other held high in a gesture of surrender. The other two manning the mortar appeared shocked, slowly raising their hands, just boys they looked. Henri's training made him leave them under cover of the Legionnaire while he worked his way from wall to wall around the floor until he was sure there were no others.

Corporal Morel ceased covering fire when it was clear the assault was under way. Henri now signalled to him to advance with his section, and join up at the foot of the warehouse. Henri couldn't help thinking the whole operation was probably elementary for Morel after the street fighting against Franco's troops in Barcelona. Spasmodic firing continued some distance away but all seemed calm where they were.

Henri took the microphone from his wireless operator and made his contact report to Company HQ, giving the result, location, and asking for further orders. The news was that the Austrians were having difficulty in the snow conditions. Although they belonged to an alpine unit, for some inexplicable reason they were without skis. It appeared they were in the process of withdrawing.

Hearing the town of Bjerkvik was now in the hands of 13 DBLE, with few casualties, Henri realized he was shaking. Must be the excitement of the assault, and the success, he thought. Yet, he kept remembering the faces of the Austrians, so young, one dead and another dying. This was his work. Was he proud of it? He'd not killed anyone before. It was his duty. Yet, there was conflict in his reasoning, between his duty to cause death and the right of others to live. Can't dwell on that sort of thing, must concentrate on what next, was his reaction. But that conflict remained in him.

It was two weeks later when the Legion and Chasseurs units received orders to cross Rombaksfjorde, and to land on the southern edge of Narvik itself. As Henri's platoon hit the beach, he knew they were in trouble, finding themselves almost on top of enemy positions. Pinned down by artillery and machine gun fire for five hours, a miracle was called for. It arrived in the form of 13 DBLE's Commanding Officer. Magrin-Vernerey came ashore and, with submachine gun, led a charge up the slopes above the beach. Although heavily outnumbered, the legionnaires and Norwegian troops who had joined them, drove the enemy out of Narvik.

Soon afterwards, Michael Gordon-Watson arrived on the scene. He looked grim, and ten years older than when they had met at Greenock.

'Captain Gordon-Watson, sir, how has your part in the operation gone so far?' asked Henri.

The young Captain stared at Henri and then spoke calmly.

'A complete and horrible disaster.'

'Why, what happened?'

'We were trying to transfer from Leland to Bodo on a Polish passenger ship called the *Chobry*. The Battalion was all loaded in, but for some stupid reason we were stuck there for five hours. When we did get going down the fjord, a German spotter plane was circling. Of course, he must have seen us.'

Gordon-Watson paused.

'Anyway, we'd just turned in when a stick of bombs hit us. The vessel caught fire, and we had to abandon ship. We were picked up by a naval vessel. But the terrible thing was that we soon discovered that one bomb had killed all the key officers. Our Commanding Officer, the Second-in-Command, the Adjutant and three of the Company Commanders. A freak. It could never happen in battle.'

'I suppose not,' Henri muttered.

'I was the senior officer left on his feet, so I had to take command for a while. Hardly a Guardsman was touched. They were at the other end of the ship. We thought we'd lost three of them, but our Sar'nt Major rescued them.'

He paused again, looking away.

'The men behaved magnificently, very steady, but finding we'd lost all our senior people like that was quite horrible. The Micks are like a family and it's hard to get over something like that.'

The young Captain was a brave enough man, with the Military Cross, but he was obviously very shaken.

Henri could not help thinking of Rooky.

'That's an unbelievably disastrous thing to have happened. What about Padre Rooker?'

'Oh, he's okay. Matter of fact, he helped in the rescue of a number of wounded on-board, and supervised their transfer to a destroyer. There were gallant things done that night, and some were his.'

Henri nodded. 'I wouldn't have expected anything else from Rooky,' he said almost to himself.

Gordon-Watson continued.

'We then re-formed under a new CO and saw action near Pothus. We held out for two days against heavy German attacks, and then withdrew when outflanked.

'What an experience. Now I understand we've all been combined into one corps under the command of General Auchinleck.'

'Not a moment too soon. Incidentally, are you aware of what's going on in Belgium? German tanks are pouring through the Low Countries, and into France.' Henri looked surprised.

Gordon-Watson went on. 'We're all ordered back to Glasgow as soon as we can pull out. We have to abandon our Norwegian friends.'

'All our losses for nothing,' said Henri. 'We lost seven officers, five NCOs and 55 legionnaires.'

Henri learnt that the French government wanted all trained forces back for the defence of France. Dan Duff was at hand to manage the embarkation of 13 DBLE back to vessels for the return to Britain. General Béthouart was said to have exclaimed, after arriving back in the UK, that Duff was the only British officer with any understanding of amphibious warfare.

Henri was pleased when he heard that Dan had been awarded a Distinguished Service Cross for heroism, having rescued the wounded from an ammunition ship sunk during the landings, and returning under fire to a stranded landing vessel to bring the men ashore. They said goodbye on the dock at Greenock.

'Dan, congratulations on your DSC. Thank you for everything you did for us French.'

'Thanks. Damn waste of men and equipment if you ask me. Your unit did well, was an inspiration to us all. I was with Michael Gordon-Watson just now. He quoted from the war diary of the 1st Battalion Irish Guards that your landing at Bjerkvik "was accomplished successfully by the Legion who landed in magnificent style and showed how highly trained and what fine troops they were." Well done.'

Henri was surprised, pausing before saying 'I think we all learnt lessons.'

'Yes. For me, the most serious was the importance of signals intelligence,' said Duff. 'The way the enemy seemed to know our movements. I just heard one of our carriers has been sunk, the *Glorious*. Seems she returned to Norway to take back the Hurricanes she previously shipped over. Never realized the *Scharnhorst* was there. Blown out of the water. The crew abandoned ship, and almost all perished because no one heard of the sinking. Somehow, the enemy knew where she was. How could that happen? The German Navy's intelligence is uncanny.'

4

13 DBLE found themselves, along with other French units, in lines of Nissen huts close by the remains of the once stately pile of Trentham Park. Henri was listening to their commanding officer Lt. Col. Magrin-Vernerey, and his adjutant Captain Pierre Koenig, addressing the officers in the make-shift mess room soon after their arrival.

'Some of you will have read in the English press the call just broadcast by Brigadier General de Gaulle to the French nation. We decided to go to London and meet the General, which we did yesterday. General Béthouart was there and has returned with us, and tomorrow evening will address a parade of all French troops here at Trentham Park. He will present you with the choice of returning to the forces in French North Africa, or of joining the Free French forces of de Gaulle.'

The room was silent, everyone still. Henri knew this would be a turning point in his professional career, in his life. That it would present a dilemma to him and his fellow officers, a decision to be faced up to. And not the kind anyone was expecting.

⋆⋅⊱⊰⋅⋆

It was exactly six o'clock the next day as General Béthouart, accompanied by a senior British officer, mounted a low dais facing the assembled company of more than one thousand French troops. Béthouart stepped one pace forward. 'Soldiers of France, comrades. Many of you were with me in Norway. You did your duty, we delivered what was expected of us, we fought alongside our allies. Circumstances beyond our control caused the French government to call us back to defend the homeland, too late as it turned out.

'As you know, most of the French troops evacuated from Dunkirk to this country were transferred back immediately to France to continue the fight. Nevertheless, Marshal Pétain and Pierre Laval have announced an armistice under which all French forces will cease the fight against Germany. German forces will occupy the northern half of our nation and also all the Atlantic seaboard including Bordeaux. Below that line will be the so-called Free Zone. The French government, to be based in the town of Vichy, will continue to have civil jurisdiction over all of Metropolitan France, and France overseas. With Le Maréchal as President and Monsieur Laval as Foreign Minister, this will include Algeria and all other overseas territories from Syria to Djibouti, Senegal to Indochina.'

The General paused before continuing, and Henri could sense the tension among the troops around him.

'You will have heard that a French officer, Brigadier General Charles de Gaulle, has arrived in Britain and proclaimed himself leader of "Free French forces". He has pledged to continue the fight against Germany, and also Italy which declared war on France and Britain just before the Armistice was signed. De Gaulle may not be known to many of you. It is unclear what he can achieve, given that German forces may well now invade Britain. Every man will be given a summary of General de Gaulle's further address broadcast by the BBC. The new government in Vichy has found General de Gaulle guilty of treason.

'I am asking you whether you wish to return to the unoccupied sector of France where you may be demobilized, or whether you want to stay here and join the so-called Free French forces under General de Gaulle. We will re-assemble on parade at 9am tomorrow morning.'

As the parade dismissed, Henri helped himself to one of the printed sheets, reading de Gaulle's latest address as he walked back to the huts:

It is absurd to consider the fight as over. Yes, we have been heavily defeated. A bad military system, the mistakes made in leading the operations, the government's spirit of abandon have all made us lose the Battle of France. But we still have a large Empire, an intact fleet, a lot of gold, we still have allies with immense resources.

If the forces of freedom finally prevail over those of slavery, what would be the fate of a France which submitted to the enemy? Honour, common sense, and the superior interests of the Nation command to all the free French to continue fighting wherever they are and however they can.

I, General de Gaulle, am starting this national task here in England. I invite all French soldiers of the armies of land, sea and air, I invite the engineers and workers specialized in armament who are on British soil or could go there.

I invite the leaders, the soldiers, the sailors, the pilots of the French forces of land, sea and air, wherever they may be, to get in touch with me. I invite all the French who want to remain free to listen to me and to follow me.

Long live a free and independent France!

Back in the officers' mess, he noticed that two groups were forming. That to which Henri gravitated was made up of a handful of officers, mainly 13 DBLE, who seemed likely to join the Free French forces. The remainder, the larger group, gave the impression of resignation, mitigated by the expectation of soon being reunited with their families and loved ones. Their discussions were emotional. 'Britain's either going to deal with Hitler in similar fashion, or else it'll be invaded with little chance of repelling this incredible German war machine,' said one of them.

'My parents live in Lyon in the new Free Zone, under the new Vichy regime, and are going to need help,' said another.

'I've plans to marry my girlfriend who lives in Clermont-Ferrand. Her father's a senior manager at Michelin. It'd be madness to stay here, maybe fighting on British soil and perhaps even losing one's life in doing so,' said a third.

Henri went to his room, sat on the bed, thinking through the options. His parents and sister Françoise would be in occupied Bordeaux, out of reach. His grandparents and most of his old schoolfriends were here in England. If there was really the chance that a free France would fight on against Nazism, wouldn't his father want him to play his part?

The next morning was cool, dry and bright. The French forces at Trentham Park formed up in their units. At nine o'clock precisely, the parade was drawn to attention. The General addressed the assembled company.

'I am going to ask those who wish to join Free French forces and remain for the present in Britain, to step forward now.'

Henri didn't need a lead, he'd made up his mind, albeit with a heavy heart. He stepped one pace forward. About half of the Legion officers did the same, as did the majority of legionnaires. But among the Chasseurs and other French units on parade, only a few men moved. Overall, the majority from Metropolitan France voted to return home. From 13 DBLE, names were noted by the platoon NCOs. The parade was given the order to dismiss.

Afterwards, a number of Legion NCOs, mostly Spanish but also two Germans who as Jews had left their country in the late 1930s to join the Legion in North Africa, came up to Henri and shook his hand. One was Corporal Juan Morel, from Barcelona.

Henri heard the final count. In 13 DBLE, nine hundred out of the original one thousand six hundred legionnaires decided to join the Free French, the remainder opting to leave for Morocco as part of the Armée d'Afrique, now under Vichy France. He and his compatriots went to Aldershot to join the other Free French forces. As soon as he arrived, he was summoned by the Adjutant, Captain Koenig, with whom Henri had developed a good relationship during and after the Narvik expedition.

'Henri, I'm so pleased you've decided to stay with us. Settle yourself in, and then I have a request which should keep you busy for a few days. The Colonel needs a liaison officer to maintain contact with the first unit of the new Free French Air Force, which is based at Odiham, near here and commanded by Commandant Lionel de Marmier.'

RAF Odiham, July 1940

Henri and his British Army driver arrived at the airfield the next morning. A sentry lifted the barrier and they drove over to the administrative block close by. As they got out of the car, Henri saw a familiar face walking across towards them. 'I can tell a South African second row forward anywhere' he called out to him. 'What the hell are you doing here, Bill?'

'I should ask you the same thing, Henri,' said Bill Lomberg as they thumped one another on the back.

The South African in RAF uniform, tall and broad shoul-dered, was grinning from ear to ear. 'Quite a lot's happened since we finished school together.'

'You can say that again,' laughed Henri. 'What have you been up to?'

'I was with a squadron of Hurricanes in northern France when the German panzers arrived in May. We were shot up and I had to crash-land. Managed to get to Amiens, and the parents of a French pilot friend, Pierre. We made it to Boulogne. Pierre's now here with the Free French flyers.' He paused. 'What about you? Thought you were trying for the French Foreign Legion. Looks like you made it,' he said as he looked up at Henri's white kepi.

'Yes, it was touch-and-go to make the top grade at Saint-Cyr, but I somehow managed it. Probably helped that several genera-tions of de Rocheforts did the same.'

'Brilliant,' said Bill. 'Must have been tough. I'd not have thought you an obvious choice for that kind of soldiering. Seen any action yet?'

Henri hesitated. 'I joined a newly formed Legion unit, 13th Demi-Brigade. We were sent to the north of Norway, landed at Narvik. Drove the Boche out.'

'Yes, heard about that adventure, well done.'

Henri suddenly remembered something. 'Bill, you won't believe it but Rooky, Dom Brendan Rooker, was there as well. He's a chaplain with the Irish Guards, who were part of the Narvik invasion force.'

'That's incredible,' exclaimed Bill. 'Rooky always seemed to have a soft spot for us three musketeers. Do you remember that discussion in his study on the last night of term?'

'What, about the Church and the moral law in time of war. How the Church will manage the dilemma of whether to speak out about the Nazis and their treatment of the Jews. Yes, I won't forget that. He was so damned serious about it.'

There was silence for a moment. Bill's face seemed to darken. 'And, what about the third musketeer?'

'You mean Leo Beckendorf,' said Henri. 'With an English mother, like me. Always said he would join the Luftwaffe.'

'And he did,' said Bill. 'We continued to correspond, right up to a year ago when war broke out. I've no idea what happened to him afterwards.' He stopped, seemed to be thinking for a moment. 'I'm to take you to meet the RAF CO, and also the French boss, Commandant de Marmier. When that's over, let's have a beer in the mess.'

⟶ ⊙ ⟵

Bill introduced Henri to his friend, Pierre, with whom he'd made his escape from France. The three of them were up against the bar of the officers' mess, surrounded by walls bearing pictures of epic air battles and fighter aces of the 1914 War. 'You know, my father flew one of those string-bags for the French Armée de l'air,' said Henri.

'A miracle that he lived to have you,' said Bill.

'So, why are you here,' said Henri to his old schoolfriend.

'They sent me to Odiham to train the French on the Hurricane. Having flown the plane in France, I suppose I was an obvious choice. Your pilots have some of their own planes which they flew over in the first group, a fortnight ago when France and Germany signed the Armistice. They arrived from Bordeaux-Mérignac. The RAF has provided Hurricanes with ground crews.'

'What's that fighter plane over there?' said Henri, catching sight through the window of a modern fighter aircraft he didn't recognize.'

Pierre was listening. 'That's the Dewoitine D.520, brand new, only a couple of squadrons had them before the Armistice. It's one of three Dewoitines which flew over here. The rest seem to have escaped to French North Africa. Fast aircraft, but handling unpredictable.'

There was a pause while they sipped their beer. Then Bill said, 'Henri, what about your twin sister, Françoise, wasn't that her name? The week I spent with your family in Bordeaux a year ago, I took a real liking to Françoise.'

'Well, you'll have to get shot down behind enemy lines if you want to see her now. I've not heard from her or our parents since France collapsed. Bordeaux is now occupied by the Germans, and they say the Boche are being kind to everyone in these early days. No doubt that will change.'

Henri turned to the Frenchman. 'Pierre, forgive me for asking, but I'm looking for a way of getting a letter home to my parents and sister over there, explaining why I've decided to remain in England. Could you help?'

Pierre looked thoughtful for a moment, then laughed, 'There's no air mail in that direction. But I know of French trawlers still ferrying military personnel back to Bordeaux. I think I could fix something. Let me have it, and I'll see what I can do.'

Henri knew it could be a long time before he saw his family again, and felt a surge of grief swell through him as he sealed down the envelope and handed it over.

◈

The Quatorze Juillet parade, Bastille Day, was suddenly upon them. Henri spotted Pierre in the French Air Force contingent. They marched together. 'So it's the London streets this year,' shouted one to the other. 'Makes a change from the Champs

Elysées. You know the official French government in Vichy regards us all as traitors.'

'Yes, heartening isn't it that so many French civilians have turned up to give us a good cheer. Look at those posters on the walls saying "A tous les Français". Must be de Gaulle's appeal to the French people over the BBC.'

After the parade, and a broadcast speech by Winston Churchill, Colonel Magrin-Vernerey addressed his legionnaires. 'You put up a good show today. We have much to prove to our English allies, this is only the beginning.'

<hr />

Henri and his fellow junior officers in 13 DBLE did not have to wait long for some action. Together in the mess one evening before dinner, the Colonel walked in. All were silent, sensing that he had something important to share with them.

Magrin-Vernerey walked stiffly across the room, on the one hand heavily incapacitated, on the other every bit the soldier. He laid his black kepi on the bar and turned towards the officers he now knew so well.

'Gentlemen. We have a job to do. We're going to Africa.'

5

Elisabeth Steiner was unsure whom to believe. No family to turn
to. It was the night of glass and fire two and a half years before
that was the turning point. Till then, hope overcame fear. People
were human even if the government wasn't. Morality would
prevail. Then came that night, when the authorities stood back,
allowed the fires to burn. People turned the other way. That
changed everything, the cruel truth was laid bare. No future for
those of her Jewish ancestry. Being banned from some professions was one thing. Being deprived of one's business and liveli-
hood, threatened with removal to ghettos and camps, was the
game changer. Rumours of terrible things happening in Poland,
now stories of murder behind the lines in the Ukraine. No one
was going to stand up for them.

Were her father with her, perhaps it would be different. He
could have returned from France when war looked inevitable.
Yet, could you blame him for not deserting his colleagues at
the Institute in Paris? He never pretended he was not of Jewish
descent, even though the family were Catholics.

His department at the Institut Pasteur was officially for
research into vaccines. Elisabeth knew there was more to it.
That night she heard him talking to the visitor at their home
in Neuilly. Father's soft voice as always. The other, animated
and persuasive. 'Give it up, get away while you can. The
Americans want you.' Something about quantities, and effect

on population. The means of delivery. The need for France to develop the substances to deter its enemies from deploying the same.

Unable to sleep, trying to reconcile the logic. If what her father was working on was many more times powerful than gas in the previous war, if millions of civilians were threatened, neither side would resort to it. That's what her father was saying. Did he really believe it?

⊷⊷◉⊶⊶

Back in Germany, now on her own. Why didn't she stay in Paris? Because Germany was her home country, and where she could train as a doctor. To be with her friends from student days, the urge to join them in the war effort? Maybe all those things. Her nursing training at the American Hospital in Neuilly mustn't be wasted. Her family was gone, safe in America. It was her choice to be back in Germany. After all, she was German. Yet now she felt threatened. She remembered, her father warned her, but she didn't listen. She couldn't hide that rebellious streak.

Eighteen months later, the threat was real. In her new work as a qualified nurse at the hospital in Munich, no one seemed to suspect. Outside, however, it was different. Among her Jewish friends, there was talk of people going missing. Rumours of resettlement in Poland. The Nuremberg laws said those with Jewish grandparents were to be considered Jews themselves, regardless of the religion they practised. Too late to escape, they said.

Who could she turn to? Perhaps the priest she knew well, Father Ambrose. He came with them when they went hiking, camping in the Bavarian Alps. Somehow he was sympathetic, worried for Elisabeth and her young Jewish friends. How should she put it to him? Best to make the approach after Mass on Sunday, fix a time to see him privately.

They went into the sacristy, a room off to the side of the main altar in the parish church. She came directly from the hospital, still in her white uniform, work over for the day. Her fair hair tied up under the nurse's cap. No make-up. Father Ambrose was waiting for her. She loved the kindly look he always gave her. Like now as he showed her into the room.

She glanced around, knowing that the vestments were kept in a special chest. That must be it, with wide drawers running down one side of the room. There was a crucifix on the far wall and a print of Jesus and the Sacred Heart opposite.

He showed her to one of the two chairs at a small table, offering her a glass of mint tea which she gratefully accepted as she sat down on one of the chairs. Presumably to put her at ease, he remarked on how pleased he was with her regular attendance at the services in his parish. He then asked her about her family, why she seemed to be alone in Munich. 'Perhaps you'd like to tell me something of your background, Elisabeth. Where does the Steiner family come from?'

'We're from Odessa, originally. Grain merchants, that's what my grandparents did.' Elisabeth wasn't sure whether he was aware of her Jewish origins. 'Moved to Munich when the Tsar was kicking out the Jews, start of the century. We're Catholics, as you know. My father converted when he married my mother.'

'Ah, my child. That must be a problem for you. They have the records, the Nazis. Will know who your grandparents were. Do you have any ideas as to how you can avoid trouble for yourself?'

'Not specifically, Father. Except that last night, I started to think about what another nurse said to me at the hospital.

More an exclamation than a suggestion. We were assigned to the operating theatre. A woman was brought in after a truck knocked her down as she ran for a tram by the entrance to the Englischer Garten. A hopeless case. The two surgeons tried to massage her heart, to bring her back, but the injuries were too great. As the porter wheeled the trolley away, the theatre nurse just said it. 'What a loss. She was our age, a life in front of her. Her identity snuffed out.'

'That's tragic,' said the priest. 'And set you thinking?'

'Yes. It was the expression "Her identity snuffed out." The words wouldn't go away. Then, it came to me. Couldn't I become that person?'

Father Ambrose said nothing, just waited for her to continue.

'I know there would be problems. What about the dead woman's family? They would be told. There'd be a funeral. Official records would show everything. So, how could it be done?' She paused. 'Do you see such cases in a city like Munich, Father? Young women dying from accidents or illness.'

'Well, sometimes, I suppose.' He was now looking serious. 'So, you want to disappear, escape the records of your ancestors. I can understand that,' said the priest. 'To swap identities with another? That sounds almost like fantasy. Adopting someone else's identity, is that possible? There must be an easier way.'

'There was an escape line, Father. I heard about it. The Gestapo closed in on the organizers, executed them as traitors. Caught the escapees at the rail station in Belgrade, sent them to the camps.'

'Let's think it through,' said the priest. 'Suppose I'm called to give the last rites to a dying woman.' He paused, seeming hesitant, unsure where this was leading him. 'Somehow I find her papers. We falsify the death certificate, entering your name and details. What then?'

'You're thinking about her family, aren't you? What if they report the dead woman has gone missing. She needs to be from another part of Germany, so no inquiries are made. She mustn't be missed locally.'

'If the relations find out she died here, they will be asked to identify the body. You will be the person pronounced dead,' said the priest.

'And me. I become the dead woman. The deceased's papers are mine. My own family left France for America. They won't know.' Elisabeth stopped to think. 'So, what happens to the dead body with my identity? With your help, it would just be buried. A tombstone with my name on.'

There was silence for a few moments. Then the priest seemed to have decided. 'I'm chaplain to the nuns in a convent at Garmisch. There's a very sick young nun, suffering from tuberculosis.'

Elisabeth froze, knowing what was to come.

'She just returned from hospital. On a stretcher. They say she needs the mountain air, but not much can be done. I've been helping her. I was with her yesterday. She'll have her just reward in heaven, and that will come soon. Lovely, brave person, devoted to her faith.' He stopped, looked up at Elisabeth. 'The Reverend Mother tells me this sick nun was an orphan, brought up by the same order in north Germany.' He paused, an intense look in his eyes. 'You must be ready when I tell you I have given her the last rites.'

'So you mean...' said Elisabeth, hesitating.

'Her name is Theresa Krüger. She's going to die, soon.'

6

Crete, May 1941

Leo Beckendorf sat shoulder to shoulder with his men along the corrugated fuselage of the Ju 52 transport aircraft as it took off from an airfield on the Greek mainland. The noise and vibration did not prevent his mind from returning to that fateful day in Munich, not long after leaving school. The Luftwaffe medical officer in charge of the examination of recruits was sitting behind his desk, staring at the file marked Leo Beckendorf, which lay open before him.

'So you're only half German, educated in England and with an English mother. What a mixture, good job the Luftwaffe doesn't fly on the right-hand side of the road. Not that you're going to fly anyway.'

Leo started with surprise, as he stood erect in front of the desk.

'I don't understand, sir. I thought that my application was accepted subject only to medical examination.'

The MO looked at him, then down at the file, and back at him.

'The eye tests you underwent indicate a degree of colour blindness. It's forbidden for anyone who shows such symptons to be accepted for pilot training.'

Leo felt sick, said nothing.

'This result need not end your ambition to become a Luftwaffe officer,' continued the MO. 'As you know, there's not only the technical branch of the force where engineering-minded recruits are directed, but also the flak and airfield defence branch.'

It was clear from Leo's dejected stare that he was in a state of shock, his ambition to fly the Luftwaffe's exciting new aircraft dashed by those few words. Before he was able to respond, the MO, observing his intense disappointment, interjected.

'There's one other option, the *Fallschirmjäger*, the Luftwaffe's parachute troops. Some time ago, Reichsmarschall Goering ordered an analysis of developments the Russians were making with airborne troops. The Reichsmarschall then appointed Colonel Kurt Student, a pilot in the last war, to form the first Luftwaffe airborne force.'

The MO stopped and regarded Leo for a long moment, taking in his short but well-built physique, under the boyish face and fair hair.

'I'd say from your physical profile, that you would be suited to the new force. What do you think?'

Leo thought carefully before responding. Should he become a soldier, albeit in the Luftwaffe, just because his eyesight didn't match the standards set for pilot training? Maybe a complete change of direction would be better, such as tanks. The panzer regiments seemed to be the big thing in the modern German Army. On the other hand, he'd heard of Goering's new parachute regiment which combined the excitement of flying with the promise of a new form of warfare. Here he was, being offered an opportunity many of his contemporaries would jump at. So much for his rivalry at school with Bill Lomberg, over which fighter aircraft they planned to fly would be the best. Too bad, he'd made up his mind.

'Sir, I'm willing to consider this option. Thank you. What do I have to do next?'

'It'll mean a further evaluation of your suitability. The criteria for entering the *Fallschirmjäger* are demanding, but you would be given a fair chance.'

◆━◎━◆

That was two years ago. Now, Leo was suddenly jerked back to reality as his platoon sergeant touched his arm, swivelling his body round so he could see out of the rectangular window of the plane, pointing down as the outline of the island of Crete came into view out on the horizon.

Leo knew the ultimate test was almost upon him. He remembered his first jump at Parachute School III, Braunschweig-Broitzem. Standing third in line leading to the open door of a Junkers Ju 52 tri-motor transport plane, like the one he was now in. Attaching the static line to the rail under the roof of the plane, feeling it was secure, holding his nerves in hand as he waited his turn. The grin from the dispatcher when the moment came, a strong slap on the back along with the shout 'Los', and out of the door and into space. Pulled up abruptly as the parachute cord was automatically pulled. A very short time before the ground was rushing up to meet him. Calling on the experience gained in the training hangar, the knees bent on contact with the ground, rolling over onto shoulders and back. A sense of elation swept over him. Five more jumps followed, and the coveted Luftwaffe parachutist badge was his.

The explosion of anti-aircraft shells broke the monotonous roar of the Ju 52's three engines, and Leo was brought back with a jolt to the part he was to play in this giant airborne attack on Crete. The island only sparsely garrisoned by British and New Zealand troops, they were told, and they were confident of rapid success. Leo prayed, hoping that was true.

He double-checked his parachute harness was securely attached to the static line running under the roof of the fuselage. His platoon lined up behind him, doing the same. Leo knew some of them from the drop on Rotterdam. Others were making their first drop into enemy territory. He tried not to think of the reception waiting for them below.

The dispatcher opened the side door of the plane and the blast of the slipstream howled at them. The orange light was on. Ten seconds, then on came the green. 'Los!' shouted the dispatcher, slapping him on the back as Leo threw himself out into space. A sudden blast of air, roaring of the engines, as he was flung away behind the aircraft. He felt the line go taught, jerking open his parachute. He was free, starting to float downwards. An astonishing sight of hundreds of aircraft flying in parallel lines abreast, disgorging paratroopers, the sky a mass of men and canopies. He saw the containers containing their machine guns and mortars, falling separately under their own parachutes. Some with three-coloured chutes dropping the small mountain guns. Leo just carried his revolver and a couple of grenades. He knew the first vital task after landing was to make for a container and arm himself with an MP 40 submachine gun.

Below him, he heard gunfire. There was the dropping zone, Maleme airfield, strewn with gliders which landed the mountain troops earlier. The runways were clear to see, hills surrounding the space. Deep blue of the Mediterranean in the distance. Almost down, enemy troops were firing up at them. About to hit the ground, one of hundreds of *Fallschirmjäger*, he saw several of his comrades being hit by rifle fire from the defenders, bodies contorting and going limp. The ground was coming up at him fast.

The shock as his legs bent on contact with the hard ground, and as he rolled on his shoulders. He knew there wasn't a moment to lose. Must release his parachute which was straining in the wind, and find a container. Where was the nearest? About thirty metres away. Head and body bent double, he made towards it. There was another *Fallschirmjäger* going for the same one. He hesitated, about to alter course for another, when the man jerked up in a spasm of pain, hit by a rifle shot. Leo kept going, reaching the container and releasing the clip. He grabbed the weapon and stuffed clips of ammunition into his smock and webbing.

Must remember his training. Leave the wounded man to the medical orderlies dropped with them. Make for cover. There wasn't any. Had to reach the perimeter of the airfield. Others were doing the same, running toward the scrubland. Almost there, he saw one of the enemy beside a crashed glider, on one knee and shooting upwards. Leo threw himself down and worked his way towards the target. His submachine gun didn't have much range, nothing like a service rifle. Must get nearer. There was another glider close by. Could he put it between himself and the target? It was close enough, and he took cover behind it. Now to get the bastard before he was spotted. Well aware the only mode of fire with the MP 40 was fully automatic, he knew the relatively low rate of fire enabled single shots with controlled squeezes on the trigger. Range about 120 metres, he judged. Two shots brought him down.

Not the first time he'd killed a man, he thought. Those Dutch troops fought hard at Rotterdam, drove us off the airfield at first. Yet he still felt the shock of ending a man's life, almost in the cold. It was the enemy or himself. That was where war overtook the law.

In the high grass beyond the perimeter, Leo went to gather in his Platoon. Several of the men were close by, there being little wind during the drop. The mortar team were with their weapon. The radio operator had recovered his equipment. But there were losses. The defenders, dug in on the sides of the surrounding hills, wrought havoc on the descending para-troopers, and on those escaping their harness and making for the weapons canisters. A field dressing station was being assem-bled, large red cross draped over the tent.

Leo realized the enemy was expecting them. There were a lot more defenders than the intelligence people told them there would be before they took off from Greece. What's going to happen, thought Leo. They could be annihilated if the British artillery were strengthened. This was the role of the para-trooper. You fought with what you carried. No armoured vehicles. Supplies from the air only. There was supposed to be a sea landing also, to give them the support of light tanks. No sign of that. Their orders were to secure the airfield so that more troops and equipment could be flown in. To do that, they must clear the surrounding cover, particularly the large hill where the defences were strongest.

'Scherber's dead.' The voice behind him was instantly recog-nizable, that of the 3rd Regiment's CO, von der Heydte talking to the Adjutant. 'General Meindl has been shot in the chest, we don't know whether he'll pull through.'

'It's been a slaughter. Who's going to take over the Battalion from Scherber?'

'Treves will take command, until we sort it out,' replied von der Heydte. He didn't seem to mind Leo overhearing, half looking at him as he spoke. 'We have to contain the situation here, survive the night. Reinforcements are expected tomorrow. Maleme is critical to this whole operation. If we can drive out the New Zealanders defending it, armoured vehicles and tanks can be flown in.'

He lay on his side with one hand touching the MP 40, on what he'd been told was Hill 107, overlooking Maleme airfield. Very early morning following the day of the drop. The first glimmer of dawn could just be made out. He felt a hand on his shoulder, his Platoon Sergeant whispering in his ear. 'The New Zealanders have disappeared. The word's been passed from position to position. It's extraordinary. They had us at their mercy.'

'They certainly did,' muttered Leo. The horror of the previous day invaded his mind. Hundreds more New Zealand infantry defending the airfield and in the surrounding hills than they'd been told.

'That New Zealander we captured,' said the Sergeant. 'He said it was like the start of the duck shooting season. Our weapons being dropped in separate containers, men shot as they tried to get to them.'

'None of the more senior officers have survived,' commented Leo, as he thought of Lieutenant Horst Treves taking command of the Battalion, not his favourite among fellow officers. He stood up as others were now doing, to get a better look. The airfield was littered with the wrecks of Ju 52s and gliders, but no enemy defenders in sight.

Major von der Heydte, came forward to confer with Treves, Leo and the other company and platoon commanders. 'We're to receive reinforcements of *Fallschirmjäger* today. Colonel Ramcke is now in command and is standing by to drop with five hundred paratroopers previously held in reserve. Nearly four hundred of you died yesterday, out of the six hundred in the Battalion. Must grab the opportunity to take control of the airfield right away, so we can fly in more troops and heavier equipment. Before the enemy counterattacks.'

By evening, Leo was watching German transport aircraft flying in reinforcements and light tanks. In a day of high drama, make or break for both sides, the reinforced *Fallschirmjäger* took control of the airfield. The New Zealanders counterattacked, but not at full strength. It seemed they were also expecting a seaborne landing.

The next day, Colonel Ramcke called together all officers who were still on their feet. Von der Heydte introduced him individually to the survivors, including Leo.

'Gentlemen,' the Colonel said. 'I'm aware of the very heavy casualties you have suffered. It's become clear that Allied forces were three times the number that our intelligence services predicted. But we now have our hands on most of the key objectives on Crete, and signs are that the British and New Zealand forces are preparing to evacuate. Resistance may not end with their departure. We're encountering stiff partisan activity. Cretan civilians, some in uniform and armbands, have joined the fight. Be on your guard. We must be ruthless in controlling terrorist activity.'

The next day, there were stories circulating of killings of comrades by Cretan civilians. Mutilated bodies of *Fallschirmjäger* were discovered. Apparently, Goering was aware of this development and was instructing Ramcke to undertake reprisals.

Close to the village of Kondomari, only two kilometers from Maleme, corpses of several *Fallschirmjäger* of Leo's regiment were found, killed by civilians armed with primitive weapons.

Oberleutnant Treves was detailed to take a detachment, including Leo, and go to Kondomari to take reprisals.

Leo froze when he read the order. He was suddenly aware of the dividing line between the ruthlessness of the Nazi regime and the basic morality he'd been brought up to believe in. He didn't discuss his feelings with fellow officers, least of all Treves. The fact was their comrades had been savagely killed, adding to the extraordinary loss of life in the original drop. It was unthinkable that in front of his men who had lost so many of their friends, he should refuse to obey orders. And yet he knew what he was to do was wrong, and somehow a turning point for him in the way he saw his part in the conflict.

Treves briefed the party. 'First we round up all the villagers, then select at least twenty of the men and march them into an olive grove, out of the way of the others. Volunteers for the firing squad, fifteen of you please?' A number of *Fallschirmjäger* stepped forward. 'Good. You will position yourselves in two ranks, seven standing and seven kneeling in front. Choose the closest peasant as your target.' He paused, and looked directly at Leo. 'Lieutenant Beckendorf, bring sufficient ammunition for your revolver to finish off any not dead.' Leo would never forget the look in Treves's eyes as he stared at him, challenging, sneering, reading Leo's thoughts.

They left the vehicles outside of the village, fanning out and positioning themselves in a large circle to block anyone running away. It was evening, and the peasant men were standing in small groups by the church and at the tavern as Treves's group closed in. The mood of the villagers was sullen. The women were sitting on chairs outside their homes. The day's work was over.

The round-up was brutal, arbitrary. The paratroopers went for a man each and marched them with hands behind the head towards the agreed point at the far end of the village. Leo found himself looking at an older man already selected by a paratrooper. The kind but somehow rebellious face looked hard at him. Leo was surprised the man made no attempt to plead for mercy. An olive grove close to the village was where it was going to happen. Twenty hostages altogether, lined up facing the firing squad. Silence for a moment. Leo noticed his man make the sign of the cross from right to left shoulder, Orthodox style. Then the order from Treves, 'At the word Fire, one shot at a time.' The firing squad raised their service rifles. A pause. 'Fire.' The fusillade shattered the peace of the evening. Several second shots, then silence. Leo went forward, revolver in hand, checking each body. When he arrived at the older man, there was blood trickling from his mouth. He couldn't see the wound. His eyes still showed defiance. Leo thought he couldn't do it. He could feel the gaze of Treves and the others on him. His mind went to the only place still open to him, and he asked God for forgiveness. He looked in the man's eyes, and shot him in the side of the head.

⊷═◉═◗═⊷

'Lieutenant Beckendorf, do come in.' Major von der Heydte was sitting in a canvas chair on the verandah of the villa, and waved Leo over to join him.

'Thank you, sir.'

'This house was requisitioned with the help of the local mayor. Let's hope the partisans leave us alone.' There was an odd look in the eyes of Leo's CO. 'We've been on Crete for two weeks now. Seems an age since that awful battle for Maleme. We've taken a lot of prisoners, but a large number of the British and New Zealanders have got away, courtesy of their Royal Navy.'

'They lost a lot of ships, as I understand, sir.'

'Yes, but their evacuation efforts show that even though the Luftwaffe control the air space, the British Navy dominates this end of the Mediterranean.' He poured Leo a glass of lemonade. 'Now, I wanted to talk about something else.' The CO paused. 'Lieutenant, the terrible losses we suffered during the drop are generating a lot of heat. They tell me the Führer was shocked, and that's saying something. Tell me what has struck you the most about the whole operation.'

Leo wondered what this was about. Why him? Von der Heydte was asking a straight question. He'd better give a direct reply. 'There was a major intelligence failure, in my view, sir.'

'Precisely,' said the Major. 'A total balls-up with horrendous consequences. Enemy strength in numbers was three times what signals intelligence indicated. All right, they were poorly equipped, having left most of their heavy armament behind on the mainland. But they knew we were coming. Those of us who have survived have been lucky as hell not to end up in prison camps.'

'That's true, sir.'

'So, General Student has been ordered by OKW to produce a comprehensive report on what happened, including the intelligence failure, as he and we see it. He wants input from each unit involved.'

There was silence for a moment. Leo felt encouraged. This was an interesting development, and he would like to be a part of it.

'Lieutenant, I'd like to designate you coordinator of the Battalion's response, and help me to prepare the report. I recall you took an interest in wireless intercept techniques before the drop on Rotterdam. That's going to be an important element of our report, and fundamental to how the signals intelligence failure is analysed.'

Leo felt immediately interested in what his CO was saying. At the same time, he was unsure whether he was the best man for the job. 'I'd be pleased to do as you have outlined, sir. I just hope I can deliver a report which will help those higher up. To establish what went wrong, that is.'

'I'm sure you will Lieutenant Beckendorf. You will report directly to me on this mission. You'll have a letter of authority signed by me and another from Colonel Ramcke. We only have two weeks. Now, let's have a glass of Sekt.'

⊷⟫⊷⟪⊷

Leo couldn't wait to get stuck into the task. He needed something to take his mind off the reprisals at Kondomari, about which he was still greatly disturbed. In spite of the trauma of the slaughter of two-thirds of his unit on the day of the landing, he couldn't accept the execution of randomly selected civilians. He knew Goering and Student gave the order not only because the Cretan population was showing they weren't going to lie down even when the British were gone. Every indication was they would fight on in savage revenge for the capture of their homeland, unless harsh retribution was taken to show them the consequences. But to him that was morally unacceptable, and might quite likely have the opposite effect. He couldn't help remembering what Rooky said when he invited him and his two school chums, Henri and Bill, for a drink in his study on that last day of term. How they discussed the way the moral law could be suspended in time of war.

⊷⟫⊷⟪⊷

The task even took Leo back to the mainland, to the signals intelligence unit responsible for intercepting enemy communications.

On Crete, he talked to those who interrogated prisoners. The knowledge of the impending attack by parachute troops, the dates predicted, how enemy strength was assessed, was clearly known by the defenders in advance.

The report complete and reviewed by Leo's CO and higher command on the island, it was dispatched to General Student. Shortly afterwards, the Battalion received orders to return to Germany. Elements of the division were to be sent to bolster the German forces laying siege to Leningrad. In his case, after some most welcome leave spent with his family in and around Berlin, he heard he was to be promoted to Captain and posted to Rome, to the headquarters of Wehrmacht Army Group South. Before that, he was to undertake a training course for prospective intelligence officers. From an interview with an officer of the Abwehr, German military intelligence, Leo realized this was to be more than just another course. It was to be his first insight into the secret war.

Lauf, Bavaria, August 1941

A cluster of high wireless masts and some large red brick buildings. It looked unimportant, almost deserted. The Corporal in the guardroom by the wire gate was expecting him. Taken to an office in an administrative building, Leo immediately came to attention. He found himself face to face with a rather unassuming man in the uniform of a lieutenant colonel. The Nazi salute he gave was not always the practice in the *Fallschirmjäger*. Just a reflex action when one encountered a senior officer, probably from Berlin and a Party member,

'Hauptmann Beckendorf,' said the Colonel. 'A pleasure to meet you. My name is Metting. Come over here and make yourself comfortable,' he said, waving an arm towards a table and chairs. The room was stark, nothing on the walls, just a coal stove in the corner. 'Have some coffee.' He poured Leo a cup, and pushed it towards him. 'You may be wondering why you've been sent here, and what this place is.'

'I was handed a written order to report here, sir, but with no explanation. Just before the end of my intelligence officers' course. Before that, I was interviewed by an officer in military intelligence. He seemed to be checking on my background, and my views on the war at this point.'

'Yes, we've been looking for someone for a special assignment. I read your report on the signals intelligence failure before the drop on Crete. I was impressed by your interpretation of what happened. You seem to have the right aptitude for the world I work in. And you're fluent in English.'

Leo was going to say something about his English mother and education, but thought the better of it.

'What we're going to propose, Herr Hauptmann, will place you in an unusual position of trust. Naturally, you've been trained to give nothing away to the enemy, never to take risks in terms of passing on information. But in the role we'd like you to fill, you'll learn of things which you can't speak to anyone about. Not even your loved ones.' He stopped for his words to sink in.

'Yes, sir, I understand that secrecy is paramount.'

'Well then, Captain, let's start at square one, the importance of wireless interception. Without it there would be no code breaking. Cryptology depends on a source of signals information. And to obtain that you must have interception. Places like where we are now.'

'Yes, I can see that,' said Leo, his interest aroused.

'Listening in on the enemy's signals. Signals transmitted when there's no battle under way but the enemy is planning an attack or withdrawal. And when battle has commenced, and the enemy is sending tactical messages between its headquarters and front line units.' The Colonel paused, and Leo thought he would make a point.

'That's certainly a part of operations which interests me, sir. When we dropped on Crete, the British and New Zealanders were much stronger in numbers than our intelligence people predicted. Two-thirds of my battalion were killed on the first day. You read my report. I heard it said the order to go in would never have been given, were the truth known beforehand.'

Metting looked at Leo for a moment, muttering 'Ah, the truth, that's what it's about. My life is all about finding out the truth. And yours will be too,' the Colonel added, as he got up from his chair and started to pace around the room. Somehow he seemed undecided on how far he should take this young officer into his confidence. 'Captain, as you probably realize, signals intercepts are made at varying levels in the enemy's command structure. From learning what spare part is need for an armoured vehicle, to the date on which a major offensive is to be launched. From the replacements needed to bring a platoon up to strength, to the arrival of a new infantry division.'

The Colonel sat down again, poured them both more coffee from the flask on the table. Then suddenly, he switched the conversation to the specific. Leo noticed him tense up, as his hands came together, and there was a strange look in his eyes as he stared hard at the young officer. 'What I'm going to tell you, Captain Beckendorf, is strictly for your ears only.' He waited for the words to sink in.

'I understand, sir, and give you my undertaking that anything you tell me will go no further.'

'Well then, Captain. The difference now is that we have access to information from an independent source. Our signals intelligence is capturing the enemy's strategic planning for its armies in Africa and the Middle East, which we are able to pass on to Field Marshal Kesselring and to General Rommel. It is giving them extraordinary insight into the enemy's strategy, and data on the British order of battle. The information is remarkable, more powerful than any senior commander in the field would dream of receiving.' Metting paused. 'We call it Black Code.'

'Black Code,' repeated Leo. 'Sir, you say this information's from an independent source. I'm unsure what that means. Could you explain something of the background?'

'The source is the US Embassy in Cairo, or rather an official based in that embassy. I'm telling you this because you will need to know.'

'Someone spying for Germany, then?'

'No, on the contrary, the person is transmitting information to Washington in the US diplomatic code without realizing that we are intercepting the traffic, and decoding it.'

'The Black Code,' said Leo.

'Precisely.'

'But how does an official in the American Embassy know all about British military planning and order of battle?' asked Leo.

'Because the British are increasingly relying on new armaments from the United States. That's why they've opened their doors to key American diplomats, told their military commanders to disclose all, the good news and the bad. American equipment is now entering the British 8th Army. Already there are Grant heavy tanks being delivered to British armoured divisions. The gun on the Grant will penetrate the armour of the Panzer III and the larger Panzer IV.'

'That's remarkable,' said Leo, half to himself. 'Remarkable that by breaking the code of a nation we're not at war with, we can learn the critical secrets of our enemy. Can I ask how we got hold of the key to the Black Code?'

'Well,' said the Colonel. 'By a rather simple, almost obvious route. Our ally Italy was most cooperative. They sent two of their Carabinieri-trained break-in specialists into the American Embassy in Rome one night. They picked their way into the safe and pulled out the code books. The next morning our Embassy in the Eternal City was handed the key to the diplomatic cipher of the United States. The Black Code.'

'Good God,' said Leo. 'How long can this go on?'

'Until America and Germany are at war. That would be tomorrow were Roosevelt to have his way. But America's a democracy. There are any number of checks and balances built into their constitution, which hamper the President's freedom of action. Although it can't be long now.'

'So how does all that affect me, if I may ask, Colonel?'

Metting actually smiled, as he took off his small round glasses and rubbed them with his handkerchief. 'Hauptmann Beckendorf, we've decided we need someone with battle experience and an appreciation of the use of signals intelligence, as our eyes in the field. You would be our link with the signals intelligence units reporting to General Rommel. And you would be available should something unexpected happen.'

Leo thought better than to ask what that meant.

The Colonel continued. 'You'll know about General Rommel's success in the Western Desert. The arrival of the Afrika Korps to rescue our Italian allies after their defeat by the British. Everyone's surprise when Rommel attacked even before all his supplies were ashore at Tripoli. He saw the opportunity, and took it. A sudden victory by surprise and daring, causing the Allies to withdraw back to Tobruk.'

'Yes, Colonel, I read all about it. Something to be proud of.'

'Indeed. But there's another factor in Rommel's success. The Afrika Korps' Radio Intercept Company. It's made an outstanding contribution. The British seem to be incapable of radio silence. Their armoured units chatter to one another all the time. Some of their cavalry regiments, armoured reconnaissance units, seem to think they're out fox hunting. They shout hunting jargon over their wireless net. Remember the name Alfred Seebóhm. He commands the Radio Intercept Company.'

Leo listened, fascinated. This was right up his street.

'We would want you to get to know Seebóhm. His information is vital input for Rommel's decisions, but it will never be the complete picture. You would act as coordinator of all sources of intelligence flowing to the General.'

'Including information from the Black Code source,' said Leo.

'Exactly, Captain. And unlike other radio intercept companies you may have run into, Seebóhm's has cipher experts.' He paused. Then came the big question. 'Now, how do you feel about taking this on? As a front line soldier, you'll not be used to being asked, rather you'll have been ordered to take on something. In our case, we want to be sure that our man will be totally committed to the role.'

Leo was silent, digesting the proposition. It would remove him from front line command, the route to promotion. Was it a dead end to his military career? He'd be on his own, not surrounded by friends and colleagues in his regiment of the *Fallschirmjäger*. On the other hand, he found signals intelligence a fascinating field, almost a science.

Metting allowed him time, didn't interrupt his train of thought.

Finally, Leo looked up into the wizened face watching him through the small round rimless glasses.

'I would like to take it on, Colonel. Thank you for explaining the background so openly with me. I believe I can do well for you as well as for General Rommel.'

'Excellent. Let's take a walk around the facility here. Then we'll go and enjoy a good lunch at the Bergerhof, not far from here. I know your next stop is Rome and, in my view, your next boss is the best Commander-in-Chief in the Wehrmacht.'

7

As the taxi pulled out from the railway station and headed south down the familiar road, Bill's mind was on Françoise. Still no news. Her undercover work just swallowed her up. He thought of their first meeting, only a month ago. That evening at the Royal Albert Hall. It was a Free French rally, and de Gaulle was up on stage. Great singing by French from all over Britain, pledged to continue the fight. The invitation came to him from the Secret Service people for whom he'd been flying agents across the Channel. Moon flights, they called them, in the eight-day period around the full moon. They told him he'd met her before, the sister of Henri de Rochefort with whom he'd been at school, the place he was now heading for.

They didn't tell him why she was in London, nor did she. He just worked it out, with the benefit of some hindsight. The car pulled in through the school gates, up the broad drive and into the quadrangle. It felt the same and yet different. The Abbey was as always, imposing and beautiful, in the background. He was sure the services were still performed devoutly and meticulously, as he remembered them. The school, he knew, would be different. He'd heard it was over-spilling with boys from other schools. Additional prefabricated buildings were accommodating the boys evacuated from the preparatory school close to London, and other schools in bombed-out areas. Above all, the mood was sombre. Everyone was haunted by the horror of that

Saturday on the cricket field, nine boys killed, and the student pilot. And the inquest that followed, held in the school gymnasium. Then the court martial which he attended at Devonport, the flying instructor in the leading aircraft pleading guilty to wilful disregard for Admiralty Fleet orders relating to low flying. John Smith was now his friend.

Bill might be able to meet with the Head Master, and perhaps the Abbot. He was there on a personal fact-finding tour, but they probably knew he'd assisted Counsel for the Defendant in making the case for leniency.

As Bill entered the main hall of the school, he passed the school shop and noticed the typed sheet displayed close by, giving latest news of old boys and members of the Abbey community. Lists of deaths and casualties, and those missing. None of his close friends were on there. He wondered what Henri was up to, no news since he'd left for Africa with the Free French. Nor of Leo, of course, since he was on the other side. And what about Rooky? Henri said he was on the Narvik expedition at the start of the war. Perhaps the Monastic Bursar would have more information.

Back outside, walking up towards the monastery, he passed the new wartime buildings. His attention was suddenly grabbed by the monastic graveyard, identical metal crosses over the grave of each monk who'd passed on towards higher things over the past century. What held his gaze were the flowers over new graves, marked temporarily with just single names. These were the boys, he realized, nine of them.

‘It was an awful day. You'll have read about it in the press, but here are some cuttings. Also, photographs, and extracts from Hansard,’ the Bursar said as he pushed a pile across his desk towards Bill. 'The Queen Mother came to present one of the boys with the Scouts' VC, and to lay a wreath. You've seen the new graves?'

'Yes, I just walked past. A tragic sight. I was in the House of Lords Gallery when the accident was discussed. I expect you know I gave advice to the Defendant's Counsel. Because I'm supposed to be an expert on low flying the Hurricane,' he added.

'Yes, of course. I understand perfectly. So the Instructor was severely reprimanded, and dismissed his ship, whatever that means in the Fleet Air Arm.'

'Since there's a war on, I would think he'll be flying again soon. Before this tragedy, he was regarded as one of the best instructors they had. Changing the subject, do you have any news from Dom Brendan Rooker? Henri de Rochefort was in Norway with him, but I've heard nothing since. We were both in his house.'

'He's in the Western Desert, as I understand, now with the Irish Hussars. Must be having a rough time. That's where the action is.'

Bill took his leave from the Bursar. He was due back at Speke, his new posting, after the weekend. In the meantime he would stay in one of the Abbey guest rooms, and eat his meals with the community. The Benedictines were noted for their excellent food, and he wondered what to expect in wartime. Certain to be much better than the boys would be getting, he reasoned. He would walk up to the cricket pavilion and pay his respects to those who perished there only a few months before. After that, he must read his notes on navigation at sea, in readiness for his passing out tests at the Merchant Ship Fighter Unit, MSFU. All being well, the next stop would be the CAM ships, the Catapult Aircraft Merchantmen. Where he hoped he'd be seeing John Smith again.

8

Theresa felt restless as she lay in her bunk, in a cabin she was sharing with two other girls on the female deck. Her long, lithe body didn't fit comfortably in the confined space. They'd been told to remain below until they berthed. Danger of attack from the air. How effective were the large red crosses on the outside of the vessel? Seemed to work during the voyage so far. Those unfortunate boys halfway over, their troopship struck by a torpedo. At least she and the others were able to help when the poor wretches were hauled from the rafts and out of the water.

Sick with sadness, her life and friends abandoned, emotion welled up inside her. Her family even further away. She tried to think of the future, what lay before her in Africa. She knew the risks she'd have to take were nothing compared with certain deportation and slave labour if she'd stayed behind. Several months of being Theresa Krüger, now in the uniform of a Luftwaffe nurse, there was everything to go for. Through the porthole, the beautiful sea front of the city spread out before her, a legacy of pre-war Italian design and engineering.

That meeting with the Reverend Mother would always come back to her. Her welcome, the friendliness, the sympathy. The baptismal certificate of Theresa Krüger, born in Hamburg twenty-five years before. Just two years older than she was. Goodbye Elisabeth Steiner.

'We have the ration cards for food and for clothing,' Reverend Mother said. They were seated in a plain room, just a crucifix on the wall. It seemed so simple. Then the warning. 'Beware of what you say and how you appear, your attitude and manner,' she said. 'Stay clear of complications, keep a low profile. Be positive at your work.' Elisabeth knew the interviews and medical examination would be the most frightening obstacles to her escape. 'Prepare yourself, leave nothing you could trip up on.'

'Now, Theresa,' said Reverend Mother, the first time Elisabeth heard herself being addressed by her new name. 'We have a nun here, Sister Agnes, who can help you. She'll suggest your background story. She knows the difficult questions. You can trust her, and learn from her. She's an experienced nurse from the last war.'

As Reverend Mother went out to find this person, it suddenly struck the new Theresa that she mightn't be the first to be helped by these lovely people.

Reverend Mother returned after a few moments, followed by a tall stern-faced nun, well into middle age. She made the introductions, and then departed with the priest. Theresa was left alone with Sister Agnes, who did actually smile as she poured out coffee for the two of them, saying 'Reverend Mother has explained to me what you are doing, Theresa. Let's start with the change in your identity.'

'Thank you, Sister,' said Elisabeth.

Sister Agnes sat back in her chair, stroking the large crucifix on the front of her habit. 'Let me suggest how to create your cover. The story behind Theresa Krüger. Most of the usual questions about parents will not apply, since you hardly knew them. Your father, Theresa, was killed in 1918 at the battle of Amiens when you were only one year old. Your mother died a year later in the great flu epidemic.'

Elisabeth was enthralled, discovering the person she was becoming. This from a woman of the world, not just the stern, middle-aged nun who introduced herself.

'You were not adopted. Just after the war ended, there was starvation in Germany. The house of our Order in Hamburg agreed to take you in. We have the original records. You grew up with other orphans at a home we maintained close to the Convent, and you went through a Catholic schooling. You were brought up a Catholic, as I understand.' The nun's face showed up her age, years of hard work, but the lines gave way to a warmth which reassured Elisabeth.

'Yes, so I took part in the religious lessons and ceremonies when at school.'

'So that's the background story, where you came from, Theresa Krüger. You are a fine girl. Taller than most, but slim, and elegant in your movements. Attractive, and with your fair hair you aren't obviously Jewish to look at.' She paused, evidently hoping she was helping the young girl's confidence. 'Now, tell me how you came to be a trained nurse. Then we can decide how to dress it up for the interviewing officer. I understand you're thinking of joining the Luftwaffe.' The nun sat back, smiling, hands clasped in her lap.

'My father was a professor of medicine and research chemist at Freiburg University. When Hitler came to power and the Nuremberg laws were passed, he and my mother knew it was only a matter of time. He would have his job taken away, to be given to a non-Jew. He already had close links with the Pasteur Institute in Paris. His special interest was vaccines. At the time, the French were expanding their plantations in Indo-China, rubber in particular, and they offered him a position devoted to anti-malarial vaccines, sponsored by the tyre company Michelin.'

'Interesting. And what about you?' said the nun.

'I was just finishing my college education here in Munich, and was interested in medicine. My father knew the Director of the American Hospital in Neuilly, on the edge of Paris. The Director was originally a military surgeon from Baltimore, who came over to help the British Army in France early in the last war. I did two years there, training to be a nurse, and received my diploma. They made me learn English also.' She stopped, thinking whether to mention it. 'My training included the treatment of casualties from chemical warfare. My father wanted me to learn how to handle that. He seemed to know a lot about it, and helped me himself.'

'I see,' said Sister Agnes. 'After the gas used in the trenches in the 1914 War, the medical services would have to be ready if it happened again. How terrible.'

'Then, rather stupidly and against my father's wishes, I returned to Germany with ideas of becoming a doctor.'

'I'm impressed,' said the nun, her natural sternness giving way to a broad smile. 'What happened to your family when war broke out?'

'My father faced a dilemma. His work by then was very important to the French. He knew a lot, not only about vaccines, but about the use of chemical agents which could be used in warfare. He didn't want to leave France but after Pétain's deal with Hitler, the Vichy French government also classified him as a Jew. It would be madness to return here and face being sent to a concentration camp. His American friend spoke to someone in the US Embassy, and the offer of a professorship at Baltimore came through quickly. The United States still being a neutral country meant there wouldn't be any immigration problems.'

The nun looked intently at Elisabeth. 'Chemical warfare, Theresa. So far that hasn't happened, praise be to God. How did you know of his involvement in that?'

'I overheard a conversation late one night at home in Paris. My father, and a visitor trying to persuade him to leave France which was now an ally of Germany. You see, I think he thought of his research, his work, as above politics. Politics was not his concern. He thought everyone should have access to his research. In that way, governments would come to the same conclusion, that the consequences were too terrible for either side to run the risk.'

Theresa, as she now was, paused. 'So he must have decided to take the advice. After I returned to Munich, that was. He and my mother and younger sister, boarded a vessel at Le Havre and just went, to America. They asked me to join them, but I refused. My life was here and that was it. Call it foolishness, but at my age I just trusted my luck. Now I realise what a mistake I made. I'm an obstinate person, Sister.'

'I see. So there's no problem of next of kin making enquiries when you disappear, Theresa.'

'That's right. And I heard that the Luftwaffe needs nurses for North Africa, female as well as male.'

Suddenly the question came. 'How can you reconcile fighting for the Nazis with their treatment of the Jews?' The nun was now deadly serious.

'I'm German. I love Germany. I hate the Nazis, but as a nurse I will be playing my part in helping our soldiers and airmen. And of course, it's a solution to my big problem. How otherwise do I avoid deportation?'

'What about your qualifications?' asked the nun.

'I intend to keep to my true story of training at the American Hospital in Paris. The Director there is still the same one, my father's friend. He's stuck to his job, and America remains neutral. I think he'll agree to re-issue my nursing diploma in my new name, Theresa Krüger. My father told me before he left, that he would ask him to remember me, in case I needed help. He knows we're of Jewish origin.'

'Well, I don't know what to say,' exclaimed the nun. 'You're certainly bold.'

'Achtung! Achtung! Bitte aussteigen.' The ship's public address system blared out, ordering all to prepare to disembark. Theresa Krüger was up on deck in no time, kit bag dragged behind her, thankful to be out in the open and stand in line with the other nurses. Still early morning, the heat was building up. Hats on the side of their heads gave little protection from a blazing sun. Libyan Arab dockhands were securing the lines as the hospital ship made fast alongside the wharf. Trucks stood ready to transport them and their baggage to her new home, Tripoli.

'Find yourself chairs, everyone. I'm going to give you some background to the fighting out here.' The Luftwaffe officer was really good-looking, thought Theresa, as she sat next to a couple of her new friends from the voyage over. A young captain, probably even younger than he looked, the officer moved across to a map bearing small coloured flags and lines drawn in wax crayon.

'The desert war moves quickly, it's hard to know where the front line is sometimes. The airfields change hands frequently, and our forward dressing stations are always on the move. You'll start here in Tripoli, in the Wehrmacht military hospital. You have to get used to the climate and the food. Life is different out here.' There was a rustle of expectation among the nurses.

The Captain continued. 'When we arrived last January, General Rommel went on the attack immediately. The British had pushed our Italian allies out of most of Libya, and were surprised the Afrika Korps went into action so soon after arriving. We took them unawares. Our advance was spectacular, into Cyrenaica and almost to the Egyptian frontier, although the enemy held on to the port of Tobruk.'

She'd heard of Tobruk in reports on German radio and knew it was a prize they needed to win, to shorten the supply lines for the Afrika Korps.

'There have been two major enemy counterattacks since then, the British called them Battleaxe and Crusader. General Rommel hit back and we recovered most of the territory we gave up. The front line is now at Gazala, and the Egyptian frontier's not far beyond. The distances are immense, and supply lines stretch for hundreds of kilometres.'

'Any questions at this point?' There was silence. Theresa felt the excitement of being a part of Rommel's campaign, and yet the inherent conflict raged within her. She knew she would do whatever it took to win the battle ahead. Yet, ultimately this would be for Hitler and his thugs. Somehow Germany has to pass through this period, and come out of it with new leadership and fair and moral government. Meanwhile, she must remember not to draw attention to herself, not try to be praised more than the others. Just to belong, to be convinced she was doing her best. Not to be noticed for being exceptional, just recognized as part of a winning team.

The Captain went on. 'It's tough as hell for our men, Luftwaffe included. Sand flies drive everyone crazy and can cause infections. Men get sick from their salty drinking water. There are sandstorms and relentless heat. Both sides respect the Geneva Convention. If water's short, the prisoners receive the same as our support units, and the principle of equality is the same in our forward dressing stations.' He stopped to let it all sink in. The room was silent. 'When the Wehrmacht advanced into Russia, the supply to Afrika Korps of replacement tanks and aircraft reduced. The situation has improved recently, and both sides are preparing for battle along the line from Gazala on the north coast, down to Bir Hakeim in the south.' He pointed to the almost vertical line drawn on the map, between these two points.

Theresa glanced around the room, then back at the Captain. She realized this was somehow freedom. Freedom from the threat she'd felt every hour of the day and night in Munich. All right, she was in a military unit, bound to obey orders. But that spelt freedom to her.

9

Beirut, October 1941

The sound of American dance music filtered out into the street. The Lieutenant, tall and lean in uniform of the French Foreign Legion, looked hard at the powerfully built doorman with a red fez on his head. The fez bowed, and Henri strode into the night club.

'Monsieur, we are honoured to welcome you to the Club Shahrizad,' said the maître d', walking towards him with the look of expectation you would expect from someone who just lost most of his clients. 'Have you come to join friends, or can I find you a table?'

'I'm on my own,' said Henri.

The maître d' took him across the floor to a small table with two chairs. The band was starting to play a Jerome Kern number, as a waiter appeared. Henri ordered a Scotch Perrier, and surveyed the scene. A month before there must have been German officers enjoying themselves here, he thought. He knew that after his regiment and the Australians took Damascus, the Vichy troops occupying Lebanon and Syria made their way back to Algeria and Morocco. Only a valuable few decided to join the Free French. The Germans were probably back in Greece.

He was just lifting the glass when she walked out across the dance floor, in the direction of the band. His arm froze in the air for a moment. The glass got no further. Maybe it was how she walked, the way her body moved under the strapless evening gown. Or her voice as she turned around, took the microphone and started to sing.

'Fish got to swim and birds got to fly, I got to love one man till I die.'

He felt suddenly alive, entranced. Something locked his attention onto her. Nothing else mattered in that instant. Then, the spell broke, shattered by a voice beside him.

'Hello, my name's Sarah, I work here.'

He swung round, only at this moment noticing the girl now sitting in the other chair at his table. Black hair, olive skin, a great smile.

'Oh I'm so sorry,' he said, half getting to his feet. 'I didn't notice you come over. I love this sort of music. And the singer, well, she's magic. I've been away from this kind of thing for a long time.'

'Oh, that's okay. I meet all sorts in this job.'

'Do you mean you work here?'

'That's right. I dance with the clients. Especially the men on their own, like you. In romantic uniforms,' she added.

His eyes were back on the singer, who was ending the number, 'Can't stop loving that man of mine.'

'I can see you're more interested in her than me.' There was a distant look in Sarah's eyes.

'I'm sorry. Do you know her?'

'Of course, she's half French, half Lebanese. Her name is Yasmin.'

The band moved into a swing number.

'Come and dance with me,' said Sarah. 'It'll only cost you a glass of champagne. You must have earned one yourself,' she said, looking at the Free French Cross of Lorraine on Henri's Legion tunic.

They walked out onto the dance floor. There were some other couples dancing now. She moved in close to him. He couldn't remember how long it was since he'd danced with a girl. Must have been in London last summer, before they embarked with the British to head for Dakar. He felt her hand on the back of his neck, her cheek rub gently against his. The bottom of her tummy moved softly up against his crotch, and pressed itself into him. The sweet musky scent of her engulfed his senses. Somehow the tension and harshness of months of physical strain, the demands for courage in the sharp firefights, melted away.

Nothing was said until they were outside the club. He felt this girl called Sarah take his arm and walk him into the back streets of Beirut. It hardly seemed a moment before she opened the door into an apartment block and started to climb the stairs. A couple of floors up, she opened her bag, taking out a key, letting them into a small apartment.

'Is this where you live?' Rather an unnecessary question he thought, as he said it. There was a small hallway with a couple of doors leading off it. 'You know they warn us about this sort of thing in the army. We issue the men with *capotes anglaises*. I don't have any.'

She laughed. 'Chéri, you won't need anything like that. I'm just here to pleasure you.' She poured him a whisky, watching quietly while he took a gulp. 'Come over here, and I'll show you.'

Henri moved towards her. He felt her hands on his chest as she undid his tunic, tie and shirt. He tightened his grip around her waist, as she undid the buttons of his trousers and eased them off him. 'Put your hands round my head,' she said. He felt the soft rich dark hair, and stroked it. 'Push downwards gently,' she whispered. Her head slowly moved down his bare chest and tummy, and lower. He felt it stop at the hair, and her lips nuzzle up against him. He gasped.

'You like that, don't you Chéri,' she said quietly, her hands stroking the bottom of his back.

The open jeep sped along the narrow road, Sarah's sleek black hair streaming behind them. The beach spread out below in a band of pale gold, beyond it the azure of the eastern Mediterranean.

'Over there,' she said, pointing towards some large rocks, with water and a small beach just inshore from them.

He parked above, and helped her down with the large basket she'd produced when he collected her outside the apartment house that morning.

The softness of the sand under foot was a delight, as they found a place of their own. He poured out the Lebanese red wine as she produced local cheese and French bread from the basket.

'Delicious,' he exclaimed. 'What more could a soldier on leave ask for?'

'Now, there are hard-boiled eggs and some of our special Muscat grapes,' she said, one hand diving back into the basket.

Afterwards, they lay on their backs until it was too hot. 'Come on,' said Henri, and they dived into the almost still water. Back close to her on the large towel, he thought about Sarah. How he liked her. A professional, but something more, he felt. He didn't want to hurt her. But he'd decided in the couple of days since they met in the club, that he must find out more about the Shahrizad's entrancing singer.

'Yasmin, tell me about her. That's if you don't mind.'

There was a pause, before she spoke. 'Yasmin, yes. I can talk to you about her.' The way she said it was restrained, as though she was on guard. Not jealousy, but something else seemed to be making her tread carefully.

'You might not think so, but Yasmin is a posh lady. She was married to an officer in the Fusiliers Marins, the French marines. He was killed in the defence of Calais. I suppose you know about that.'

'Yes. They held out in the Citadel, fighting to the last man, alongside those light infantry the British call the Green Jackets. Truly brave, although the same couldn't be said of some of the other people there.'

'Yasmin worked in the American Embassy. Still does, but she's at Shahrizad in the evenings.'

'Why's that?'

'She just loves singing to American dance music, has a passion about it.'

'Does she have a passion for anything else?' he said, rather pointedly.

'Now then, chéri. You don't stand a chance. Yasmin's a big-time girl. There's an older chap who picks her up in a swanky car, Studebaker, I think.'

'Oh. What does he do?'

'Merchant, or something like that. Travels a lot, it seems. France, even Germany she once let slip although I don't think he'll be going there any more.

'Sarah, I know this sounds awful, but I've been challenged by my Legion friends to take her out to dinner. Apparently, none of our lot has managed it yet.'

'You're sure it stops at dinner? I'd watch out if I were you. She's quite capable of pulling a gun on you.'

He was taking a chance. But if it worked, she'd be bowled over, and he would be a hero. There was to be a Regimental Ball, given by the 13th Demi-Brigade French Foreign Legion, for Beirut potentates and their wives and any girlfriends the officers could conjure up. The regimental band didn't exist any more, so the plan was to borrow dance band musicians from Shahrizad, and their friends.

He wasn't telling Sarah anything about it. She knew he'd got to know Yasmin. It was thanks to her gallantly bringing the singer over to their table at the club one evening, and introducing him. When it happened, he felt the allure of that extraordinary woman spread over him. Why did she have that effect? She was older, obviously sophisticated, yet seemed somehow to connect with him. Sarah tactfully rose and moved on to another table.

As Yasmin spoke, her large eyes were inquiring. The blonde hair was held with ribbon behind her neck, then down over a bare shoulder. The dress tonight had thin straps with sequins over the shoulders. As she leant forward, it sagged into a deep cleavage.

'So, Lieutenant, tell me about yourself. The Légion étrangère has such a romantic reputation.'

'Not what you see on the screen, Yasmin. More hard slog and hellish training. Our legionnaires come from everywhere, even Germany. Socialists and communists escaping from the fascists, from Hitler and Franco. We're infantry, of course, so no horses, no tanks. Unusually, our Colonel is a White Russian, but the rest of us officers are French.'

'I've heard of him. Don't you call him Amilak?'

'Yes, short for Amilakvari.'

'Where have you been since the war started. Someone said your unit, 13 DBLE isn't it, was actually in Norway? That seems weird.'

'Yes, we were surprised when they told us. First of all, it was to be Finland. Then the Finns were forced into submission by the Russians. So we sailed with the British to a port up in the north of Norway, called Narvik.'

'And I suppose that ended when the Germans invaded France in May last year.' Yasmin clearly took an interest in these things, thought Henri.

'Yes. I decided to listen to de Gaulle, and stayed in England. We went to Dakar, what a mess that was. De Gaulle thought Senegal would welcome them with open arms. Instead, the Royal Navy nearly lost a battleship. The British pushed off back home. The Free French forces and de Gaulle sailed on down to Douala in the Cameroon, to meet up with Leclerc.'

'Remarkable man, Leclerc, from what I've heard,' said Yasmin. 'He's in fact a French aristocrat, you know, a Count. But changed his name after escaping from the Vichy lot. They condemned him to death as a traitor, and he wanted to protect his family who are still in France.'

'Yes, hence the name change,' said Henri. 'Anyway, we kicked our heels down there until we suddenly embarked on the long sea voyage around the Cape, and up to Eritrea on the Red Sea. The British were confronting Italian forces. We fought hard at Keren and Massawa, as part of the British victory. It helped our reputation no end. So when General Maitland Wilson launched the attack on Syria and Lebanon, we helped to lead the charge.' Henri noticed Yasmin was watching him and listening intently.

'Wasn't there a drama when you faced the Vichy French defences as you approached Damascus?' she asked. 'An Australian officer told me something about it the other day.'

'There certainly was. We found we were facing another unit of the Legion, one which was part of Vichy French forces. It was intolerable that the two of us should fight one another.

Understand that the Légion étrangère is unique. It's the only regiment that doesn't swear allegiance to France. It swears allegiance to itself. That, in spite of the officers coming from Saint-Cyr, almost all being French.'

'So, what happened?'

'Colonel Amilakvari, who took over from Magrin-Vernerey after Keren, ordered our bugler to sound 'Le Boudin'. After a few bars, he stopped and there was silence. Then, back came the same call sign from a Legion bugler on the other side. The two COs met. It was agreed there would be a ceasefire for twenty-four hours, and the Vichy forces then withdrew leaving Damascus to us. That way, the other side didn't lose face.' He gave her a wry smile.

Yasmin held his gaze, as she touched his hand. 'Oh, so gallant,' she said, shaking her head so the blonde hair fell further back on her bare shoulders.

Henri waited for his moment, then let Yasmin into the plan for his Regiment's Ball. They needed advice about whom to invite. Having made notes of the names and positions of those she seemed ready to suggest, he took the plunge. 'Will you come as my guest?'

She gave him a long curious look. 'Well, what an interesting invitation. Of course I will.' A bridge was crossed. Game on, he said to himself.

~·~

The dinner and speeches over, the band was in full swing. Amilak was doing his duty with the wife of the Mayor, no mean task. After a quickstep or two, they returned to the top table. Henri and Yasmin returned to theirs. The predictable was about to happen, Henri said to himself. Amilak was heading for their table. The Colonel nodded to Henri, introducing himself to Yasmin and asking her to dance. Yasmin looked at Henri, smiled, and rose to accompany Amilak onto the floor. The vivid green silk of her long dress shimmered under the giant chandelier. One of Henri's fellow officers across their table raised his eyebrows, giving him a look of resignation.

He didn't have to worry. Yasmin was back after a couple of numbers, and Henri knew he was still in the game. After a few dances, they walked out onto the terrace of the palace hired for the ball. The scent in the wind wafted across to them. 'That must be jasmine,' whispered Henri in her ear, and she squeezed his arm, pressing herself lightly against him.

'I can't imagine anything being more romantic than being here with you,' he said.

'Oh, Henri, what film's that line from?' There was a real spark in her sense of humour. He warmed to it, a promise of mischief, or was it somehow a warning? Mystery certainly attached to Yasmin.

⟶⟵

'There's someone I want you to meet.' Henri was surprised to hear her on the phone the next morning. Lucky he was still on leave, but already up and around the small villa he was sharing with two fellow officers, their dogs running around his feet.

'Of course,' replied Henri. 'Where and when?'

'There's a bar called Metro, on Maarad street,' said Yasmin. 'Come this evening at seven. Walk in through the bar and into the room at the back.'

'Can you tell me something about this person?'

'No, not on the phone. Come a little earlier, and I'll explain before he arrives.'

⟶⟵

Henri found his way through to the back of the Bar Metro. Certainly one of the smarter places to meet in Beirut. That was Yasmin, he thought, she wouldn't settle for anything less. Then he saw her, on one of the stools at a round table. She was reading an old French newspaper and smoking black Turkish from a silver cigarette holder. A bucket of ice on the table, and a bottle of mineral water. He kissed her on both cheeks, and said how great she looked. That earned him another kiss.

A waiter came up to them. They ordered a bottle of Château Musar, which arrived immediately and was poured out without any question of tasting.

'Chéri, you'll like Ahmed,' she said. 'He's a shareholder in Club Shahrizad. Rather secretive. A dealer of some sort. No one seems to know exactly what he deals in. He asked me about the ball the other night, and when I mentioned you in conversation, he seemed to know about your unit. He said he wanted to meet you.'

'I can't see what he'd find interesting in me,' said Henri. 'I'm not an arms dealer, you know.'

'Perhaps he wants to sell some to you,' said Yasmin. They laughed at that.

She looked back towards the entrance. 'Ah, here he is.'

A striking pale-skinned man, tall and dressed in a Western suit clearly cut by a good tailor. He could even be an actor, thought Henri, looking at the white trilby.

'Yasmin, my darling,' he said, embracing her. 'And Lieutenant de Rochefort. I'm so honoured to meet you. Everyone's talking about the Free French forces here.'

'There aren't so many of us, Monsieur, but we like to punch above our weight,' said Henri. 'Have a glass of this excellent wine, or perhaps something else?'

'Do call me Ahmed, Lieutenant, everyone does. I usually take an Arak at this time each day,' he said, looking at the waiter who was standing waiting. 'With some of that ice. I walked from my office.'

'Ahmed,' said Yasmin, 'your office is only round the corner.'

Ahmed grinned, and moved on. 'It's been a busy day. I have business in Egypt, but it's so difficult to get anything done. The controls on movement are tough.' The waiter brought the Arak, and Ahmed added some ice. Taking a sip, he said 'Lieutenant, when do you leave for Egypt?'

Henri showed his surprise. 'Forgive me, but it's not the practice to discuss movement of military units when there's a war on. I have to obey the rules,' he said rather stiffly.

'But there aren't any rules in Beirut, Lieutenant de Rochefort. And it's easy to deduce that now you have liberated Syria and Lebanon, the way is clear for you to join the British 8th Army. I'm sure they'll welcome troops of your calibre with open arms.'

'That's very flattering, Ahmed, but you'll appreciate I'm just a junior officer among many. I'm not told the big picture and, even if I was free to speak with outsiders, I'd have little knowledge of what's in the minds of our commanders.'

Ahmed was silent for a moment. 'I understand, forgive me. I always leap to the point, and push out the boundaries. It's a failing I have.' He seemed to bring himself to the point he wanted to make. 'Lieutenant, I deal in artefacts, and am something of an expert on icons. That is, icons of the Eastern Orthodox churches. I operate in a very private market, and that requires me to travel. As you can imagine, travel between countries is now very difficult. No one trusts anyone when there's a war on.'

'I can well imagine that,' said Henri.

'The immediate problem I have is with this client in Cairo. I have an ancient icon which I have to get to him. I was thinking that you, Lieutenant, might be persuaded to take it with you when you head in that direction.'

Henri didn't know how to respond. What if he was found with the thing in his baggage? He could be accused of smuggling contraband into a war zone? While he was trying to find an excuse not to help, Ahmed continued.

'The icon used to belong to the Monastery of St Catherine in Sinai. The Russians took it in the last century. I bought it from a Polish officer here, because I have a client in Cairo who I know will buy it if I can get it to him. He's a wealthy philanthropist dedicated to returning valuable artefacts to where they belong.'

'What will he do with it?' Yasmin suddenly said.

'Why, he will give it back to St Catherine's Monastery. That's the sort of thing he does.'

Henri was not a naturally suspicious person. But he wondered how authentic all this was. He was conscious that Ahmed was looking at him intently. Was he reading Henri's thoughts. Was he testing him to see whether it was a problem of principle to the French Legionnaire? Or was it a matter of price, of a fee?

'How big is the icon?' said Henri. 'What is it an image of?'

'About half a metre in height. Of St Catherine of Alexandria, with her left hand resting on the wheel she was tied to.'

'It would be difficult, and I'm unsure I can take the risk. If I were found to be carrying contraband, I could lose my commission.'

There was a long silence. Yasmin broke it. 'Suppose it were to be accompanied by a letter from the Patriarch of Antioch? He is head of the Maronite Church here. Maybe he would be willing to authenticate your mission, expressing thanks to you for delivering the sacred icon to its proper owner, via Ahmed's client in Cairo?'

'Of course,' said Ahmed. 'That surely would be the perfect *laissez-passer*. Could you arrange that, chérie?'

'I don't see why not. The Patriarch has always been close to my family. I'd be happy to try.'

Turning to Henri, Ahmed said 'My client is somewhat idiosyncratic. He lives on a houseboat. I would give you the address, easy to find. What do you say?'

Henri was distracted imperceptibly by Yasmin. So far, for instance at the ball and when he took her home afterwards, she drew back. Now, somehow, she was signalling to him that this might change. What was it? Just a movement, her hand very lightly on his thigh. The look she was giving him. He could not decide. 'Ahmed, let me think about it. I'll tell you tomorrow whether I can take the risk.'

He saw Ahmed breathe in deeply. 'Lieutenant Henri, you are an understanding person. And a prudent one. A person I can trust. He paused, smiling. Now, I propose we go to a small restaurant, Lebanese cooking and, to prepare you for Cairo, just the possibility of some belly dancing.'

10

'Ah, Hauptmann Beckendorf, I heard about the exploits of you and your *Fallschirmjäger* friends at Crete. A cruel affair, terrible losses. But you took the island, when it looked like you were doomed. I'm pleased to have you in my new team here.'

Leo was at attention, his brain on high alert, as the great man spoke to him. He'd already met Kesselring briefly after the taking of Rotterdam, Leo's first experience of action. Now the newly appointed Oberbefehlshaber Sud, Commander-in-Chief of the German forces in Southern Europe and the Mediterranean, was establishing his HQ just southeast of the Eternal City. The great man moved on to welcome other new arrivals.

As everyone took their seats, a hush fell over the room. Kesselring walked over to a map of the Mediterranean between Italy and North Africa.

'Gentlemen, first of all some background. You'll appreciate that following the armistice with France, the French overseas possessions remained under the administration of the new French government led by Maréchal Pétain. At the beginning of June this year, British and Commonwealth troops invaded Syria, and marched on Beirut and Damascus. Britain was reacting to the Luftwaffe's use of Vichy French airfields in Syria. By all accounts the Vichy French forces fought hard but were outnumbered, and so that sphere of Vichy influence has evaporated. Is everyone with me?'

There was a chorus in the affirmative. The Field Marshal continued.

'General Rommel and his Afrika Korps came to the rescue of our Italian ally in Libya early this year. Rommel soon detected a weakening in British firepower as they transferred troops and armour to Greece, and rapidly took the initiative and pushed them back. However, the British and Australians have held on to Tobruk, and we badly need that port to supply the Afrika Korps. The distances over there are immense, and as General Rommel advances over hundreds of kilometres, the problem grows massively, particularly in fuel for his panzers. We could be in Cairo in a short time, ready to take the Suez Canal, Iraq and the oil the Reich so badly needs. But the British have the strongest naval forces in the Mediterranean, and the supply ships to Rommel's ports of entry are highly vulnerable.'

Kesselring paused, changing to a smaller-scale map of the Mediterranean from Sicily to Libya.

'It's the island of Malta which fascinates me. So small, but astride our shipping lanes to Africa. It's from there that the British naval commander Admiral Cunningham can launch surface and submarine attacks on our supply ships. The Italian Regia Aeronautica have been attempting to destroy the massive port facilities on Malta. Our submarines operating from Taranto have just sunk the battleship *Barham*. The Luftwaffe Fliegerkorps II will be in Sicily shortly, but I have my doubts as to whether air and submarine attack will deliver the solution. The British are not fighting in Russia like we are, and they can concentrate much of their resources down here. One way or the other they will hold on to the Middle East, unless.' He paused. 'Unless we take Malta.'

There was total silence for a brief moment, and then spontaneous clapping.

The Commander-in-Chief went into some detail on related matters, and the conference then ended. As Leo rose to leave, a familiar face came towards him, and he jumped to attention and saluted. 'Colonel Metting, sir,' he said.

'Captain, we meet again. I must say, this is a more inspiring place than that listening station at Lauf.'

'Yes, sir, except for the Bavarian mountains, and that splendid lunch you gave me.'

'It was a pleasure. Now, could you please come with me, the Field Marshal wants to speak with us.'

Leo was immediately on guard. Why would Kesselring want to speak with him, surely he had more important people to see? His mind searched for traps, mistakes he might have made back from when he was commissioned.

⊶⊷

Metting led Leo to a small office and as they entered, Kesselring looked up from a table he was seated at and gestured to them to join him.

'Gentlemen, I hope my presentation just now was of use to you in understanding the big picture and where our objectives lie. Captain Beckendorf, officially you have been posted here with the Ramcke team to train the newly established Italian parachute troops, their "Folgore Division". Folgore means "lightning" and the division will include airborne troops originally trained in Libya before the war. Major-General Ramcke is arriving soon to take command and you and selected *Fallschirmjäger* will assist him and conduct the training jointly with Italian instructors.'

Leo knew better than to ask what the strategic objective of the new force would be, but from the earlier reference to Malta, it was clear to him that the island was at the top of the list.

'Captain, I'm aware that Colonel Metting has already discussed with you an intelligence assignment. Monitoring signals interception in Libya and Egypt will be interesting, to say the least. However, I have an additional job for you, which also involves total secrecy. By total secrecy, I mean that only you, Colonel Metting and myself will know anything about what I'm referring to.'

Leo was intrigued, pleased that he'd been selected for some special task in addition to what Metting previously described to him at the Lauf station. He merely said 'I understand, Field Marshal.'

Kesselring gestured to the Colonel.

'Colonel Metting is Second-in-Command of the OKW/Chiffrierabteilung, the High Command's cryptologic centre. Colonel, please could you explain the project to Captain Beckendorf.'

The Colonel removed his steel-rimmed spectacles. He looked hard at Leo, his face showing no sign of emotion and, as he started to speak, it was in a monotone as though a machine was talking.

'Captain, you'll be aware of the method by which coded messages are sent between commanders and field operations in the Wehrmacht. We call the encoding process "Enigma". It is generally believed that it's impossible for the enemy to break the codes generated by the Enigma machines. The sending and receiving of these messages takes time because they are transmitted in Morse.'

Leo nodded his head. 'Yes, I've had personal experience of the operation of Enigma transmissions.'

Metting sat back in his chair, his arms folded. He glanced at Kesselring, then back to Leo. 'Captain, not everyone in the Wehrmacht accepts that the Enigma codes cannot in some way be broken, even though they are generated at random by the rotors and key settings of the Enigma machines. Several such machines have been recovered by the British from our surface ships and U-boats.' He paused, then continued. 'Partly for that reason, and partly because a more rapid transmission system is required, the German High Command, OKW, has had a new system developed for its own use by C. Lorenz AG in Berlin. Lorenz has designed a machine called the SZ-40, and we have two of them on test here at the Headquarters of Army Group South. They are called Geheimschreiber, or Secret Writer.'

Kesselring interjected at this point. 'Thank you, Colonel, and I know that you want to show the Captain the machines and explain how they work. Before you do that, I have a little more to say to our friend here.'

Leo stiffened.

'Captain Beckendorf, the High Command proposes to employ the Geheimschreiber system solely for communications between the Führer's OKW and his most senior commanders in the field. There's to be such a link between OKW and me here in Rome. I want you to assume overall responsibility for its security. You will instruct the Lorenz representative here, and the small number of military personnel directly involved, on how the facility is to be protected. And when the time comes for us to leave Rome, you will arrange for its safe removal to my new HQ. It's imperative that a Geheimschreiber does not fall into the hands of the enemy. If a machine cannot be evacuated, then it must be destroyed so that the enemy can't reconstruct it. You'll have direct access to me on all related matters. No one is to have any knowledge of the installation and its purpose, other than those authorized personally by me. Is that absolutely clear?'

Deep down in himself, Leo understood that any failure on his behalf would be the end of his career as an officer. Kesselring could not have made the position clearer. 'Yes, Field Marshal, I understand perfectly' was his response.

With that, Kesselring rose, shook hands with Leo and the Colonel, and departed. Metting turned to Leo and said, 'Let's go and inspect the installation, and I'll introduce you to the engineer from Lorenz.'

They walked out of the main HQ building and towards a bunker about four hundred metres away, ostensibly built for air raid protection. They entered and the Colonel led Leo down a short passageway. With his own key, he unlocked a door and went into a room without windows. In the centre of the room were two tables and on each stood a machine. An Army Signals NCO stood beside each machine. A technician in a white coat bearing his employer's name, C. Lorenz AG, came forward to greet them.

The Colonel started to explain.

'These are the new Geheimschreiber machines, one for sending and one for receiving. As you will observe, the basis of the machine is a teleprinter. Regular teleprinters are connected by land-line, but the SZ-40 is connected to OKW by wireless. The code is generated at the sending end and read at the receiving end by these in-line encryption devices.' He pointed out the machine's twelve rotors. The messages are typed up in clear with a paper tape perforator, and then fed at high speed into the teleprinter. The encoded messages can be sent and received much faster than if Morse transmissions were used, as happens with Enigma. In every link, such as this one between OKW and Army Group South, there are four machines - two at each end, one for sending and one for receiving.' He then performed a demonstration of the process.

Leo asked a number of questions. Reflecting that he was now responsible for the security of the installation in all its aspects, he said to the Colonel, 'Would the capture of an SZ-40 in itself compromise the integrity of such an advanced coding system?'

Metting ran his hand over his face, clearly considering his response. 'Possession of the machine wouldn't in itself enable the enemy to interpret the messages. However, knowledge of how it was constructed and the method by which messages were input and encoded could help solve the codes if procedures weren't strictly followed by the operators. For example, should a message be repeated without altering the rotor settings, and the content of the message amended, then it could theoretically be possible for a third party to break the code.'

Leo thought through the devastating consequences an interception of Geheimschreiber messages could have, should the enemy learn the strategic intentions of the Führer and OKW before a major offensive. Responsibility for safeguarding these machines was one thing, but knowing that if he failed then conceivably the Führer's most secret messages might be read by the enemy, was more than horrifying.

⊷⊷⊙⊶⊶

Clearly, Metting was not finished with Leo. They were seated again in the room where they met with Kesselring an hour earlier. 'There's something else I should advise you of, Captain, so you have the full picture of our intelligence capability in the Mediterranean theatre. I explained to you at Lauf about OKW/ Chi's interception of American diplomatic messages, via the Black Code. And the Afrika Korps' signals intercept capability. Field Marshall Kesselring just charged you with securing his Lorenz messaging link with OKW. To complete the matrix, I need to take you into our confidence on what the Kriegsmarine has been doing.'

Leo was surprised. Why would they want to involve him in matters naval? He'd never had anything to do with the German Navy. His surprise must have showed.

Metting continued. 'I expect you remember the invasion of Norway, just before the *Blitzkrieg* and your parachute drop into Holland.'

'Yes, I certainly do,' said Leo.

'Well, while the British and French were withdrawing from Norway, in spite of taking Narvik, the Kriegsmarine and Royal Navy were fighting it out. The culmination of these naval battles was the sinking of the British aircraft carrier *Glorious*. The British put this disaster down to bad luck, that *Glorious* and her two destroyers had run into our battleships *Scharnhorst* and *Gneisenau*. The truth is different, although a closely guarded secret. Let me tell you.'

Metting got up and started pacing the room, before continuing. 'The signals interception and code-breaking department of the Kriegsmarine is known as B-Dienst. They started to break the codes used by the British navy before the war started. The claim that *Scharnhorst* saw the smoke from the *Glorious* on the horizon and closed in and sank her by gunfire, is only the end of the story. What really happened is that B-Dienst picked up the position of *Glorious* by intercepting and decoding Royal Navy signals.'

'I see,' said Leo.

'She was there originally to fly off Hurricane fighters which were to land on Norwegian airfields. Later, to take them off again because of the British withdrawal. B-Dienst was tracking her. After she was sunk, Goebbels made fantastic propaganda, even showing in German cinemas newsreel of the sinking,'

Leo knew what this could mean. 'So can we track the movement of enemy capital ships and convoys in the Mediterranean?'

Metting almost smiled. 'Have you heard of the *Ark Royal*?'

Leo thought for a second. 'The aircraft carrier that we sunk more than once?'

Metting almost smiled again. 'The Ark, as the British sailors call her, is a lucky ship. The Royal Navy's much more disciplined than the 8th Army in controlling wireless usage.'

'And so?' said Leo.

'Just wait. You may be surprised.'

11

Cairo, November 1941

There it was, one of many houseboats at El Agouza, in the Giza district. Henri didn't have the icon with him, left behind in the strong room at Shepheard's Hotel. An elementary precaution in case of trouble, as Ahmed put it when passing the package over to him at their last meeting in Beirut. Together with it was the *laissez-passer* from the Patriarch.

There was the gangplank leading to the boat, just as Ahmed described. No one on deck. No answer to his shout. He was ready with the password he'd memorized. No option but to explore the vessel. There were steps down below the cockpit, and he took them slowly. A galley, two berths in the bows and another in the stern, everything shipshape. As he climbed back up to the open deck, a large figure blocked out the light, another behind.

'On the deck with your hands on your head,' said a voice. He saw the polished boots first, then found himself facing a British military policeman in red-topped cap and holding a Browning service revolver. The man behind him was in civilian clothes. 'I'm going to search you,' the policeman said when Henri was up on deck, and did so thoroughly. Henri was in uniform, as was the rule.

'We'd like to ask you a few questions, if we may,' said the other politely. 'Best we go to my office. We've a car just over there. Here's my ID. He showed a printed card in his wallet stating the holder was a British Army captain in a department marked simply as SME Cairo. They climbed into an open Humber 4 × 4 and set off back towards the city. The game was up. What would happen? When they interrogated him it would make sense to stick to the truth, and face any consequences, he reasoned.

It was a villa rather than office building, with no obvious military or police presence. In the Al Maadi district, a suburb to the south of Cairo, on the east bank of the Nile. Except Henri knew General Headquarters Middle East was close by in Garden City. He'd studied a map of the area before setting off that morning. The military policeman took his leave, and an orderly brought a large brown teapot and mugs on a tray into the room, where the two of them sat down at a small bridge table with worn baize surface.

'Help yourself to tea, Lieutenant, said the Captain. He offered him a cigarette, which Henri declined. 'Could you give me your name and unit, please. I see you're French Foreign Legion and part of the Free French Division. I'd also like to know how you got here and what you were doing at the houseboat.'

Must keep it short and to the point, thought Henri. They were waiting for someone at the boat. How much did they already know? He would be straightforward, not appear devious. 'My name is Henri de Rochefort, Lieutenant in the French Foreign Legion. My unit is 13th Demi-Brigade. We were part of General Maitland-Wilson's force which advanced into Syria and Lebanon last summer. After the armistice, we were granted leave. That was followed by a period of training, prior to transferring here last week to join 8th Army.'

'So what took you to the houseboat, if I may ask?'

'Before I left Beirut, I was asked by someone introduced by a friend, and indirectly by the Patriarch there, to deliver a package when I arrived in Cairo. The houseboat was the address of the intended recipient.'

'And to whom were you to deliver this package, and what was in it?'

'To the client of my friend's associate in Lebanon. I was told the recipient was a wealthy Egyptian philanthropist. In the package was an icon. I understand that it's destined for the Monastery of St Catherine in Sinai, where it properly belongs. The icon is of St Catherine.'

'You don't have it with you.'

'No, it's in the strong room of the hotel where I'm staying, Shepheard's. I'm on four days' leave, have to be back at my unit on Tuesday.'

'I think we should both take a look at this package, if you don't mind. I just need some additional information, and then we'll take the car over to Shepheard's.'

<hr />

Henri felt he was being grilled alive by the heat of mid-morning, as they bowled along in the large open car. The Captain was friendly enough, as he turned his head round towards Henri on the rear seat. 'Lieutenant, I must congratulate you on your perfect English.'

'Thank you. My mother is British, father French. We're a Bordeaux family. I went to school in England.'

'Now that's unusual.' There was genuine surprise in the Captain's voice.

Henri went straight to the concierge when they arrived at the hotel, and withdrew the package from the strong room. 'I'd prefer we open this and look at the icon in my room, if that's okay,' said Henri.

Once inside the rather poky single room, he opened the package and passed the contents to the Captain.

'Certainly beautiful' was the response. 'Doubt if it's original, but I'm no expert. Very heavy.'

There was a short silence. Henri always thought it was heavy for its size.

'The frame and back are pretty solid,' said the Captain. He pulled out a penknife. 'I won't do it any harm. Was just wondering if the back comes off without forcing.' Henri said nothing as the Captain applied some pressure to the edge of the frame. It came apart without much difficulty. 'Ah, what do we have here?'

'My God,' Henri blurted out. He was shocked. Inside a false rear to the frame was a thin compartment containing a large number of white English five pound notes. Even more incredible were the coins lying flat and covering the whole face of the compartment, gold sovereigns.

'Lieutenant,' said the Captain, his mood was now changed for the worse. 'You must realize this lands you in an awkward position. Currency smuggling is a very serious offence.'

'I'd simply no idea there was any money concealed in the frame,' said Henri. He was now deadly nervous, shaking. What would happen to him? The consequences could be disastrous. It might mean a court martial. The French divisional staff would assume he was in the know, receiving a reward for bringing the money into Egypt. He'd really been taken by that smooth bastard Ahmed.

'Let's go straight back to my office, with all of this,' said the Captain, folding up the package. 'We'll find some lunch for you. I have to consult with my colleagues. Then there will have to be a full interrogation.'

They were now in a larger room in the villa. Behind a desk was another man, also in plain clothes, who introduced himself as James Robertson. The interrogation took three hours, the Captain sitting in the background and taking notes throughout. Every question Henri could imagine. His family background, education, army training, the Narvik landings, and the trek from French West Africa via Eritrea to Syria. He held nothing back. What would be the point? Stupid to hide anything.

Henri concluded Robertson was a patient man, meticulous in his questioning, returning to the same subject from a different direction time and again. He was checking that the same answer was emerging to the same question put another way. His relationship with Yasmin was prised out of him. 'So erotic a woman, it was natural for you to be drawn to her, the relationship to become intimate. That's how it happened, you must have been intoxicated by her sexuality?'

The inevitable conclusion was being drawn. Robertson arrived at it gently. But when finally he delivered it, there was suddenly a hardness in his manner, threatening you could say. 'At best, any court would decide you agreed to act as courier for the package because your lover used her best favours to encourage you. To persuade you to accept the request of this Ahmed character. The letter from the Patriarch would count for little.'

The interrogation finished for the day. The Captain was gathering his notes together. Robertson was friendly again, but firm, as he smiled at Henri. 'Lieutenant, we would like you to spend the night here. We'll advise the hotel that you've been called away. We have our own cook, he'll look after you. Tomorrow, we'll decide what's going to happen. It'll be in your best interest to cooperate with us.'

Breakfast arrived in his room. Not exactly a cell, but a military policeman on duty in the corridor outside. A bad night. Constant anxiety about what was to be his fate. What would it do to his army career, to his life for that matter?

Back in the room where the interrogation took place, Robertson was already behind his desk, the Captain close by, when a police sergeant brought Henri in. They all shook hands, perhaps in deference to his French uniform. Not a bad start, given they might be about to hand him over to the Egyptian police or an even worse fate. Have they decided what to do with me? Would they have already checked up on his service record? Dear God, help me, he prayed.

'Lieutenant de Rochefort,' Robertson started. 'Your case interests us, as you'll have gathered from the detail we went into yesterday. You're in a serious position. The consequences of what you've done could be disastrous for your status in the Free French forces, and a prison term could be on the cards.' He paused. Henri's hopes descended to rock bottom.

'I recognize the seriousness of the situation, sir,' he replied, submitting to the worst, a sick feeling inside him.

'We've reviewed carefully your situation in the light of what we so far know,' Robertson went on. 'We have a proposition to put to you. What we have to say must be strictly confidential between us.'

'Yes, I fully understand, I agree to that,' said Henri, almost whispering his response. Could there somehow be a way out of this? He just hoped for a miracle.

After a pause, Robertson drew himself up, as though he'd decided to cross into new territory. 'First of all, Lieutenant, I should explain who we are. Like the Deuxième Bureau in France, Britain also has a counterespionage service. In a large occupied territory like Egypt, there's a branch of that service and we are it. For obvious reasons, I can't give you any real detail of our activities.'

'I understand,' said Henri.

'Counterespionage out here is concerned with agents of the Abwehr, Germany's military intelligence service, and of its Italian equivalent. Coming to the point, we believe that the money which you brought from Beirut was intended for a German spy under the control of the Abwehr. They have controlling stations in countries allied or friendly to the Nazis, for instance in Rome and Istanbul, and in occupied territories like Greece.'

German military intelligence, Abwehr agents. Henri's despair turned into fear. He remained silent. The conversation was moving in an unexpected direction.

'What we propose is that you spend a few months at General Headquarters in Cairo, as part of the small Free French liaison team being established there. During this time, you would be available to us to do some undercover work. Your Commanding Officer in 13 DBLE would be advised accordingly. All being well, you would return to your unit after say three months, and nothing further would be said about the mess you've got yourself into.'

Henri was staggered. 'Thank you, sir. I appreciate the opportunity to make amends. I was a fool, and allowed myself to be taken for a ride. The least I can do is help track down enemy sympathizers here in Egypt.'

'I was hoping you'd take it that way, Lieutenant. You'll need some basic instruction from us. We wouldn't propose a change of identity, but you would be posing as a civilian much of the time. First of all, we'll help you to fix up accommodation. The people at GHQ can organize that.'

Henri was amazed. Relief flooded through him. Then anxiety. He would have to trust these people. What would they let him in for? Not much he could do about it. This was the only way out.

'Thank you.' Henri paused. He felt he must ask for some idea of what was going to be asked of him. 'Would you able to give me an idea of how I can help?' he said.

Robertson sat back in his chair, looking across the room to the Captain, and then back at Henri. 'I'll give you a flavor of what we are up against. Our intelligence people have alerted us to a pending Abwehr operation to insert a spy and radio operator into Cairo. They will attempt to enter Egypt by circumventing the southernmost point in our defence line which runs from Gazala on the coast, down to Bir Hakeim. We man a wireless intercept station at Bir Hakeim. Coincidentally, the Free French may be taking responsibility for the defences in that area.'

'I heard something about that,' said Henri. 'So, perhaps it will be necessary to intercept them. And take them out.'

'Intercept, yes. But living spies can often be more useful than dead ones. We don't expect any Afrika Korps protection for the convoy. We're told it will consist of a small number of Ford trucks. They want to be perceived as a non-military expedition, and plan on navigating the soft sand desert surface in the south, where the war doesn't go. Armoured vehicles can't operate in those conditions. However, we have something else in mind which might interest you. Let's get together again with one or two of my colleagues tomorrow.'

⊷▰▰◅

Robertson was sitting with a couple of others as Henri was shown into the same office, and they all rose to meet him. There was coffee on the table, and the atmosphere was relatively relaxed. He'd thought a lot about the discussion the day before. Counter-intelligence in Cairo sounded intriguing, and he assumed that SME was the Middle East offshoot of Britain's MI5.

'Lieutenant de Rochefort,' said Robertson after making the introductions, 'there's one specific area of concern where we believe you could assist us.'

'But of course,' said Henri.

'A certain French lady is spending some time in Cairo. She's a journalist, working mainly for the American press. Her name is Mercure, Noelle Mercure. Her mother was a well known physicist, Annette Mercure.'

'Yes, I think I've heard of her.'

'Noelle Mercure's a fascinating person. A beautiful woman, calm and intellectual. Apparently educated to be a scientist like her mother, in fact she's very different from her. Artistic and, as I said, a journalist.' He paused. 'She's also a fine pianist.'

'Sounds a remarkable person,' said Henri.

'She is that. An independent voice. Her readership is the American public, in a neutral country. When France fell, she escaped to London and joined de Gaulle. We think you should get to know her. She's ten years older than you, but both of you being French and on the same side in the war, she's likely to tell you more than she would us.'

'What is it you want to find out, sir?'

'Well, although she's sympathetic to our cause, Noelle Mercure has other friends and contacts in Egypt.'

'Oh, what sort of friends?' asked Henri.

One of the others present spoke up. 'Lieutenant, there is an underground nationalist movement among educated young Egyptians. Mademoiselle Mercure's job brings her into contact with them. After all, she's looking for stories for her American readers. She probably searches them out. We've read some of what she writes in the *New York Herald Tribune*. They're not anti-British articles, but remember the Americans don't like colonialism. We treat Egypt like a colony while this war's on.'

'Yes, that figures.' He was beginning to see where this was leading.

Robertson remarked 'You know, there are many French in Egypt, and among them are Vichy sympathizers. There're still plenty of them, even after the defeat of the Vichy Army of the Levant. Your victory in Syria and Lebanon. They don't trust us and think Britain is out to grab French possessions overseas. They mix with anti-British Egyptians who are plotting for the day when they can win independence. In the meantime, any chance to send information out of the country, and to Rommel, is gratefully accepted. One of those actively involved is a young Egyptian Army officer, Anwar Sadat.

'I know what you're saying, sir. Very few of the Vichy troops we defeated and offered a home to, have joined us. Most have gone back to Algeria, Morocco and France itself.'

There was a lull in the conversation. Then Robertson said 'We'd like you to find out more about the Egyptian trouble-makers. Hopefully, being French and with the assistance of Noelle Mercure, you could feed back to us some very useful intelligence. I think she'll appreciate that you represent the sharp end of de Gaulle's influence and treat you as an ally.' He paused, looking at Henri and the others, with a gleam in his eye. 'Here's what I propose.'

Henri ran through Robertson's instructions. Follow them to the letter, he'd been told. Speak French at all times, wear mostly civilian clothes, read Egyptian newspapers, and so on. Mix with the French population, make notes of their political leanings. Identify those he suspected to have Vichy leanings, concentrate on them. Who are their Egyptian friends? Noelle hates Vichy, but she knows Egyptians in the circle Sadat moves in. Ask her to lunch. Be open with her, she's on our side but her job is to capture the zeitgeist among the anti-British. Her employers, particularly the *Herald Tribune*, want that information so their editors can run articles such as wouldn't appear in the British press. If she takes to you, encourage her. She's on her own. She'll welcome friendship from someone on her political wavelength. Steer clear of the fleshpots. There'll be spivs after your money, pimps and blackmailers. They'll have you into the belly dancer clubs in no time. If you're sucked down that avenue, you'll soon be a write-off.'

'That's the office of United Press, over there,' said the driver, pulling into the kerb and pointing across the road.

'Right, you can drop me here,' said Henri, not wanting to be seen arriving in a British Army vehicle. Walking into UPI was entering neutral territory.

A smart Egyptian girl in carefully ironed white cotton blouse looked up at him from behind the reception desk.

'My name is de Rochefort. I would like to see Mademoiselle Mercure, please,' said Henri.

'Can I tell her what it's about please, sir?'

'You can tell her that I have recently arrived from Algiers, and have some useful information about the political situation there.'

He waited over in a corner of the room where there were copies of American newspapers lying on a table. The latest he could find was about two weeks old, and he was scanning the pages when a frosted glass door behind Reception opened and a woman came out into the waiting area. His first impression was of a business-like, almost stern manner. She was small in height and very thin, with full features and sleek black hair cut short above the neck.

'I'm Noelle Mercure,' she said, as she came over to him. 'You wanted to see me?' The voice was soft but inquiring, in best French diction. He noticed her eyes, large and dark as they took him in.

Henri introduced himself. He didn't feel hesitant but was on guard, conscious of a woman at least ten years older than he was. And, he suspected, a lot more sophisticated and socially aware.

'I arrived the other day from Beirut, but have been in Algiers until recently. I thought you might be interested to hear about what's going on there. Perhaps we could talk over lunch? He paused. 'Today, if you could spare the time.'

She looked at him in a very direct way, almost a stare. The dark eyes expressive, and yet giving away nothing of her thoughts. Just a hint of surprise. He was in plain clothes, looking like any other European in Cairo. But he'd been careful, for this occasion, to wear in his lapel a small Cross of Lorraine. The symbol of the Free French, a signal to her of what side he was on.

'Give me half an hour to complete a filing with New York, and I'll join you. Would the restaurant terrace at Shepheard's be okay? It's nearby and I've work to do afterwards.'

'Perfect,' said Henri. 'See you there, shortly.'

⊷⊶

Reading a *Tribune* he'd brought with him from the UPI office, Henri wasn't conscious she'd arrived until he realized she was standing there by his table. Jumping to his feet, he knocked his head on the parasol above. She actually laughed, as he gathered himself together and pulled out a chair for her. The waiter appeared at once, and they ordered chilled lemonade.

The conversation was soon on Algiers and the Vichy regime under Admiral Darlan. He explained that the Americans, although neutral, were regarded as pro the British. The British, in their turn, were thought to be operating undercover agents and saboteurs. The Free French sympathizers were being watched, and kept their powder dry. In general, the population was very anti-British, the memory of Mers-el-Kébir still fresh in everyone's mind.

They helped themselves to lunch from the cold buffet, and he answered most of her questions adequately, he felt, pleased he'd paid full attention to the briefing by Robertson and his friends. Coffee arrived. He was looking into those amazing dark eyes as he spoke, trying to detect any real interest towards him. She seemed the epitome of the sophisticated Parisienne.

'Mademoiselle.'

'Yes?' she said in an expectant way, or was it his imagination?

'Let's meet again. How about dinner in a couple of days' time? We could continue our discussions, and perhaps you could tell me a little of what you've learnt about Egypt.'

She stared at him for a moment. 'Yes, I'd enjoy that.'

He sensed just a flicker of excitement in the way she said it.

⋯

He saw the maître d' first, heading for his table. She walked a little behind, aside of him. Purposefully, a confident woman, yet at the same time restrained and elegant. So different in appearance from their lunchtime meeting a couple of days before. A short red dress, white jacket over the shoulders.

Henri rose and they shook hands, rather formally, but there was just the suggestion of a smile on her beautifully made-up but otherwise serious face. Again, he was amazed by her eyes, pools of darkness. She sank down into the banquette which curved around part of the table, facing him obliquely. The wine waiter was there right away. 'A glass of champagne, Madame, Monsieur?' and they both nodded their assent.

'Blind date in Cairo' was her opening remark, before he'd said anything. 'I suppose anything goes in a city like this in the middle of a war.'

'I'm sorry to be so forward,' said Henri.

She actually smiled properly, showing off the fullness of her features. 'Thanks for coming up with the idea. Dinner here at Kit Kat is a treat, and the chance to dance.'

Henri felt a little inadequate, up against this older and sophisticated woman. 'My excuse is that I have an inquisitive mind. I'm meant to be a soldier, but I've an interest in people of all sorts. When I heard you were a journalist, I realized we might have something to offer one another.'

'Great idea, Henri,' she said.

'Let's order. We should try some of the fish perhaps.'

'I agree. Pan-fried Nile perch is an obvious choice, and I see there's a *dorade*.' She leant towards him to point out the dish in the fish section.

He was aware at once of the scent she used, almost erotic to his starved senses. The waiter brought him back to earth, and they decided on the *dorade*, with a Sancerre.

'I was told by an Egyptian friend that you were writing an article on how de Gaulle has developed his political influence in Africa,' said Henri. 'You might like to hear where my unit has been in the past year. It rather reflects the story of the General and the Free French since June 1940.'

'Go ahead, right up my street.' Her long fingers lifted the wine glass. 'Mm, delicious.'

While they ate, he took her through the exploits of 13 DBLE, from the disaster of Dakar to Doula and meeting with Leclerc. From Keren in Eritrea to Damascus. She pulled out a notebook and silver pencil from her evening bag, and made notes. He noticed again the slender long fingers, a pianist's fingers.

'You went straight to London when Pétain signed the Armistice, didn't you,' said Henri. 'Must have been a dangerous trip. Brave thing to do. I found myself there already, at Trentham Park after Norway.'

'Thanks. The choice came easily for me. The Vichy people were shits, and still are. They've revoked my French nationality. And I'm the daughter of a French Nobel Prize winner.'

'I know your mother was famous for her work, and probably died from the effects of it.'

She gave him a long look, seeming to accept him more. The conversation moved the way he'd been hoping, to Egypt and its peoples. From there, it was an easy step into politics.

She sat back, and said suddenly 'We're both French, so it's easier for us to understand the aspirations of the young educated Egyptians, students and professionals. They want their country to play its part as an independent nation, at least when the war in Africa's over. Easier for us to understand, than for the British to accept, I mean.'

'Are they a threat to the British?' he asked.

'Yes, although only in the undercover sense at the moment. You know, I've met certain characters, even young Egyptian Army officers, who would subvert the Allied war effort given half the chance.'

'You mean, by passing information, spying?'

'Certainly. Rommel is a real threat, he could advance across Egypt if he receives the supplies and equipment he needs. These people see him as their chance. Many of them admire the Germans. Where that country has come from since the chaos following the 1914 War.'

'Do they have leaders? The King and the rich pashas seem to toe the line with Britain. Would I know their names?'

'I don't know. One is Anwar Sadat, a young Egyptian Army officer. He's formed an inner circle of like-minded army people. If they could be harnessed by the Germans as Rommel advances, they could pass a lot of critical information to the enemy.'

The dancing was beginning, a few couples on the small floor. Noelle looked across at the band as it swung into a Gershwin favourite, and the singer sang 'Oh Sweet and Lovely, Lady be Good.' She touched him on the arm as she slowly removed her jacket, revealing the curve of her beautiful shoulders. They made towards the dancers without saying anything. She turned towards him, that dark look in her eyes as he put his arm around her narrow waist. When he pulled her slightly to him, she pressed her body gently against his, her sleek black hair touching his cheek. She felt as light as she looked.

Out on the water, some time later, they leant back against the cushions as the small boat glided along the banks of the Nile. A whisky bottle and soda syphon rested nearby. The club attendant served as barman as well as skipper.

'Kit Kat's an odd name for a night club,' said Henri. 'Hope this chap knows where he's going.'

'I like travelling, Henri. You know something? I've Polish blood in me. In this war the Poles are always on the move, kicked out of their country by the Germans and the Russians.'

'Yes, I heard about the thousands who made their way to Iran, with their families. Many of the chaps are already trained soldiers and are joining 8th Army.'

He felt her hand over his, the pressure of her long fingers as they moved in his. 'I'm on a sort of world tour, you know.

In Egypt for a couple of months, filing my articles back to the States. Then on to India to do the same. After that, Singapore.'

Henri leant towards her. 'Oh, I'd hoped this was the beginning of a long friendship.'

'Nobody makes plans in the world we live in.'

Was there a finality in the way she said that? No doubt he'd find out.

'Would you take me back home?' she said suddenly. 'If your friend puts us ashore here, there should be a taxi.'

'Of course,' said Henri, leaning across to the attendant and giving him the instruction.

⟶≫◍◍≪⟵

He wasn't expecting to be asked in. Nor was he. Noelle went straight to the door of the bungalow and unlocked it, standing aside for him to walk in.

'I'll fix us a drink,' she said as she went over to a glass cabinet. Handing the drink to him, she led the way into the sitting room and slid back the screen opening onto a veranda. The cool night air was on his face as he followed her out. When she turned round he saw in the semi-darkness that the thin straps of her dress were now down resting on her arms, and the top of the red cotton garment was sagging and revealing the mounds of her breasts. They were not large but the impact on him of their beauty made him want her suddenly. His pulse was racing, excitement flooding through him.

'Come and hold me, darling,' she said.

Henri moved towards her as she took a couple of steps to him, and he took her in his arms. He kissed her gently, touching her tongue with his, feeling the warm softness of her body press against him under the dress.

A few moments after, she pulled back slightly and took his arm, guiding him back indoors and through to the room beyond. To the left was a bed surrounded by mosquito netting which she swept aside. Opposite were the windows which in daylight would look out towards the river.

Noelle turned round to face him. She put both her arms down her sides and began to lift slowly the hem of her dress. Henri took the hem in his hands and lifted the garment up and over her head. The short petticoat underneath slipped down to her waist, uncovering her breasts. He felt her fingers unbutton his shirt and then his trousers. The petticoat slipped down around her ankles and she stepped out of it, her body now entirely naked. His hands were either side of her thighs, and he helped her up onto the bed. He now wanted her desperately. The attraction of her body was overwhelming all his other senses, as he moved over her. The climax when it came for him was not just the intense pleasure of love, but also release from the punishment and fears of two years of warfare.

⊸➤◉ ◉◅⊸

Noelle lay back, seemingly luxuriating in the aftermath of their lovemaking. He watched her stretch her arms above her head, her breasts rising as her tight tummy pushed away towards her legs.

'You are truly beautiful, my darling,' he said, kissing her lightly on the forehead.

'And you have a soldier's body,' she said, looking up at him. 'Scars and bone. You make love with gentleness and restraint.'

They talked about themselves, not about war and politics. At least until Henri asked whether he could meet some of her politically minded friends, particularly the Egyptian ones. He wasn't sure what she would think his motives were, but too bad, she'd say and do what she wanted.

'There's a group that meets each week,' she said. 'They might be suspicious of you. I could take you, we could try. It's all talk and no action most of the time. But since Rommel arrived on the doorstep, the tone has changed. Some of the military types talk privately amongst themselves.'

'Any indication whether they're working on something specific?'

'Well, one thing they talk about is SALAM. I think that's code for an Abwehr spy who goes by the name of Hussein Gaffar. They don't think much of him. Seems he spends a lot of time with a belly dancer they don't trust, known to have links with the Egyptian royal family and the British.'

'I'd like to give it a go. Can we go together? You could say I'm from the *Tribune*'s Paris office.'

She was quiet. After some hesitation, she replied 'I'm not sure. If they're suspicious of you, they're going to cut both of us out, and I'll lose an important source of information. Better you leave it to me. I'll feed back to you what I learn.' She turned towards him. 'I wonder who you're working for?'

'Trust me,' he said. 'We're on the same side.'

12

Western Mediterranean, November 1941

Bill looked forward from the bridge of the Catapult Aircraft Merchant ship, towards the ramp protruding beyond the bows. In between was the Hurricane, resting on a trolley forming the rocket-powered catapult. He remembered the prototype of the device on his first day at Speke, where he reported after volunteering for the Merchant Ship Fighter Unit, MSFU for short. That was soon after John Smith's court martial. When they met a few days later for a beer, John was still badly shaken from his part in the accident on the cricket fields of St Gregory's. Bill was asking how he felt about his future in the Fleet Air Arm.

'Frankly, after pleading guilty and being dismissed my ship, I don't think I have a future,' said John.

'Well, I wondered whether you'd be interested in what I'm now up to,' said Bill.

John looked surprised. 'So, what's that?'

'I volunteered to train pilots for the launch of Hurricanes by catapult from merchant ships, CAM ships they call them.'

'Good God. How are they going to organize that?' John looked sceptical.

'It was an Admiralty idea, and a few Fleet Air Arm Sea Hurricane pilots like you are involved. But most of them will be RAF. They'll only fly two or three combat missions from CAM ships, before the pilots return to normal flying duties. It's thought that a longer gap than that runs the risk of pilots losing their skills.'

John was looking less gloomy now, his interest clearly stimulated by what Bill was saying.

'Training is at Speke, just outside Liverpool. You could say it's tantamount to suicide. You're fired by a rocket-propelled catapult mounted on a merchantman far out at sea. You shoot down what you can, and when your fuel is used up you bail out or ditch in the drink, and hope you'll be picked up. It's mainly about solving the Condor problem.'

'Oh, what's the Condor problem?' asked John.

'It's the area of ocean too far out for our land-based aircraft to reach. The Condor's a very long-range Luftwaffe aircraft operating from Bordeaux-Mérignac, which seeks out the convoys when they enter that space. They're part of the Kriegsmarine's signals intelligence network, reporting convoy movements to the U-boats. We don't have the escort carriers yet to enable our fighters to go after them.'

John appeared to be thinking hard, head in hands as he stared into space. 'So, one would stand by day after day on the CAM ship until a Condor was sighted or found on a radar track. Then it would be up into the Hurricane, blast off, and start the climb up towards the enemy.'

'Who is armed,' said Bill. 'If it's a Condor, with three machine guns and forward cannon.'

'Okay. So, after shooting down the Condor, one would bail out or ditch, and hope someone notices.'

'You've got it, John. Depending how much fuel remains in the tanks, you would look around for any other target to take out.

'As far as I'm concerned, I'd volunteer if that persuaded the Admiralty to lift its ban on me flying.'

'Great. Just make a written application to be considered. There's always a shortage of pilots. I think you'd stand a good chance. You can mention me, and I'll help if I can.'

Bill's attention went back to the convoy, now two days after forming up in the Atlantic, and passing Gibraltar into the Med. He was with John, the two being the Hurricane pilots on a CAM ship assigned to a Force H Malta convoy. Their cargo was food and fuel. John would pilot the Hurricane, Bill acting both as back-up and Fighter Direction Officer. Both were surprised when ordered to join an MSFU mission in the Mediterranean. Most CAM ships operated out in the North Atlantic. They weren't told much, but everyone assumed the destination was Malta. That usually meant carriers providing the convoy with air cover. Yet, Bill heard from a more senior RAF contact that part of the convoy's mission was to fly off Hurricanes to bolster the island's meagre air defences. Presumably, he reasoned, all the carrying capacity of a carrier would be taken up by the Hurricanes to be flown off when they were close enough to Malta.

Suddenly, the door onto the bridge opened and the signals officer entered in a hurry. 'We've received an RDF message from the cruiser, sir. Bearing 035, range 30 miles, altitude 10,000 feet. Probably a Ju 88 spying on us,' he added. Not having radar themselves, they relied on the closest cruiser to pass on the sighting.

Bill moved fast. 'Pilot to aircraft,' he ordered down the speaker tube. Conditions were fine, little wave height, light swell, wind speed no more than Force 2. 'Okay,' he snapped to the signals officer. He knew the mechanics would have fired up the Hurricane's engine at least once that morning, and that

John would be climbing into the aircraft. 'I'll vector him to the target,' he said as he went over to the Bigsworth board, ready to track the incoming plane. The attached parallel pantograph arm was to compute speed of the enemy, and then the heading and speed required for the fighter to intercept.

Bill heard John start the aircraft's already warm Merlin. He knew a crew member would remove the pins, show them to the pilot, and take them to the Catapult Duty Officer.

The pilot applied thirty degrees of flap and set the rudder at one-third right.

Bill felt the ship's Captain manoeuvre the vessel into the wind.

The routine was embedded in his mind. First Mate, acting as CDO, waves his blue flag indicating he's ready to launch upon a signal from the pilot. The pilot opens full throttle, presses his head against the head-rest, lowering his left hand as a signal to launch.

The CDO would be waiting for the bow to rise from the trough of the light swell, hand on the switch to fire the catapult rockets.

Bill watched as the rockets blasted the Hurricane away from him along the ramp, saw it hurtle into space and start to climb. 'Fighter Director to Hurricane, are you receiving me?' he said into the microphone. No answer. He repeated the call, and this time the response crackled back from the receiver on the bridge.

'Hurricane to Fighter Director, receiving you loud and clear.'

'Turn to starboard eighteen degrees. Maintain rate of climb. You should see bandit in one minute. Bill was thinking what John was probably thinking. Hoping the enemy didn't see the flash from the rockets firing.

'I have sight of him,' replied John, shortly afterwards. Will climb up behind and into sun.'

Bill knew he was hoping to attack the raider from above and with the sun behind him.

'It's a single Ju 88, reconnaissance flight. I'll get him before he radios the convoy's position.'

'Okay. Will stand by. Good luck. Out.' Bill knew it all rested on John, now. Two challenges faced him. To overpower the German aircraft which had a top speed slightly less than John's old Hurricane, and then to bail out safely and be recovered by one of the convoy escort vessels. Out on deck it was just possible to see the Ju 88. Crew on many of the convoy vessels would be staring up there, willing John on.

Several minutes later, suddenly the muffled but unmistakable clatter of heavy machine gun fire, a long way up. Both planes were losing altitude. Even if John hadn't surprised his opponent all the way, he had the edge over him in terms of speed and in positioning if he'd been able to climb above and into sun. On the other hand, the Ju 88 with a crew of four would have at least one gunner engaging him, as John swooped in from behind.

More gunfire. The two planes were now clearly visible as their vapour trails looped through the clear Mediterranean sky. Suddenly, dark smoke competed with the white vapour. Bill felt a halt in the combined breathing of hundreds of watching sailors. Whose smoke was it? The Ju 88 was twin-engined, so only one would be emitting smoke and it might not be fatal. It could creep back to Sicily, if left alone. The Hurricane had nowhere to go except downwards if it lost power on its only engine. And no spare crew to fight a fire on-board.

The two planes broke away from one another. It was clear that the smoke was coming from the twin-engined plane. Was that the murmur of a cheer, Bill thought he heard? Then, silence, just the noise of ships' engines and the wash against the hulls as he looked upwards. John wasn't finished yet. The Hurricane banked round a full three hundred degrees and returned to business, its machine guns distinct enough now for everyone to hear unless they were wearing blast and ear protection.

Suddenly a flash, distinct in spite of the bright sunshine. The raider just blew up and disintegrated. No parachutes.

That was real, prolonged cheering, Bill heard. So now, it's challenge number two, he thought. Would John bail out straight away? It was rumoured to be an old Battle of Britain Hurricane. No, he seemed to be bringing down the aircraft. After a minute or so, he was already low, heading towards the *Ark Royal* at the rear of the convoy. The Hurricane came in from behind at about one thousand feet and, as it passed over the carrier towards the CAM ship on the port bank of the convoy, there was the victory roll. Another rumble of cheering.

He realized John was preparing to ditch the aircraft. Bill remembered what he'd said the day before, better to save the plane if he could. Malta could do with another Hurricane, if it could be winched onto a convoy vessel before sinking.

He watched, fascinated, making a quick prayer to the Almighty. John banked away again and then throttled right back, flaps down, as he came back in, wheels still up of course. The engine air scoop under the fuselage was the problem. Easy to end up with the plane's nose in the water and the tail in the air. In he came, lower and lower. Contact, the plane bouncing in a cloud of spray. Down again, just a slight bounce this time. Then the water was pulling it to a sudden stop. The superbly sturdy construction of the Hurricane holding it together. The nose went down, up came the tail.

A launch, already lowered by the cruiser nearby, was already on its way. Bill saw John pulling at the perspex canopy above his head. It only opened a foot or so, then jammed. The pilot pulled furiously at it. The cruiser was almost alongside. The crane used for seaplanes swung out amidships. There were two naval divers in the water, trying to work a steel hawser down and underneath the airframe. If they couldn't get him out, they'd have to hold the fuselage above the surface.

❖

Bill held onto the guy-wire of a Hurricane fighter on the flight deck, feeling the early morning sun, the salt and strong wind on his face. A familiar figure appeared from down below, where other aircraft were parked on the two hangar decks. He waved over the Fleet Air Arm officer.

'Fantastic sight isn't it, John?' Bill shouted. 'Bet you weren't expecting to end your mission on the *Ark Royal*.' The destroyer screen was creaming through the choppy water on either side of the carrier, spray up over the bows of the escort vessels, their sonars listening for that fatal echo. Ahead of the Ark was *Argus* with more Hurricanes. Soon it would be the turn of radar, as the two carriers approached the range of enemy fighter bombers based on Sicily.

'It was my lucky day,' said John. 'Glad those cruiser boys were on the ball. Crane, divers, what more could a ditched pilot stuck in his cockpit expect.'

'Well, you did provide them with their best entertainment for some time,' laughed Bill. 'I think you can be pretty sure the Navy will look after you from now on.' He knew the memory of the tragedy on the cricket fields would still be fresh in John's mind. But the former flying instructor would be accepted back into the mainstream from now on.

'The enemy keeps claiming they've sunk the *Ark Royal*,' John shouted. 'Yet here she is, ploughing through the Med at twenty knots, carrying Hurricanes to relieve Malta.'

'I know. The crew says the Ark's a lucky ship. What a way for us two to return to Gibraltar. The CAM ship will hopefully make it back later if it survives the rest of the trip, and back. It's got to be hellish risky, this convoy,' said Bill. 'Not sure why they've codenamed it "Perpetual". I don't mean it's just risky for the chaps who are going to fly their Hurricanes off the carriers with barely enough fuel to reach the island.' They both knew that some months previously, twelve Hurricanes flew off the carrier *Argus*, heading for Malta. That eight of them ran out of fuel and ditched in the sea, only one pilot saved. 'It's also a calculated gamble to deploy the Ark to transport them.'

'Yes,' said John. 'I've heard the story of enemy submarines transferred from the Atlantic to the western Med. Every U-boat commander must be out to sink the *Ark Royal*. But Malta's starved of everything, and they're being blown to pieces. They must have the fighters and pilots to stop those bombers.' Anyway, how do you feel about your latest posting?'

'Mixed feelings. I hate leaving friends, and that means leaving Hurricanes as well. But I have this opportunity. Been selected for a new aircraft. Won't be in service for some time, but it will outfly anything Jerry can put up.'

'Lucky man. I've heard rumours about the plane.'

There was a pause as they both looked around them. Bill then said, with a certain finality, 'Latest Met's okay. Tomorrow morning it is, for the Hurricanes to fly off. Yours will take a bit longer to get to Malta. But they'll be pleased to have it.'

⇥⊙⇤

Bill felt the flight deck heave to port, as the carrier pulled out from the line of the main force. The Ark was positioning herself for launching aircraft. Destroyers moved with her, *Legion* and *Gurkha* maintaining their station, critical for the screen. A roar of engine noise and whack of the catapult as the first Hurricane surged forward to launch, the others lined up awaiting their turn.

All away, climbing to join the two Blenheims sent from Malta to lead them to the island. Now it was back to training. No let up. The flight deck already pointing west after launching the aircraft into wind. Ahead, Admiral Somerville's flagship *Malaya*, the other carrier *Argus*, the destroyer screen around them. A short rising sea, that's why speed was down to sixteen knots. More than that and the destroyers would be in trouble. The whack of the catapult, there went a Swordfish to maintain the anti-submarine patrol. It was all action. Deck landing training ordered by Maund, the Ark's Captain, and Admiral Somerville, hard taskmasters.

Suddenly, a massive explosion. The few aircraft remaining on the flight deck bounced as the Ark seemed to whiplash. Surely it couldn't be a torpedo? No warning. What else could it be? Why were the destroyers swinging away. Must be to search for the submarine. The Ark began to list, and to slow down. Other destroyers now circling them.

Not far to Gib, thought Bill. Some crew taken off by the destroyers. He and John ordered to go with them. Fighter pilots were the least they needed in the struggle to save the Ark. Now on-board *Hermione*, he could see the carrier was under tow, even making some way under her own engines. More ships around, must have come from Gib to increase protection. The crump of depth charges to put off new attacks. Everyone expected they would get her there.

Two in the morning. A turn for the worse. The Ark was losing steam. Fire in the boiler room, someone said. That meant the generators would fail, with loss of electric power. Admiral Somerville in a motor launch alongside. Captain Maund taken off. The list was now thirty-five degrees to starboard. Towlines being dropped.

Six in the morning. The list was even worse. Swordfish aircraft began to slide across the deck. All ships standing back.

She was on her side now, lying there. She'd held on long enough for her entire complement to be taken off. Then, very slowly, she turned over. So tired, she had to find rest, her duty done.

⊹►═◄ ►═◄⊹

The Rock loomed on the horizon. *Hermione* seemed to put on extra steam at the sight. All on-board were silent, the crew doing their work seemingly automatically, those rescued from the Ark deep in their thoughts. Without the *Ark Royal*, part of their lives was gone. In Bill, there was something nagging him, something he couldn't reconcile in his inquisitive mind. Like the loss of *Glorious* and her Hurricanes after Norway, how did the enemy know where they were?

13

Libyan Desert, May 1942

Henri was surprised and shocked when the note from Noelle arrived out of the blue. Three months in the desert without leave was plenty of time to think about her. He couldn't pretend the news was unexpected. After all, the letters between them were spasmodic. Yet he'd been kidding himself she would still be there when he returned to Cairo, whenever that would be. Now he knew Noelle Mercure was gone, on the way to India. The last letter was loving and sensitive. There would always be something special between them. But she was moving on, the next leg in the tour she did tell him about when they were lying back on the cushions in the boat on the Nile. He could always reach her via one of the overseas offices of UPI or the *Herald Tribune*, she wrote.

He wrenched himself back to the present. The wind and the dust with it blew as though from a blast furnace. God, it's hot, thought Henri. What a contrast from the snow and ice of Norway two years ago. A lot had happened since then, ending with his stint at GHQ in Cairo and the undercover work for British counterespionage. That ended when Robertson told him 13 DBLE needed him for their deployment at Bir Hakeim.

Abruptly, he focused back on the task before him, the briefing he was to give. He must put up a good show. The Humber 4 × 4 staff car which the British sent for him, stopped at the entrance to the wired off camp. The British sentry saluted and waved him through to the circle of tents and dugouts that formed the British 150th Infantry Brigade's headquarters, in the 'box' it occupied south of Gazala.

Entering the largest tent, Henri heard the authoritative voice of Brigadier Clive Haydon, CO of the Brigade.

'Lieutenant, come in and join us.' To his officers around him, he said, 'Gentlemen, may I present Legionnaire Lieutenant Henri de Rochefort of the 1st Free French Division.' Then turning to Henri, 'we can only offer you 8th Army tea and bread and jam, nothing stronger than that, I'm afraid.'

Henri saluted. 'I'm honoured to be with you, sir.' He was conscious of his junior rank, maybe the British were expecting at least a Captain to present himself for such a briefing, but the advantage of a fluent English speaker was overriding. He took in the battalion commanders and others officers present, knowing that the infantry regiments represented were from the northeast of England. He risked a light-hearted response, 'We French are said to have delicate tastes, but your ability to produce fresh baked bread in the desert is legendary. They say Rommel's men will risk all to capture one of your field bakeries.'

Brigadier Haydon smiled, as an aide produced a canvas chair for Henri. 'Make yourself comfortable. Your General Koenig said he would send a liaison officer to enlighten us on what the Free French can do to hold up Rommel if he decides to outflank us at the southern end of this Gazala line. Our Brigade here forms the next defensive box to the north of yours at Bir Hakeim. Start with the make-up and disposition of your force, and your supply position.'

Henri was well prepared. 'As you say, sir, we are the last and most southern box in 8th Army's Gazala line, 15 miles south of you. Bir Hakeim is the site of a derelict Turkish fort. We've worked hard for three months to build up the defences, there being no help from the natural layout of the place. The largest component of our force is two French Foreign Legion battalions, experienced troops including former Spanish Republican fighters who are committed anti-fascists.'

'I can imagine,' growled the Brigadier.

'The legionnaires are commanded by French officers, and 13 DBLE as this unit is called, has already seen action in Norway, French Africa and Syria. Then there are two battalions of colonial infantry plus the Marine Fusiliers, a regiment of artillery, and a transport company. The support units are from French Equatorial Africa. They are not what I understand Mr Churchill once referred to as "bouches inutiles", useless mouths. They'll fight if called upon.'

There was some laughter from those in the audience.

'Total strength is 3,700 men and...' he paused and looked at the top of the large tent, 'three women. We are well trained and looking for the chance to prove we're up to the best that Rommel can throw at us. Also there's a British Naval Commander, said to be over seventy years old.'

'Who on earth's that?' exclaimed the Brigadier.

'Admiral Sir Walter Cowan Bt, RN retired was his full title, I believe, but in order to join up again, he apparently took the lower rank of Commander.' There was a stir among those present. Brigadier Haydon thought for a moment.

'Of course, Tich Cowan, commanded a battle cruiser at Jutland, and in 1919 he kept the Baltic open to the new Baltic states, particularly Estonia, and was awarded a baronetcy. I once heard him talk at my club. He retired from the Royal Navy years ago. It's unbelievable that he's out here. What about artillery and anti-tank?'

'We have 54 of the soixante-quinze, the 75s, and a few of the new British 6-pounder anti-tank guns, 18 Bofors anti-aircraft guns manned by the Fusiliers Marins battalion but without operating instructions, ample shells and other ammunition, and food for 10 days.' Henri felt a steady stare and intensity of interest from the assembled company.

Clive Haydon sat back, looking hard at the young French Lieutenant. 'When you try to hold this position and are encircled by German and Italian armour, sooner or later you'll have to give yourselves up since we're unlikely to be able to help.'

Henri looked around at them all. 'You know, we French have nothing more to lose but everything to prove, and we recognize that the tactical positioning of our force can present a major obstacle for Rommel, to which he'll commit strong forces to annihilate. Provided we receive water and whatever supplies you can send in, plus the RAF, we can hold up the Axis forces for at least a week. That should give 8th Army valuable time to re-position its formations according to how the battle develops.'

Haydon seemed to relax somewhat. Henri wondered whether he'd convinced him. The Brigadier commented. 'Let me give you some background on why the ability of the French to hold out at Bir Hakeim is so important to the whole front. General Ritchie is concentrating 8th Army strength in the path of the expected push by Axis forces towards Gazala, and of course Tobruk. With the Mediterranean seaboard on our right flank, we have a good chance of holding him while we prepare new defences on the Egyptian border. However, our left flank is at risk from one of Rommel's encircling manoeuvres. This is why the make-up of your force, and your supply position, is of paramount importance to us. We'll rely on you holding out.'

The Brigadier didn't show his anxiety, just paused for their precarious situation to soak in. 'Now, Lieutenant de Rochefort, do you have any specific requests, other than instructions for your Bofors, which we will supply?'

'Well, our liaison with the RAF is going to be vital. We expect heavy Stuka dive bombing when things hot up, and would appreciate your stressing at the highest level the importance of rapid response when we call for air support. Also, if the supply situation deteriorates, we may come to depend on air drops, particularly of water. And there's one other thing. We have a Catholic bias in terms of the religion of our troops including the Spanish legionnaires, but only one chaplain, a Czechoslovak. A daily Mass is needed, aside from the importance of counselling young soldiers and administering the last rites to those who are not going to make it. Would you be able to help, sir?'

Haydon turned to the assembled company. 'Gentlemen, any ideas?'

A battalion commander spoke up. 'The 8th Hussars have two RC padres, one just finishing his induction into the life out here. The senior could be released as that would still leave enough in 7th Armoured Div, it being at one brigade strength right now. We can take Lieutenant de Rochefort back there and find out.'

The Brigadier ended the meeting, and each of those present shook hands with Henri. One or two said 'Bonne chance.'

Henri thought to himself, the way the French would put it is 'Bon courage.'

⊷⊶

He heard the gruff exclamation from over his shoulder, as he entered the tented HQ inside the 8th Hussars laager. 'Rochefort, what are you doing here?' At first he was surprised by the tall figure who faced him, in battledress with black buttons. Then he recognized Rooky, Dom Brendan Rooker, his house master at school in England, and whom he'd run into before departing for Norway.

'Father, marvellous to see you again. I thought you were with the Irish Guards.'

'I was transferred out here after Narvik. I gather you're short of a padre. I can understand that you French and any Poles with you would need a Catholic chaplain. But surely your Spanish legionnaires who fought on the Republican side, are unlikely to want me around, given that the Catholic Church in Spain sided with Franco.'

Henri was surprised. 'Yes, maybe, but their true hatred is for fascists, and belief in salvation through Christ is deep down in their make-up.'

'My Spanish is okay, but French modest. Anyway, all Catholics understand the Latin Mass, thanks be to God.'

Henri briefly explained to Rooky the situation at Bir Hakeim. 'If Rommel does decide to swing around 8th Army's left flank, he's going to have to deal with us. There seems to be an even chance that he will, so I have to warn you that you may well not get out alive.'

The padre grinned at his former pupil. 'Oh well, then you'll have to give me the last rites, I'll show you how. I think I could free myself up in a couple of days. Have you time for a chat now, before you return to your unit?'

'Certainly.'

They made their way down a line of armoured vehicles, mainly British equipment and, by the look of them, in poor condition. Henri recalled much had been said about the pending arrival of tanks from the United States, and he did see a handful of the larger Grant heavy tanks.

'I've been out here a long time,' said Rooky, 'most of it with the 8th Hussars in 7th Armoured. It was a thrilling experience to start with, pursuing the Italians. Then the German Afrika Korps arrived to bail out their allies, and with them came Erwin Rommel. I was sent to Greece, but that's another story. After my return, I found the going was much tougher, with powerful German armour and some excellent Italian units which had found new heart. We ended up here but there was a lot of advance and retreat in between, and of course the defence of Tobruk.'

'Yes,' said Henri, 'Tobruk seems to have become something of a legend, Rommel must badly need that port.'

'You can say that again. The 8th Hussars took heavy casualties, particularly during the Sidi Rasegh battles, and the Commanding Officer Peter Sandbach was killed. My work on encouraging the men in their fighting for a better world gave way to administering last rites to those on their way to the next,' he said grimly. 'Then Gerald "Smash" Kilkelly returned from Syria to take over as CO of the Regiment in February. Anyway, enough of my experiences, what've you been up to since Norway?'

Henri looked at his old house master and religious mentor. 'After Narvik and the collapse in France, some French troops and officers elected to stay in England and continue the fight. I sailed from Liverpool with 13 DBLE, and a powerful Royal Navy force with de Gaulle and General Spears on-board. The objective was to persuade the Vichy French at Dakar to join the Free French.'

'And you got a bloody nose,' said Rooky.

'Yes, total failure.'

Henri explained how even de Gaulle had to accept he wasn't wanted there. But that from then on things went much better, the Royal Navy leaving them at Douala in French Cameroon where they received a great welcome from the locals. General Leclerc, who'd escaped from France to join de Gaulle, was the Governor down there. Then after suppressing the Vichy forces in Chad, they sailed round the Cape and up to Port Sudan. The British there were suspicious of them because they were legionnaires and reputed to be unruly.

'They didn't like our habits, for example that we already had operating a "bordel mobile de campagne", which is what we call our Legion brothel.'

Rooky laughed.

'We followed the British force into Eritrea, and went into action against the Italians. We fought well at Keren and the British were suddenly impressed. After the Italians had surrendered at Massawa, we trekked across the Sinai and into Palestine. Then it was on to Vichy-held Syria. We took Damascus, and the armistice was announced.

Henri saw the Humber 4 × 4 drive up, ready to take him back to Bir Hakeim. 'Can I pick you up here at 10am in two days' time?'

'Whatever you say, Lieutenant,' said Rooky, clearly intrigued by the challenge before them.

14

Silence in the desert for a change, as they drove the 15 miles back to Bir Hakeim. Entering the Free French stronghold through the labyrinth of wire, deep minefields and anti-tank defences, Henri took Rooky straight to HQ to introduce him to General Koenig. He'd already briefed Koenig on his conference with Brigadier Haydon, and mentioned that he'd found an extra padre.

'So, Father,' said the General to Rooky, 'delighted you can join us. Meet my Chief of Staff, Colonel Masson,' and he motioned to the tough-looking officer beside him. 'We're a multi-racial community here at Bir Hakeim. Even some British helping to man our anti-aircraft defences, along with two nurses, an Admiral, and Miss Travers, my driver. Show Père Rooker around, Lieutenant, he might well have operational as well as spiritual advice to give us. I understand, Father, you're an infantry veteran of the 1914 War.'

'I know something about trenches and dugouts, General, and have a strong respect for the 75s which I've already noticed in your artillery batteries.'

Taking their leave from Koenig, they went off to find Corporal Morel and a jeep.

'Corporal Morel,' said Henri. 'I want you to look after Père Rooker while he's with us. He was in Norway, at Narvik.' The Legionnaire Corporal came to attention and saluted smartly.

'Now, let's introduce the Padre to the unit commanders,' said Henri. There was a grinding of gears as the Corporal engaged four wheel drive to help them through the sand. Rooky sat next to him, his arm holding onto the windscreen and one leg up on the side of the jeep. Henri squatted in the back and shouted in the padre's ear.

'Three months here, Father, has given us plenty of time to prepare. General Koenig's experience in the last war is reflected in the way everything, personnel, armaments, vehicles, has been dug into the hard ground to a minimum depth of one metre. The minefields have been laid in triangles, V formation, from one defensive position to each neighbouring position, with channels for motorized patrols. When Rommel strikes we'll live and fight from individual dugouts, one per man. A slit trench is useless. The German tanks can drive along them, then turn inside the trench and wipe out the occupants.'

'Is the strategy purely defensive?' asked Rooky.

'Absolutely not. We send out powerful patrols to harass and confuse the enemy, adopting the Jock column principle of a combined unit of motorized infantry and artillery. It's our view that when Rommel launches his expected attack, he'll bank on outflanking the Allied left flank here in the south. It'll be our job to hold him off our box, and attack his formations from the rear as he circles around us.'

Henri's CO saw them coming. Lt. Col. Prince Dimitri Amilakvari, originally a fugitive from the Russian Revolution and Commanding Officer of 13th Demi-Brigade, in black kepi, was turned out as though on parade at Les Invalides. He shook hands with Rooky and introduced him to three of his company commanders, de Sairigné, Messmer and Lamaze.

As they climbed back into the jeep, Rooky looked almost amused. 'How can a chap look like that in the desert front line?'

Henri grinned. 'Amilak once told me that when one risks appearing before God, one must be properly dressed.'

He continued. 'As well as 13 DBLE, we have two battalions of colonial troops constituting the infantry "demi-brigade de marche" under Colonel Robert de Roux. You'll meet him in due course. Right now we're heading for the Marine Fusiliers who man our anti-aircraft defenses, along with a British troop from the City of London Yeomanry. They're under the command of Commandant Amyot d'Inville, an interesting character. His minesweeper helped in the evacuation from Dunkirk, but was sunk underneath him. He remained in England and signed up with General de Gaulle. Like many in the FF units, he has his own dog, called Bob.'

The tour completed, Rooky commented 'I'm amazed how independently minded everyone is. It must be their different backgrounds. They're so enthusiastic, and ready for the fight. I'll do everything I can for those who want a priest, and pray for those who don't.'

⊷═◈═⊶

'All troops to combat positions!' Henri awoke to the bugle call and these shouted words. Rommel must be launching his offensive further up the Gazala line. A feint at the centre to draw the British armour, so he could then sweep around Bir Hakeim in the south.

His mind focused immediately on what was to come. This was going to be the big test. Norway was tough while it lasted, but he was only under fire briefly. Now it could be a battle lasting several days. He mustn't crack. You could be unnerved solely by the intensity of air attack and artillery fire.

As he and his platoon moved to their individual foxholes, he heard it. The drone of approaching enemy aircraft. He crouched into the hole, wishing it to protect him, braced himself as the screaming sirens started, meaning the first wave of Stuka dive bombers. Silence as the bombs were released. A few seconds' wait. Then the ground beneath him shuddered as they exploded, a hurricane of dirt and rock tore over him. Henri didn't look up at the aircraft, he was saying his prayers more fervently than before a beating at school. The heat was intense, yet he was shivering. He forced himself to concentrate, must remain steady if he expected that of his men. Ready for orders when the enemy's ground attack started.

He could just see them, the Ariete rolling into the southern part of the French stronghold. The Italians were driving their tanks forward without support, the barrage from the quick-firing French 75s was so intense the Italian infantry couldn't dismount to deal with the defending gun emplacements. Henri and his legionnaires stayed right where they were, in their foxholes.

'They've lost half their tanks,' shouted Henri's company commander, Captain Lamaze, less than an hour later. 'They're withdrawing.'

Henri's platoon sergeant suddenly exclaimed, 'Look at that,' pointing to the south. To his horror, Henri saw RAF fighter bombers diving on the abandoned Italian tanks in the French lines, mistaking them for active Axis armour, with bombs and machine gun fire carving up the French positions. Lamaze and Henri were called immediately to the command post, and ordered to take a detachment of engineers and blow up the disabled tanks. Chief of Staff Masson appeared at the entrance to the bunker, 'The Englishman, Commander Cowan, he's been taken prisoner, captured after fighting an Italian tank crew with only a revolver. Just before his 71st birthday.' Henri couldn't stop himself saying in English, 'Remarkable man, once an Admiral, still a baronet, what an example.'

———

Back from dealing with the abandoned tanks, there was bad news from Masson. 'The British tank units behind us were surprised by the Afrika Korps panzers in their sweep around the bottom of the line. 7th Armoured was warned, but the staff didn't react. No-one told their formations, some equipped with Grant tanks. Now the Afrika Korps is behind us. 7th Armoured's HQ was overrun, and its commander, General Messervy, taken prisoner.'

Masson continued. 'General Koenig says we must take the initiative. Another Jock column is to be sent out as soon as possible, to engage the German tanks from the rear.'

———

The next day, Amilakvari walked into the field hospital, where Henri was with Rooky and the medical team. 'Lieutenant de Rochefort, kindly inform the medical services that the British 150th Brigade, to the north of us, has been destroyed. Brigadier Haydon's been killed, the rest have surrendered. They defended until their supplies and ammunition were exhausted. There may be vehicles bringing in casualties.' He paused, and Henri knew what he was going to say. 'That leaves us encircled and under siege.'

He was shocked. Having met with Clive Haydon and his officers only a few days before, their loss meant much more to him than a statistic. That one conference in their Brigade HQ tent was enough to form a bond with those friendly soldiers from the north-east of England. Now, many were killed or wounded, and the remainder prisoners.

His thoughts were interrupted by Colonel Masson, who was followed by the extraordinary sight of Captain de Sairigné leading in two blindfolded enemy officers. General Koenig arrived at the same moment.

'These two Italian gentlemen advanced on us with a white flag,' de Sairigné said, 'they speak no French, nor English.'

A long silence. Then, one of the Italians spoke slowly in his own language. 'If you hand yourselves over, then as prisoners of the Italians who respect the Free French, you will be well treated as our POWs. If you refuse, Rommel will annihilate you.'

Everyone understood the gist of this message.

Koenig spoke. 'We're not here to give ourselves up. Go back to your General, great soldiers, and tell him that. Au revoir messieurs.' De Sairigné re-bound their eyes and marched them back through the lines.

⟶▬▬◁

As if to confirm their plight, the next day, Rommel was sighted as he passed by the top point of the northerly "V" minefield, in his armoured command vehicle. The siege was on.

Shortly afterwards, with Henri and his platoon dug in on the edge of the minefields, two British POWs carrying a white flag, walked towards them. They carried two copies of an ultimatum, in telegraph format and handwritten in German. It was signed by General Rommel:

> *To the troops of Bir Hakeim. Further resistance will only lead to pointless blood-letting. You will suffer the same fate as the two English brigades which were at Got el Ualeb and which were destroyed the day before yesterday – we will cease fighting as soon as you show the white flag and come towards us unarmed. Signed: Rommel, General Oberst.*

Henri took the copies of the message to Colonel Amilakvari who read the content, handing one of the copies to General Koenig who was standing beside him. The General looked up from the form. 'Rommel's clearly angry that the Free French are proving an obstacle to his plan to roll up the 8th Army from the south.'

They looked at the General. Koenig's response was to order an artillery barrage against the armoured vehicles facing them.

<hr>

Amilakvari called 13th Demi-Brigade officers to his command post. As always, the former Russian aristocrat was immaculate in his turn-out as he looked each one of them in the eyes. 'Just a few weeks ago, we celebrated our feast day, the anniversary of the Legion's great fight seventy-nine years ago at Camarón in Mexico. General Koenig asked us to show by our own example, our respect for those legionnaires at Camarón. I replied that those of us who are foreigners could never do enough to express our gratitude to France, which means Free France, for what she has done for us during the past century.'

Henri could feel the tension as the Legion commander went on. 'This battle has been under way for several days now. Rommel's forces are having supply problems further north due to the damage our Jock columns have been inflicting behind his lines, and a terrific battle is under way in what is being called the "Cauldron". He's going to have to take Bir Hakeim if he is to encircle 8th Army. We and our other French comrades here know what's expected of us. We have to hold him.'

Sure enough, at 8 o'clock the following morning, all hell broke loose. Henri was just then at General Koenig's command post. There were shouts as the field telephone reports came in. 'Afrika Korps, they're attacking from the south. Italians, attacking from the north.' A message from Headquarters, 8th

Army, confirmed that Rommel was down in the south, taking personal command of the attack on Bir Hakeim.

⟡

Henri stared at Rooky who was describing a slaughter overhead by Me 109 fighters shooting down South African Kittyhawks.

'The RAF are certainly doing what they can, attacking Axis ground forces,' said Henri. You can see burning wrecks all around Bir Hakeim. I'll tell you, Koenig just sent a message to the RAF Desert Air Force Command, "Bravo! Merci pour la RAF. Koenig", which brought the immediate reply "Merci pour le sport. Tedder".'

⟡

Amilakvari sat in a canvas chair, the Legion officers and some senior NCOs around him. They knew that after ten days of battle, the strain was showing everywhere.

'As you'll have heard, Rommel's got the upper hand, and 8th Army is pulling back. If we can hold on another couple of days, they should be able to extricate most of their forces and start the withdrawal into Egypt.' There was silence in the tent.

The Colonel continued. 'The supply position is critical. In two days' time, we'll be out of ammunition. We're already short of water despite an RAF drop of nearly two hundred litres, mainly for the wounded. As you know, the daily ration is down from one and a half litres per man, to one cupful.'

There was a murmur among the assembled company, only too aware of the situation.

'General Koenig has received orders from 8th Army Headquarters to break out tomorrow night, and some initial planning on the direction of exit through the minefields has been done.' Complete silence as everyone felt the shock of this announcement. 'We'll head for a rendezvous point south-west of Bir Hakeim where we'll be met by the British, the Rifle Brigade and KRR whom we know and trust.' He paused, and looked around the group before continuing.

'The General insists it be a fighting retreat. Some of you will remember Norway, where we left behind all our *matériel*. He's pointed out that here we have wounded legionnaires of German origin, and other nationalities whom the enemy would love to get their hands on. These men have fought for us and we owe it to them to bring them out.' There was a rumble of agreement around the tent. 'There's to be a briefing of all available officers at nine o'clock this evening, at the General's command post. The order in which the various units will break out is to be confirmed then. The troops will only be informed at the last moment, to avoid damage to morale.'

<hr />

Henri, along with other officers including those who could be spared from the outlying defences, sat facing General Koenig. Alongside was Chief of Staff Masson, and Prince Amilakvari as CO of 13 DBLE, Robert Le Roux in command of the two colonial infantry battalions, and Commandant Amyot d'Inville of the Marine Fusiliers.

Koenig addressed the group. 'Gentlemen, you know why I've asked you to join me this evening. Let's go straight to the details. The break-out is not going to be a smooth operation. It has to be at night. The path through the minefields is unlikely to be broad enough to enable the rapid exit demanded. Should the Axis forces realize what's happening, they'll fire flares and light up the whole scene.'

There was some sucking in of breath as the danger faced became apparent to all.

The General explained which of the three gaps in the 'V' formation minefields should be the exit route. The gap towards the south-west was preferred, through which the Jock columns went out and came back. No enemy vehicles were sighted in that direction for some days. He added that the break-out would be in four phases. He then invited questions.

Captain Lamaze raised an arm. 'What about those unable, who aren't mobile?'

The General snapped back, 'It's going to be a fighting break-out, we're not leaving any wounded behind.'

He continued. 'In the first phase, all units will assemble in columns, en masse and in silence. Captain Gravier's sappers will create a breach two hundred metres wide through which the columns will pass.

'The second phase begins at "H" hour, when those infantry on foot will open the corridor and hold it free of enemy interference.

'The third phase is the launch of the columns of vehicles down the corridor, guarded by the infantry on the left and right.

'The fourth phase will be when the infantry on foot join the vehicle columns at the rendezvous point with British Army units. Any questions?'

Captain de Sairigné held up a hand. 'Will there be any attempt to deceive the enemy, as to the direction of our objective?'

Koenig grimaced, almost a smile. 'Yes, at the time of exit the columns of vehicles will head due west for the first ten kilometres, then turn due south to the rendezvous point. The intention is to avoid the enemy knowing our objective is south-west and launching an armoured column to destroy our infantry.'

Colonel Masson spoke up. 'We have to be sure that all company commanders are clear as to these orders. Some are missing, particularly in the north where heavy fighting has been going on all day.'

Henri knew that Pierre Messmer's company had been involved in furious combat in the north of the Bir Hakeim box, and communications with him had broken down.

The Chief of Staff continued. 'The dead must all be buried and a cross placed on each provisional grave, with the name as legible and indelible as possible, marked clearly by surrounding stones so they can be identified when we return to honour those we've left behind. Other preparations during tomorrow will include fuelling to maximum all vehicles, and destruction of those to be left behind along with supplies not required. And we burn files and records we're not taking with us.'

Henri

~~Leo~~ looked at his watch. Just before midnight. The Legion infantry was in the vanguard, waiting for the signal to move forward, at the entrance to the passage between the minefields. Behind, he could see the mass of infantry. He knew that at the rear there were two hundred vehicles drawn up in two columns. The combat vehicles in front, the service trucks, and behind them the ambulances carrying the wounded. Rooky would be in there somewhere. Around them the Bren gun carriers, to give immediate protection.

Henri's platoon and the rest of Captain Lamaze's company moved forward through the minefields. Just through the corridor, suddenly all hell let loose. He presumed the enemy was alerted by the noise of engines, or earlier by the explosions of mines being cleared. The legionnaires deployed rapidly. The firing intensified. He realized the area just beyond their exit route was occupied by enemy forces. Was this an ambush, how strong was the enemy?

An astonishing spectacle broke out above their heads. Rockets and tracer ammunition in red, green, white. Those were not signal flares, he said to himself. Must be to show the French what they were up against. More flares. On the floodlit desert surface, he could make out three lines of enemy forces ahead, groups of heavy machine guns and other automatic weapons.

Henri's platoon made contact with the opposition as they advanced steadily, destroying or neutralizing pockets of resistance. Beside him, the Adjutant went down, killed outright, a veteran Captain wearing his old helmet from the previous war. Then the worst happened. Company Commander Lamaze, charging at the head of his men in the fashion of the old Saint-Cyr-trained elite, was blown upwards, and fell forward onto the stone-littered sand. He moved to help him, calling forward a medical orderly who was at his side in no time, kneeling down to examine the body. The orderly looked up, fixed his eyes on Henri's, and shook his head to say there was nothing to be done for the Company Commander. They'd lost him. Henri remembered how Lamaze mentioned the night before that he'd just taken Communion from Rooky. Somehow a premonition he wasn't going to make it.

Henri glanced back. The Free French vehicles were streaming out of the corridor into open desert, heading indirectly for the rendezvous point. They enjoyed a degree of protection thanks to the infantry's engagement with the opposition. He'd lost some of his own men, but suddenly those remaining in his platoon were through the enemy lines. The firing immediately around them stopped. Looking around, he saw two Bren carriers heading their way. As they were almost abreast of him, he waved them down.

'Give us a lift,' said Henri.

He recognized Pierre Messmer, who called out. 'Of course, de Rochefort. Jump in, and the rest of you.'

'Thanks. We thought we'd be walking there.'

'Where's Lamaze?'

Henri told him what happened. There was a long gap in their conversation. Then Messmer explained his own experience.

'We'd no notice of the break-out until the last minute, when we managed to get back from the fighting up on the northern front. After the exit, I stopped to discuss the enemy positions with Captain Lalande, and lost touch with my men. We both made off together and walked slap into a German position. They were Boche watching the battle from a distance and not expecting a visit. The Captain speaks almost fluent German, and bluffed his way along with them. Then suddenly these two captured Bren carriers appeared and we shot them up.'

They drove on, Messmer periodically alighting to take a bearing as they headed for the rendezvous point, looking for the three red lights which would indicate the British reception committee.

'Over there,' shouted someone, and a cheer went up. The British faithful to their word, thought Henri.

'Look at that,' said Messmer. 'Must be sixty trucks and nearly as many ambulances impeccably arranged in two lines. Fantastic sight. And armoured protection. We've made it.'

Henri glanced at the time. Six in the morning, and some of their comrades already there. The convoy of wounded arrived. The mass of other vehicles slowly rolled in. He noticed some commanders stretching prudence beyond the limit, going back to pick up casualties.

Masson arrived at the rendezvous point, wounded in the head, demanding that the British commanding officer provide him with an escort so he could recover survivors still out there.

'Where's the General?' asked someone.

'He had Amilak in his car, Susan Travers driving,' said someone else. 'Hope they get through to safety somewhere.' Then word came through that Koenig and Amilakvari finally made it to a British armoured unit.

Henri asked about Rooky. He surfaced eventually and in one piece, thanks to Corporal Morel who'd stuck with him all the way.

⊷⊶

Henri and Rooky stood together three days later when Pierre Koenig addressed his surviving officers and men, now at Sidi Barrani.

'Tragically we've suffered many casualties during the escape, and lost others taken prisoner. The covering fire given by the British Light Infantry helped us avoid disaster. It may have felt like a shambles, perhaps it was, but two-thirds of those who started the battle at Bir Hakeim are still safe and will fight again.' There was a spontaneous cheer.

The General continued. 'I have here the transcript of a speech broadcast on the BBC by Maurice Schumann, General de Gaulle's Foreign Minister designate. He describes on "Radio Londres" the action at Bir Hakeim as a "rendezvous d'honneur", to stand alongside Verdun.' He paused, then with characteristic self-deprecation, added 'If you'd like my own view, I regard our performance overall as satisfactory.'

'Well,' said Rooky quietly to his former pupil, 'you can thank your lucky stars that you've a general with his feet firmly in the sand. What's next?'

'Alexandria and Cairo, for a short rest.'

'Oh,' said Rooky. 'This sudden silence in the desert won't last for long.'

15

'The battle of Gazala is over, the battle for Egypt has begun.' His hero, that's how Leo felt about Field Marshal Kesselring, stood facing his staff and senior officers of the Ramcke Brigade. He'd witnessed the Commander-in-Chief involving himself directly in the Gazala battle. When Rommel split command of his forces, taking for himself the German and Italian armoured formations to the south against the Free French forces at Bir Hakeim, the commander of the Axis forces in the north was taken prisoner. Leo was astonished when he heard that Kesselring was flying into the battle zone to take his place.

Alongside the Commander-in-Chief stood veteran parachute commander from the capture of Crete, General Ramcke.

'You have just witnessed Rommel's greatest success so far in the desert campaign. The rout of 8th Army along the Gazala line is having an important impact on our strategic thinking, and specifically on the plan to capture Malta. The Führer hasn't forgotten the carnage inflicted on the *Fallschirmjäger* in the drop on Crete.'

There was a murmur of anticipation among the group.

'After doubling back to take Tobruk, Rommel has successfully persuaded the Führer to abandon the invasion of Malta in favour of Axis forces advancing on Cairo and Suez. As a consequence, the Ramcke Parachute Brigade is being assigned to join the Afrika Korps in Egypt.'

Silence. Leo tensed up. A taste of real desert warfare. The realization in the minds of the audience. You could feel the tension in the air as this news sank in. The alternative could have been Stalingrad. Everyone knew the opening moves of the German attack on the great city on the Don were under way. Maybe it would be a walk-over but, should it not be, the Russian winter awaited the attackers.

Was Kesselring's heart in this change of plan? Malta remained critical to the Allies' attempts to block Rommel's supply lines.

The Field Marshal turned towards the not so young, but tough-looking man at his side. 'General Ramcke, please explain the detail to everyone.'

Ramcke stepped forward. 'Initially, our task is to counter the success of the British Special Air Service which has been disrupting our supply lines and attacking Luftwaffe airfields. I then expect we'll be ordered to join the main attack which'll be launched on the new Allied defensive line running from the coast down to the Qattara Depression. If Deutsche Afrika Korps and the re-trained Italian formations including the Folgore, can take Cairo, then the Suez Canal and Palestine will be wide open to us. You know what that means. The oilfields of Iraq and Iran.'

Leo realized that desert warfare would be everyone's vote, when the alternative was Stalingrad. Then his mind switched to the Geheimschreiber encryption machines. He must find the right person to take over from him, their protection was paramount. Should the British get their hands on them and break into the encryption, they would read the messages from the Führer to Rommel. That could be the end for them all.

⇥⟐⟐⇤

'Captain.' Leo felt a hand on his shoulder, as he made his way to the Mess for lunch. It was Colonel Metting, from OKW/Chi, the High Command's cryptologic centre.

'Colonel, sir.' Leo responded to Metting's Nazi salute, and his Heil Hitler. 'How good to see you again.'

'Yes, Captain. I hear you've done an excellent job in ensuring the secrecy and security of the Geheimschreiber installation, the Lorenz machines. I'm making a short visit to HQ here. There's something which the Field Marshal and I believe you could assist us with.'

Leo felt himself immediately on the alert when he heard the reference to Kesselring. 'I'd be pleased to help if I can.'

Metting led the way to a small room in the main HQ building. Coffee was brought in by an orderly, and the Colonel opened his briefcase and laid out some documents on the table between them. He looked directly at Leo, and started to speak in his machine-like monotone voice. 'Captain Beckendorf, I know you're familiar with the importance of wireless interception in this war. An outstanding example of its role is the use which General Rommel has put it to. Captain Seeböhm, commander of the Afrika Korps Radio Intercept Company, is constantly listening to British military radio traffic.'

'Yes, Colonel. I can imagine that signals interception is even more effective in desert warfare because both sides are on the move much of the time. Identifying the other side's order of battle, the location of their units, must be crucial.'

'Precisely. Rommel has to know the strength of the forces he's up against, their location, their plans, and the timing of advances and withdrawals. To deliver this need requires intelligent people trained in such specialized work. As you know, his radio intercept unit in the field is not Rommel's only source. OKW/Chi supplies him with top-secret intelligence traffic flowing from the Cairo embassy of the United States to Washington. You will recall our earlier discussion on the subject.'

'Yes, Colonel, the breaking of the US diplomatic code.'

'Correct. We read the US State Department's Black Code, as it's called, and decrypt the reports including those from the source in Cairo. Cairo's reports detail the British military status in North Africa. We then pass the information to Rommel.' Metting waited for a moment, then said 'Captain Beckendorf, we are asking you to oversee the security of General Rommel's communications with OKW and Field Marshal Kesselring.'

Leo was unsure what this really meant. On the face of it, he on his own could never manage such a broad undertaking. 'Naturally, sir, I will take on whatever you and the Field Marshal ask me to handle. My worry, though, is whether such a task is within my capabilities.'

'Captain, we're referring specifically to the Geheimschreiber machines. Two of these machines, like the Lorenz SZ-40 here, are being installed at Rommel's desert HQ. Your official role will be as General Ramcke's intelligence officer, but we want you to maintain oversight of the security of Field Marshal Rommel's long-range transmission equipment.'

'So, I would have to alert you to anything which might threaten the high-level information flowing between OKW and Rommel's HQ.'

'Exactly. Just think for a moment about the consequences of such information falling into enemy hands, at the point where we are about to take Cairo.'

16

Benghazi, June 1942

'We face an unusual situation.' The nurses were seated in the canteen of the Wehrmacht base hospital. The Luftwaffe senior medical officer faced them. 'There's a shortage of nursing teams with the forward units at the new line which the enemy is holding from El Alamein to the Qattara Depression. You know that only male medical staff are sent into the front line, normally.'

There was a murmur among the women, a tremor of expectation.

'I'm asking for volunteers. It will be hazardous, and those with dependents back in Germany should think twice before volunteering. Any of you willing to go forward should give your names to the senior Medical Officer after this briefing.'

Theresa remembered the advice from the Reverend Mother when she was preparing herself back at the convent outside Munich. 'Elisabeth, when you become Theresa, don't stand out and be noticed. Go with the crowd. Be yourself and positive with your work, but don't draw attention to yourself.

The meeting broke up. She had to decide. The consequence of her real self being found out was too terrible to think about. A Jewish woman in disguise, in a front line unit of the Afrika Korps. She would be taken and, if lucky, shot as a spy. More likely, the Gestapo would find out and move her to somewhere where they could interrogate her. She would suffer terribly before she died. Yet she knew they wouldn't be asking for female nurses unless the need was critical. Something inside her was saying she should volunteer. She wasn't encumbered with commitments back home, wherever home now was for her. The advice 'be yourself' surely meant she should do what she would normally do, were all else equal.

The MO looked up when she approached the open door. 'Ah, Fräulein Krüger, if I'm not mistaken.'

'Yes, sir,' replied Theresa. 'I have come to ask you to put me down for transfer to the front.'

Sidi Haneish, June 1942

This really is the middle of nowhere. That's what first came to Theresa's mind as the two trucks pulled alongside the tented field hospital close to the airfield. The plan was to stand by there until called on to transfer to the forward dressing stations. The impression was that Rommel was about to launch one of his lightning attacks, before 8th Army could re-build its strength. They'd just heard of his promotion to Field Marshal. All knew that after their retreat, the Allies were back at a prepared defensive line which was much shorter and therefore easier to defend than that between Gazala and Bir Hakeim.

'Welcome to Egypt,' said a parachute NCO, after they dropped from the back of the vehicles, dragging their kit with them. 'Come with me and I'll show you the air raid shelters, then the latrine tent, and finally your quarters which are in shared tents. That's the order of priority,' he added, which at least produced a laugh.

As they moved off, a transport aircraft landed, and taxied towards them in a cloud of dust. Theresa pulled the hood of her tunic up over her face, putting her head down. When she finally looked up, there was a short tough-looking paratrooper with some other passengers in uniform, walking towards them from the plane. He looked in their direction, but nothing was said. 'I bet they weren't expecting to find females here,' said one of the nurses beside her. 'Looks like we might have an interesting evening after all.'

They were to take their meals in the officers' mess tent. A group of them went in after the call went around, and there was a distinct drop in the noise of conversation as they entered. Several Luftwaffe pilots got up and invited them to join their tables. One officer wore the smock of a *Fallschirmjäger* captain, the paratrooper she saw earlier. He caught her eye, and Theresa went over to the chair he was pulling out.

'I think I saw you when our plane landed. I guess you'd just arrived,' he said, giving her a warm smile.

'Yes,' she replied. 'We had one hell of a ride by truck, from Benghazi.'

'I can imagine. You might not believe it but I flew in from Italy.'

'Some change of scene.' She didn't know why, but she added 'Strange place here to take a holiday.' Laughter all round.

'I have to leave tomorrow for the front,' he said. 'Come and help yourself to food, and Munich beer if you like it.'

'Do I just,' Theresa replied. 'That's my home town.' Immediately she realized she'd made her first mistake. Theresa Krüger was originally from Hamburg. She tried not to let her sudden anxiety show.

'My name's Leo Beckendorf,' he said as they walked over to the makeshift cafeteria.

'Oh, I'm Theresa, Theresa Krüger.' At least I got that right, she said to herself.

It was going to be cold that night, out in the open desert even in June. They'd been warned. She piled on the blankets as she said goodnight to the nurse she was sharing the tent with. Attractive man, Leo Beckendorf. To have met a man like that, right out here, was unexpected. Not that strange though, given there were soldiers everywhere, officers too. And not all were Nazis. Was he interested in her? Difficult to look attractive at the end of a day in the desert. He said he was on the way to the front. That he hoped to see her at breakfast time, before he left.

17

The French population in Alexandria gave the survivors of Bir Hakeim a great welcome, but it was in Cairo that Henri realized the Free French had indeed turned the corner in the eyes of their allies. He and a couple of fellow officers walked into an officers only bar, smart in their Foreign Legion uniform but with 8th Army black beret rather than kepi. Silence came over the assembled company, followed by appreciative 'Jolly well dones' from the British and Australian officers, and drinks all round.

'Lieutenant de Rochefort,' said the concierge at Shepheard's, when Henri collected his key. 'There's a message to call a Mr Robertson.'

James Robertson, thought Henri. They don't wait long. He went to the phone booth and dialled the number passed to him on the message form. A female answered, asking him to go straight over to Robertson's office at Grey Pillars, close by Garden City. They would send a car.

The driver dropped him outside a modern apartment building as the sun set over the Nile, and Henri made his way up the stairs until he reached the apartment number. He was shown straight away into an office where Robertson was waiting for him, in shirtsleeves and khaki drills.

'Lieutenant de Rochefort, so pleased you could drop by. It's getting late, but I've some Black Label here. What about it, and a little Perrier? Or a Pernod, of course. We respect the French culture here in Egypt.'

'A Scotch Perrier please, sir,' said Henri. 'Something we missed badly in the desert.'

Robertson made up the drinks, and waved Henri over to a couple of sofa chairs around a small table in the corner. On one wall was George VI and on the other King Farouk.

'Before we get down to business, Lieutenant, I must first say how impressed we all are with the way you dealt with Rommel at Bir Hakeim. Bloody good show. Without the delay you created in the Axis advance, we'd never have got back intact to the defensive line in Egypt.'

'Thank you, sir. It may have looked impressive but there was some magnificent defensive work further up the line, at the Knightsbridge box for instance.'

'I know. But we owe you Free French a lot.'

Robertson leant back in the chair, looking out of the window towards the west bank of the great river, before continuing. 'We know the Abwehr is re-doubling its efforts here. There's something going on in the Sinai.'

'I'm surprised,' said Henri. 'I can't believe anything happens down there.'

'You'll know something about signals intelligence by now, Lieutenant. We think the opposition might have a secret intercept station in the south of the Sinai peninsula. If that's the case, they would be in range of shipping in the Indian Ocean, not to mention the Red Sea and Gulf of Suez. It occurred to me that you'll have some leave due to you. We thought you might like to drive down and take a look.'

'Drive? How would I do that. Surely it's a desert wilderness.'

'Yes. But there's an ancient monastery there, at the biblical site of Mount Sinai. Every so often a car and trailer drive down with supplies for the monks. We can conduct aerial reconnaissance, but anything secret is not going to show itself that easily. We were wondering about the monastery itself.'

Henri thought for a moment. 'Would I be able to take an army chaplain with me? He was with us at Bir Hakeim'

'Oh, who's that?' asked Robertson.

'His name's Rooker. A Benedictine, was a monk at my school in England. Before that he was an officer in the Irish Guards.'

'I don't see why not. He might make your acceptance at the monastery more straightforward. Give you more chance to snoop around.' Robertson paused. 'We have to decide how to get you on the next supply trip. Why don't you have a word with Rooker first. He might have a religious connection here in Cairo. If you can be introduced to the Abbot of St Catherine's that way, it might raise less curiosity than if we arrange it.'

Henri was pleased. 'Certainly, I'll do that right away.'

'In the meantime,' said Robertson, 'I'm going to fix for you to spend some time tomorrow with an expert we have here on signals intelligence and intercept equipment. He'll help you with what to look out for.'

⁂

Back at the hotel, Henri contacted Rooky and brought him in for a drink. He explained the idea of a trip into Sinai.

'What an odd coincidence,' said Rooky. 'I was invited to say Mass at the RC church in Heliopolis last Sunday by a Benedictine monk I ran into. Afterwards, he asked me if I'd thought of visiting the Orthodox Monastery of St Catherine, in the Sinai Desert? He said there was a car used by the Catholic and Orthodox communities in Cairo for pastoral work.'

'That sounds just what we want,' said Henri.

'They have an allowance of fuel, and drive down every few days to the monastery as part of the lifeline between the monks and civilization. There's a trip scheduled for two days' time, and there should be space for us both since they tow a trailer behind for the supplies. The drive's about five hours.'

18

Sinai Desert, June 1942

The battered Studebaker kicked up a small dust storm as it entered the Sinai, heading for St Catherine's, a long and dusty drive. Henri used the time to think through his mission. It would make sense to take Rooky into his confidence. At roughly the half-way stage, the driver stopped in a wadi. Rooky beckoned to Henri, and together they walked a few hundred metres away into the dunes. The desert was totally still, silent. Sitting on boulders, neither said anything for a while, just surveying the expanse of sand and stone which lay before them. Rooky was the first to speak. 'I always have a respect for the Desert Fathers.'

'Who on earth are they?' said Henri.

'The first monks, you could say. They inhabited the Egyptian desert, around here. Remember, Alexandria was a centre of the early Christian Church. The Desert Fathers go back almost to the beginning, the second century. Probably came from Alexandria. Some lived in small groups, others were hermits out on their own. There's no precise history of them, just fragments of their sayings.'

'I vaguely remember you talking at school about the contemplative communities.'

'Yes. Their practices and traditions are reflected in the Rule of St Benedict. They practised contemplation, set an example for us Benedictines.' Rooky paused, thinking. 'You remember that discussion in my study on your last evening at school, with

Leo Beckendorf and Bill Lomberg. We talked about disregard of the moral law in wartime.'

'Yes, I do remember,' said Henri. 'You were concerned about how the Vatican would perform in that regard.'

'I know. I'm still worried. The Nazis are going to lose this war, but not until they've wiped out the Jews. People will ask what the Church did about it.' Rooky shifted his position on the rock he was perched on. Somehow, he knew there was something else on his ex-pupil's mind.

Then Henri spoke. 'You know, Father, I still alternate between fear and anger. I'm a bundle of nerves half the time. Many of my fellow officers seem, outwardly anyway, to get tougher as the fighting goes on. I continue to be afraid. It still takes all I've got to overcome fear, to show the example expected of me.'

Rooky smiled encouragingly at him. 'You shouldn't be ashamed of that, Henri. Courage is a gift of the Holy Spirit. You may not be born with it, but by praying, you'll be granted it. Contemplation helps you do that, and to return God's love. But contemplation demands space and silence and you must look for that, like the first Desert Fathers did here. Try to be alone and quiet each day for a few minutes, when there isn't a battle on. Meditate a little, feel the love of God flow into you, use the silence in the desert.' He smiled, got up and stretched his arms in the air. 'Better get back to the car.'

'Hang on one moment, Rooky. I've got to tell you something else.'

'Okay. Go ahead,' Rooky said, looking at him curiously.

Henri told the padre how he'd become involved with British counterespionage in Cairo, that there was more to his interest in St Catherine's than just the monastery.

'Now you do surprise me,' said Rooky. 'You're not just a soldier, but a spook also. Sounds gripping. I'll help if I can. Incidentally, what firepower have we got?'

'I brought a Thompson and some grenades, apart from my service revolver. Don't tell the driver. How about you?'

'Lieutenant, padres don't handle weapons. Of course, I have a Luger in the bottom of my case. Been there since Ypres in 1917.'

They laughed together, as they set off for the car.

◦━●━●━◦

Henri saw it suddenly as they rounded a ridge of high rock. The edifice was there before them. The driver pointed excitedly, describing the monastery buildings, and then Mount Sinai as referred to in the Book of Exodus. Stopping at the massive outer walls, he took in the monastery buildings and bell tower rising within them.

The driver rapped hard on the heavy double doors. A smiling Orthodox monk, wearing the black cylindrical *kalimavkion* on his head, revealed himself as he swung them open. The monk bowed, saying that they were expected, and took them straight to their adjoining rooms for a wash. A few minutes later, he was there waiting in the passage outside. 'Father Abbot suggested you might like a tour of the monastery to start with. He'd then like to welcome you personally. We have wireless connection with Cairo, and heard you were coming. Few visitors venture here now that the war's on our doorstep.'

Rooky murmured in Henri's ear, 'Even down here, they know that Rommel is about to pounce on Cairo.'

But Henri was focusing on the words 'wireless connection.'

Turning to the monk, Rooky said, 'It's good of you to go to all this trouble.'

The monk started off down the corridor, explaining the story of St Catherine's as he went.

'The monastery and its Church of the Transfiguration were originally built by order of the Roman Emperor Justinian, about five hundred years after Christ. The community has always been Eastern Orthodox. As we enter the church, you'll see in the apse the Byzantine mosaic dating back to 540 AD.'

The short tour didn't last long. The monk then turned to Rooky.

'As I mentioned, Father Abbot has asked to see you. May I take you to his cell?'

'Why, of course. Could we both come please since the Lieutenant here's an old friend of mine, educated by the Benedictines where I'm from in England.'

The monk smiled and nodded, and they followed him down a passage which led to the monks' private quarters. He knocked on the door of a cell, and took them into a small room containing bed, desk and some chairs. The Abbot got up from the chair behind his desk, an old thin but still powerful-looking man, bearded and with an expansive smile. He held out his hand towards Rooky, who kissed his ring. 'It's wonderful to have a Benedictine army chaplain here. Of course, our Order is Greek Orthodox, but as you know we're both able to celebrate Mass in one another's churches.' Then, turning towards Henri, he said 'I hope you have enjoyed your tour.'

'Most certainly we have,' responded Henri. 'It's remarkable. I never saw anything like it.'

The Abbot continued. 'Our sect of Christianity may have stood still during the thousand years since we split from Rome, while your church has developed over time, but we still share the same essential beliefs. When we consecrate the Eucharist, it's the Real Presence we celebrate. There's been no fundamental change between what you and we believe in, no Reformation, no destruction of the essence of the Sacrament such as brought about by Martin Luther.' He sat down heavily, lifting his habit as he did so, and clasping his hands tightly before him. He smiled at them. 'But I mustn't preach to the converted.'

'Your monastery's famous,' said Rooky. 'We're honoured to be here.'

'Strangely, there's a Foundation of St Katharine in the East End of London which is linked to us,' said the Abbot. 'You see, the St Catherine we're named after wasn't Catherine of Sienna. Rather, she was the Catherine who was tied to a wheel and set on fire. Your famous firework, the Catherine wheel, is named after her.'

Henri looked at Rooky in surprise, then back to the Abbot. 'I understand you have wireless connection with Cairo, Father Abbot.'

The Abbot hesitated, just for a second. 'Yes, we do. It's an unusual story, and we were very fortunate. I'll explain later.' He got up, and showed them out into the corridor. 'Now I'm going to tell you something and make a very unusual request. Come with me to the monastery library, please.' With that, he strode out of the cell and set off in the lead, down a series of corridors and galleries. At a large door, he grasped the handle and led them into a vaulted room where the walls were made up of bookshelves and ladders. At one end, there were three monks working on illuminated manuscripts in what was obviously the scriptorium. He asked them to leave. Father Abbot then turned to Rooky.

'I'm sure your monastery has a library and that in there are treasures, perhaps very old treasures. Well, here "old" is relative. What I mean is that this monastery has stood on the same site for one thousand five hundred years, and some of its books date back to Rome and to the first millennium after Christ. There are some of the oldest manuscripts in the world here. This is where the "Codex Sinaiticus", written in Greek and one of the four most ancient Christian bibles, was kept until the late nineteenth century. Thereafter, a large part of the Codex resided in St Petersburg, until 1933 when Bolshevik Russia sold it to the British Museum. Stalin wanted dollars to buy arms.'

'Yes,' said Rooky. 'I learnt a little of that history in my studies for the priesthood.'

'However, remarked the Abbot, 'there are still some folios of that Codex remaining here, and we're concerned as to what might happen to them if British forces have to withdraw behind the Suez Canal and across Sinai. Most of the remainder of the Codex is in Germany, and their troops may well be instructed to take what we have back to Germany. Our community regards the British as the more appropriate custodian.'

'By which you mean we're more likely to return the folios to you when the war is over,' said Rooky.

'Precisely,' said the Abbot. 'Your country has stood by Greece in its hour of crisis when German troops invaded, and your British Museum is a centre of knowledge on the Codex Sinaiticus. We'd like to entrust what we have remaining of the Codex to you, Father Rooker, on the understanding that you will pass it to your General Alexander for transfer to London.'

With that, the Abbot rose and opened a cabinet of wide drawers. Pulling open one of the drawers, he extracted a number of sheets of vellum, covered in Greek text which he explained was of the Alexandrian variety.

'Here they are. Are you willing to accede to my request?

'Well, Father Abbot,' replied Rooky, cautiously. 'We're honoured to be chosen for such an important mission. But I have to point out that there's no absolutely safe way of transporting such a treasure to London. I will take on the task and do my best if you truly believe it's the right solution for your community, in view of the military situation. Please make it as compact a package as practicable. We'll execute an appropriate document for your records, and take the package to General Headquarters. They can decide how best to transport it to London.'

'Excellent,' said the Abbot. 'Now, the two of you must relax for a couple of hours before joining us in the refectory for supper. You are welcome to explore the monastery and its surroundings.'

⇢⊷◉⊶⇠

'What do you think?' said Henri, as they walked together and alone, along the outer walls. 'Anything strike you as odd?'

'Well, he said he would explain to us how they had wireless connection with Cairo, but he didn't,' commented Rooky.

'And what about this package, the sheets of vellum? I don't know anything about the Codex.'

Rooky paused in thought. 'As I recall, there were four original codices, original manuscripts of the Bible. One resided here until part of it was removed by a professor from Leipzig, who passed most of it on to the Tsar. What's left here is presumably what the Abbot is asking us to look after.'

'Father Abbot sounded genuine to me. I didn't get the impression he was trying to hide anything.'

'No, agreed. So, does the Abwehr have a friend here?'

'You mentioned the Desert Fathers yesterday. Maybe there's one living as a hermit somewhere around here, and supplied with food by the monastery,' Henri said, half jokingly. 'The intercept equipment could be hidden where this individual lives.'

'Okay, but if there's an agent intercepting messages, how does he pass them on?' said Rooky.

'Only two ways,' said Henri. 'By wireless, or by post which here means by Studebaker.'

—•—

Silence reigned in the refectory as they entered at the appointed hour. Henri looked around the room. Most present wore the black habit of the Orthodox monks. A couple of others wore brown. Brothers, perhaps. A sharp clap of hands by one of the monks, and everyone sat down to eat. A brother in brown walked across to a lectern, and started to read from a book. Rooky looked at Henri with a sparkle in his eye, 'I think that's *The Imitation of Christ* by Thomas à Kempis, in Greek.'

Supper finished, they walked back towards the accommodation block.

'If an agent is using the monastery's transmitter to forward intercepted messages,' said Henri, 'they would have to be transmitted in clear, with content that one would expect from such a source. Otherwise, our intelligence people in Cairo would have detected something odd.'

Rooky thought for a moment, then commented 'Unless of course they have.'

'So why would I be asked to check things out?' He paused, then answered the question himself. 'Of course, they want to know who the enemy is down here.'

Rooky was thinking, then looked up at Henri. 'If you want my opinion, it's the brother who read to us during supper. You might not have noticed, but there were small thin scars on his cheeks.'

'You're not suggesting he's an aristocratic German from one of their great universities where they fence to prove their manhood? You're mad, Rooky.'

'Well, why don't we make an inquiry or two? We have some time before returning to Cairo.'

The Abbot looked surprised, then chuckled. He repeated the question Rooky just put to him.

'Do we have any members of the community who are not Greeks? Well, the answer is yes. One of the brothers, Brother Anton, is Austrian. He speaks fluent Greek as you heard over supper last night. He was a scholar at Heidelberg originally, then escaped to Greece when the Nazis walked into Vienna. He was a Catholic, but changed to the Orthodox persuasion.'

'How interesting,' exclaimed Rooky, glancing at Henri, then back to the Abbot. 'What's his occupation here? I know the younger monks and brothers work hard during the day, as well as pray.'

'Brother Anton's great interest, where we rely on him greatly, is our wireless transmitter.'

Henri forced himself not to gasp in amazement. So Rooky was right. Brother Anton was their man. Afterwards, he and Rooky discussed the situation together in private. There was little doubt that, acting as an Abwehr wireless operator, the brother was able to intercept signals from allied shipping. He would transmit anything urgent to the Axis intelligence people by wireless, otherwise sending it to an agent in Cairo via the Studebaker.

Rooky was thinking. 'Let's ask Father Abbot if we can send a radio message to Cairo. It should give us a chance to inspect the interior of the radio room.'

'Good idea,' said Henri. 'Then I can return during the night if we think there's something that needs a closer look. Before I left Cairo my friends there gave me a crash course in British,

German and other wireless sets, so I should know what to look out for. They also gave me a miniature Minox camera.'

They went off to find Father Abbot, and explained their need to inform Cairo of when they would be returning.

'Of course, I will have Brother Anton help you,' said the Abbot. 'He'll probably be in the radio room now. He's very protective of it, doesn't allow anyone in.'

As the three of them headed out into the passage, Henri noticed the Abbot stop at an alcove where lines of large iron keys hung from hooks, small signs underneath stating the rooms to which each applied. 'Yes, he must be there,' he said, and strode off down the passage.

Brother Anton took some time to answer the Abbot's knock on the door of the radio room. Suddenly it swung open and the tall strong figure of the Brother stood there, earphones around his neck, long brown habit stretching down to just above the ankles, a knotted rope around the waist. The Abbot explained their request.

'Please write down on this message pad what you want sent. I will convert it into Morse and send it,' said Brother Anton, picking up a pad from beside the door. Henri interjected. 'Could I come in, please, since there may be a reply.'

The Brother hesitated, clearly not wanting them in his lair. Thinking the better of it, he stepped aside and they went in.

Henri saw a table on which sat a British Number 11 transceiver. Just behind to the right was a large wooden cabinet with double doors, locked but with a key in the lock. On the left was a desk bearing what looked like message pads, instruction manuals and notebooks. Above that, on the wall, was a map of the Red Sea and Gulf of Suez, and another of the Sinai.

'So what do you think,' said Rooky to Henri, when they were back in one of their rooms.

'I would like to see what's in that large cabinet,' said Henri. 'It shouldn't be too difficult to prise the lock open, even if I can't find the key. And on the desk, written on a message pad, there were what looked to me like coordinates. Could be positions of vessels at sea.' He paused. 'I'm going back in, after midnight.'

'Okay, I'll follow you and stand outside in case anyone comes our way. So I can warn you.'

⊷⊷⊶⊷

Henri felt his way to the alcove outside the Abbot's cell. Where's that key? He risked a brief beam from the flashlight in his hand. There was the small sign underneath, marked as key to the radio room. He took it silently from its hook and moved on down the passage. Rooky was several paces behind.

There was the door. He flashed the light briefly on the handle and lock, inserting the key. Now for it. There was a faint creak as the lock turned and he pushed open the heavy door.

Henri advanced into the room. In front of him was the British-made transmitter, the desk and the large stand-alone cabinet. There was no sign of the key to the cabinet, and he examined its lock, which looked straightforward. Extracting from his pocket the small tool Robertson's people gave him during his training in Cairo, he inserted it into the lock. Almost at once, the bolt moved and then released the doors. He stood silent for a moment. All well, no sound from anywhere. His heart was pumping fast.

He shone the light at the bulky equipment on the shelving inside the cabinet. At once he realized this was not standard gear. He looked it over, searching for a manufacturer's plate. On the right side at the bottom, he saw the word Siemens, and a part number and date stamped on the plate. With flashlight close to it, he used the Minox in the hope there was sufficient exposure to record an image. To him, and from what he'd been shown in Cairo, it looked like listening equipment used by German signals intelligence.

He closed the cabinet and rolled the lock forward to secure it.

Henri moved over to the table, illuminating the notes and message pads. Yes, what he saw confirmed his earlier suspicions. There were columns headed by geographic region, such as Gulf of Suez, and down the left vertical margin the type of vessel and flag identity. In the centre boxes were coordinates of latitude and longitude together with dates.

Suddenly there was light. He swung round and Brother Anton was facing him, holding a large oil lamp.

'So, Legionnaire Lieutenant, I see you're a wireless enthusiast. Someone after my own heart,' said the Brother in a sneering voice. 'Give me those papers.' His hand was pointing at the sheets of coordinates.

'Not yet,' said Henri, quietly. 'First, let's call the Abbot, so he can hear what you have to say. You, Brother Anton, clearly have two vocations. First, a brother of the Orthodox persuasion, and second an agent of the Abwehr.' Henri realized the Brother must have entered the room through another door, a disguised opening.

Brother Anton placed the oil lamp on the floor with his left arm, distracting Henri for a second. As he did so, his right arm went under his habit and burst out of it holding a foil. The swing of his arm lifted the narrow sword upwards. Henri only had a split second to move sideways as the sword came sweeping down. The weapon slashed along the side of Henri's left arm and a spasm of pain shot through him.

Henri's nervous system and the pump of adrenalin drove him in a frantic lunge at the lower part of the habit. The two of them crashed to the floor.

The Brother was on his feet before Henri. The sword arm went up and was about to slash at his head, when there was a loud report, a sharp crack.

Brother Anton's arm stopped in the air, the sword clattering to the floor. He crumpled into a heap. Then silence.

Henri was hardly conscious of the wound to his arm, such was the shock of what happened in such a small space of time. He tried to recover himself, looked down and saw blood spurting from the damaged arteries. At the same time, Rooky was beside him, tearing off his shirt. 'Quick, I'm putting this around your arm above the wound, going to be very tight, a tourniquet, may hurt like hell.

Then, another lantern, this time in the doorway. One of the monks must have heard the gunshot.

Rooky looked up. 'Father, please bring Fr Abbot, and the monk in charge of first aid. At once.'

The monk disappeared, at speed.

'Now, Henri, get this in your head. You shot Brother Anton. This is your Luger,' he said, putting the weapon into Henri's good hand. Monks don't shoot other monks, particularly with a Luger.'

Henri gasped. 'My God, Rooky, you saved my life. Where did you shoot him?'

I aimed for the head, short range, from the doorway. I was watching you from there. Lucky he didn't come up from behind me. Hopefully, you've only a flesh wound and the tendons aren't damaged. You can show your wound to the Heidelberg fencing alumni. They may award you an honorary degree. Now let's have a look at our friend. Dead, I fear. Ah, yes, small hole in the temple, to go with the two scars on his cheeks. That's the beauty of the Luger, small calibre, high muzzle velocity. Doesn't make a mess.'

At that moment, the Abbot burst in.

Rooky did the explaining, showing him the listening equipment and lists of vessels and coordinates. And of course, the sword and Henri's wounds and newly acquired Luger.

Although there was no doctor at St Catherine's, it turned out there was a trained medical orderly in the community. He gave Henri a jab of morphine and cleaned up the wound. There was some discussion as to what should happen to the corpse. In the end, a short service was held the following morning in the abbey church, after which Brother Anton and coffin were loaded into the back of the Studebaker.

Rooky and Henri decided that Fr Abbot and the community should be absolved from any responsibility for what happened, and undertook to arrange matters in Cairo to that effect. Fr Abbot was overwhelmed with thanks for their understanding, stressing the importance of the monastery's reputation. Rooky assured him that the package containing the folios of the Codex Sinaiticus would be delivered to General Alexander.

19

The corpse in its coffin was deposited at the morgue of the General Hospital, where Henri's wound was dressed and he was assured that his arm should regain its full use.

At Shepheard's, Henri and Rooky were to part company. Henri knew that his mentor was now was to re-join 7th Armoured Division, to be attached to the temporarily merged 4th/8th Hussars. Thanking him once more for what he'd done for the Free French, he knelt and received Rooky's blessing. In the car, on the way to see Robertson at Grey Pillars, the memories of his schooling flooded back. Where was Bill now? Was Leo really in the Luftwaffe? They were both survivors, he was sure. All three would never forget Rooky's guiding hand, exemplified by that discussion between him and the padre in the Sinai.

⟶▸⊜◂⟵

Rooky went to his room and opened his bag, taking out the package entrusted to him. Sitting at the desk, he started to write to his old friend Harold Alexander, Commander-in-Chief of Middle East Command. He called for a dispatch rider and instructed him to take the letter addressed to the C-in-C, and to part with it only to the General's ADC.

He didn't have to wait long for a response. The next day was August 15, the Feast of the Assumption, and Rooky was to say Mass at the Armenian Catholic Church of the Assumption.

When he returned to Shepheard's, a staff car was waiting for him. The driver announced that Rooky was required immediately at General Headquarters Middle East.

They drove through the narrow streets until arriving at the wired-off area in Garden City. The car passed through the outer barrier with just a salute as the sentries recognized the vehicle and its driver, and proceeded to what had been blocks of recently constructed apartments.

The high level of security at one block suggested occupation by the top brass. Rooky was waved in, and after a few minutes only, General Alexander's ADC appeared. The young officer saluted, leading Rooky through to a large office at the back of the building. There was a conference table and maps both on tables and on the walls. The Commander-in-Chief, immaculate, sharp, and exuding friendliness, turned to welcome his visitor.

'Rooky, all this time in the desert has certainly cleansed your body to match the soul,' he said, looking the padre up and down. 'You do look fit. Coffee or tea, or something stronger?' They sat down in a couple of sofa chairs in a corner of the room, as an orderly served them.

'Congratulations on your appointment. At least it's warmer here than when I was at Narvik with the Micks,' said Rooky.

'I'd forgotten you were there,' said the General. 'Bloody awful show that was, the 1st Battalion losing its senior officers, all at once. Now I understand you're returning to the Irish Hussars. It seems an age since you were with my battalion during Ludendorff's offensive,' said the General. 'I say mine, but although I had the temporary rank of Lieutenant Colonel, my substantive rank was only Captain.'

'I remember well, Alex,' said Rooky.

'That was when my low opinion of Pétain was formed,' said the C-in-C. 'The German storm troopers attacked at the point where British and French forces met along the line. We needed the French to bring in reserves and Pétain was very slow to act. Thank God Marshal Foch stepped in. Then you went off to the Benedictines. Pretty brave effort to come back and spend all this time here in the thick of it.'

'Not really,' said Rooky. 'Remember Father Browne, Alex, one of our padres in Flanders? Two MCs, wounded several times, and gassed. You can call that brave.'

Alex looked hard at Rooky. 'Yes, you're right. Father Browne was a hero. And there was his photography, what a talent. But you've done well, Rooky.'

'Actually, I've just shot dead a monk.'

'You've what?'

'I'm meant to be an unarmed padre, though when things get tough there's the odd stretcher to carry. I was witness to a brother at the Monastery of St Catherine in Sinai attempting to drive a foil through my Foreign Legion friend who does under-cover work for MI5's offshoot here.'

'Good grief. Who was this Brother, what was he up to?'

Rooky explained the story to the Commander-in-Chief.

'If you're just an unarmed padre, how did you dispose of this Abwehr agent?'

'With the Luger I took off a German officer we took prisoner in 1917,' said Rooky. 'Just never got around to turning it in. It got lost at the bottom of my suitcase, with a few clips of 9mm ammo. Officially, my French friend shot the brother with his Luger.'

'I don't want to know any more,' the General said ruefully. 'How did you find the Free French in battle?'

'They must be as good as any unit you've got, superbly disciplined and officered.'

The General nodded. 'You know I've only this moment taken over here. Winston's visit last week was really a watershed. The withdrawal from the Gazala line back into Egypt generated a major flap in Cairo. Wholesale evacuation of staffs, burning of documents, withdrawal of money from the banks. Those who've been enjoying the sweet life for the past two years suddenly got the wind up.'

'But the mood's changed, hasn't it,' said Rooky.

'Yes. When the public heard Churchill's orders, and Monty's as the new 8th Army Commander, that there was to be no more retreat, the mood changed. Cairo now has the feel of a military city knowing what's expected of it. Yet, every day the strangest things happen, not least of which is your letter saying you have part of the Codex Sinaiticus in your hotel room.'

'Well, I couldn't refuse the Abbot at St Catherine's, and it was he who insisted I should deliver the Codex to you. Actually, it isn't in my room, it's here,' Rooky said as he pulled the sheets of vellum from his briefcase and passed them to Alexander. My obvious concern is how we get them to the British Museum. I'm not sure how good you are in Alexandrian Greek script, but he told me this is mainly New Testament.'

Alexander laughed. 'I take your word for it. I'm no classicist, went to Sandhurst rather than Oxbridge. But to be serious for a moment, the least dangerous route is through the Canal, and round the Cape. That takes time but the Codex has been around already for fifteen hundred years, so time's not of the essence.'

'We can't afford to lose it to the bottom of the ocean, or to the enemy for that matter,' said Rooky. Couldn't we give the package to someone in our confidence to take to London, but address it to the Vatican? If it falls into German or Italian hands, they're likely to hand it over to the Pope. They'd look inside, but if we forge a covering note from the Abbot of St Catherine's to the Pope, it would probably get to the Vatican.'

That agreed, Alexander gave the package to his ADC, instructing him to find a government courier.

Rooky set off to take up his chaplain duties with the merged 4th/8th Hussars. Both regiments suffered such a mauling that putting the two together was the pragmatic solution. From what the C-in-C told him, General Bernard Montgomery was about to have a dramatic impact on the morale and fighting efficiency of 8th Army.

20

The message from Metting sounded distinctly odd. 'German public radio station just broadcast radio play with actor depicting American military attaché in Cairo and referring to *gute Quelle*.' Leo knew this was how Rommel referred to the information intercepted from the US Embassy. Metting's message continued 'Likely will trigger immediate investigation by British including seeking out and capture of Radio Intercept Company.'

Leo was already not comfortable with the security of the Company. Any outsider would find a lot more than basic signals intelligence going on in the unit. He'd been horrified to hear that Geheimschreiber machines, in addition to those at Rommel's HQ, were being installed at Seeböhm's Intercept Company's field unit. The Company was dug in on a ridge close to the coast, less than a mile behind the front line. Ideal for signals interception, but vulnerable to any breakthrough by the enemy. He'd already noticed reconnaissance flights by the RAF. Afrika Korps forces were on the offensive in the south, and defence of the front where Seeböhm's Company was located depended on Italian infantry.

Wakened the next day by a heavy artillery barrage, Leo was up and over to the Company's HQ tent in a flash. Inside, to the left of the entrance, was a signals NCO operating an Enigma machine. Seeböhm was there, a worried look on his face. 'No movements from their front line troops yet, but evidence of tanks assembling behind them,' said Seeböhm.

'Who're we facing?' asked Leo.

'Australians, back from rest period in Palestine. Veterans, the best. Worse than that, our Italian friends are feeling the strain. The inexperienced ones are upset by the artillery barrage. They say they're too lightly armed to defend the position against an armoured attack.'

'There're about two hundred in your Company. If we're raided, we have only rifles and machine guns. No anti-tank. The Italians' anti-tank armament is too light to stop anything other than the Honeys.' He was sorry for the Italians. They could fight well, but their equipment was lousy.

'Better prepare for the worst,' Seeböhm muttered. This time I'm determined to fight it out. Not going to be criticized again by that colonel who accused us of pulling back when the going got tough.'

'Yes, that was grossly unfair, especially as you couldn't tell him the truth about what the Company was up to.' Leo remembered the moment, a couple of weeks before when a colonel on the Afrika Korps staff accused Seeböhm and his team of cowardice when they withdrew to preserve the integrity of their unit.

'What's that?' said Seeböhm, looking round. There was a commotion at the entrance to the tent. An Italian NCO was trying to enter, shouting out 'It's the Australians. They're surging up the ridge towards us, British tanks behind them.'

Seeböhm turned to a lieutenant next to him. 'Clear the secure bunker and take the Geheimschreiber machines and keys back to Division HQ, with the operating team,' he said. 'Also the Enigma and its operator.' He turned to Leo. 'The rest of us will fight it out.'

To Leo, it looked hopeless. His job was to avoid a disaster like this. If Seeböhm's Company was overrun, Rommel would lose a crucial intelligence advantage which helped him reach Egypt. Worse than that if the British got their hands on the Geheimschreiber. He dashed outside and helped load the armoured half-track with its valuable cargo. He had to do more to protect it, and detailed a veteran Afrika Korps sergeant and heavy machine gun crew to join the lieutenant on-board. A radio truck was to follow, together with an Italian armoured vehicle.

There was the scream of a tank shell, and he glanced back at the HQ tent. It exploded on the edge of the shallow sand bunker into which the large tent was dug. He rushed forward, and helped to drag Seeböhm out. It was clear he was seriously wounded. A medical orderly rushed forward with a stretcher, and Leo went back to the dressing station with them.

'Got to save him,' he said to the MO and nurse assisting him.

The MO took one long experienced look at the wounded man, and shook his head at Leo. 'I doubt he'll make it. He needs expert medical attention as soon as possible. The Allies have that capability with their forward units. We have also, with the Afrika Korps panzers in the south, but not up here.'

Leo knew he'd have to decide. The position of the Intercept Company was hopeless. Enemy infantry and tanks were about to overrun them. The enemy's assault looked deliberate and specific, not part of a general attack. It would be everyone for himself. Seeböhm and the other seriously wounded would normally be sent to a field hospital in the rear. But the Radio Intercept Officer on whom Rommel depended, was in such poor shape that the MO didn't think he'd survive the journey.

He thought it through. Best chance of Seeböhm's life being saved was to be taken prisoner and properly treated by an Allied medical team. He'd be given a chance to live and recover. The Radio Intercept Company was being destroyed. Even if it was put together again, only Seeböhm knew how to exploit its potential. Not just so Rommel could maintain that extra tactical edge in the desert, but to interface with the Black Code messages from Cairo.

This is a crossroads for me, thought Leo. This man's life can be saved. But then, with whom might he share his secrets? Or I could effectively kill him, by ordering that he be transferred back to base hospital fifty kilometres behind our lines. He would die in silence, his secrets would go with him.

All this went through Leo's mind. He decided. Seeböhm's life must come first.

Only afterwards did he look up and see her. The nurse from the airfield at Sidi Haneish. She was staring at him, intensely. It was Theresa.

⊶⊷⊙⊶⊷

A short firefight, further casualties, then the senior German officer still on his feet ordered those who could to fight their way out. Seeböhm and some others were left at the dressing station with an orderly who volunteered to stay behind under red and white hospital flag.

The nurses were ordered back, although Theresa said she wanted to stay with the wounded. Leo persuaded her. 'You can do more good with our forces than in a POW camp. Come on, into this Italian truck.'

'If you say so,' she replied. 'What if the RAF pounce on us?'

'We'll jump out the back and find whatever cover there is,' he said.

Silence, as the truck rolled unsteadily over the stony desert surface towards the Italian divisional HQ.

Suddenly he asked her 'What made you decide on Africa with the Luftwaffe?'

'Oh, I was on my own. I've no parents, you see. Having been trained as a nurse, I knew I was qualified to do something meaningful in the war. Heard the Luftwaffe needed people for their medical services in Africa. That was after seeing the news-reels of Rommel's success out here.'

'I can imagine. Hope you haven't been disappointed. We've come a long way. Cairo's so near, and yet ...' Leo paused.

'You sound hesitant. Can't we push on and get there, fast?'

'The troops and airmen, they're exhausted. The supply lines can't cope. Distances back to the ports are unbelievably long. On top of that, only half the shipping gets through, the other half goes to the bottom of the Mediterranean.'

'What about you, what's your background?' said Theresa.

'My parents live near Berlin. Don't spread it around, but I went to school in England.'

'You're kidding me.' She laughed out loud. 'How come?'

'My mother's English. I know it sounds weird, but there are lots of cases like me. I have two great friends, or did have, who were at school with me. One is French with an English mother, like me. The other's South African.'

'Oh, what are their names?'

'Henri and Bill.'

Theresa touched his shoulder. 'You were cut up about having to leave behind the head of that signals unit to the enemy, weren't you? I admired you for how you handled it. Are you going to be in trouble for losing the position?'

'The position? It's the loss of that communications company that's the disaster. Thanks anyway for the kind words.'

Their eyes met. More than kind words, he felt like adding. There was more between them than that.

Back at Italian Division HQ, Leo knew the worst might be still to come. Alfred Gause, Rommel's Chief of Staff, stood there, as if waiting. Leo never saw him look so serious. The look was direct, penetrating. 'The Geheimschreiber's been taken. They ran into an enemy reconnaissance unit.'

Gause, one of the very few who knew of the existence of the Geheimschreiber machines in Afrika Korps. Who knew that Leo was the person responsible for their security. The implication of what just happened rushed up on Leo. Not only had the Intercept Company been destroyed, its commander seriously wounded and in the hands of the enemy, but he Leo sent back the top-secret encoding machines without sufficient cover.

Leo wasn't regretting his decision to leave Seeböhm behind. The man made an immense contribution to Axis success in the desert campaign. He deserved the best treatment he could get, the chance to live. Rather, it was his failure to find an armoured escort for the equipment, capable of resisting attack. And yet, was there more to his own thinking, driving that decision. Was he ready to admit to it, even privately to himself? Was there something down among his innermost thoughts, to do with the rights and the wrongs of the side he was fighting on?

He could tell from Gause's words that he was in trouble. Would he be pulled out of Africa, sent back to Italy, or even Germany, his military career in jeopardy?

21

Sidi Haneish, July 1942

Back at the field hospital, Theresa was able to think through the events at Tel el Eisa. Leo's concern over the loss of the communications company and its commander. His views on the overstretched position of the Afrika Korps and its Italian allies. If what he said was correct, and knowing the enemy was being re-equipped by America, could this lead to catastrophe? The word was that Germany faced a decisive battle in Russia. Stalingrad was a new name to her until it started to appear in communiqués to Wehrmacht forces. A massive city on the Volga, the key to Stalin's southern flank. Her fellow doctors and nurses were saying that Paulus's 6th Army and Manstein in the Caucasus were being given priority. They would receive the new tanks and guns, not to mention aircraft for the Luftwaffe there. Yet their own equipment in Egypt was constantly being withdrawn for repair. How long would this go on?

Then there was Leo. Theresa felt something special about this paratrooper. He looked a hard man, but she'd bet that underneath he could be human, and more than that. The last thing she'd expected was to run into someone like this, when people around her were crying out in pain, dying. That must be war. Yet, she needed to be close to someone. She'd been on her guard for so long, frightened to get too close to her nursing friends, let alone with men. Where was this relationship going to lead, was there any way they could stick together in a world like this?

22

They were in trouble from the start. From the 8th Army brief-
ings, Henri knew it was going to be the decisive battle. They
were to cross a plain of soft sand on the very edge of the Qattara
Depression, at the southern-most point of the line running
down from El Alamein on the coast. Heavier vehicles began to
get bogged down. No option but to abandon them, as the two
Legion battalions pressed forward towards their objective. Now it
was night, and the sappers were entering the minefields. First the
Allied minefields, poorly mapped. Worse still, the Italians planted
false trails and signs. Once through, then on into the enemy's. He
knew the objective, a mountain ridge called Qaret el Himeimat.
Orders were to take it by storming an almost sheer face.

Sudden disaster, the Free French wireless net suddenly packed
up. That meant no artillery support. The CO, Amilakvari,
ordered one battalion to attack but they were beaten back by
heavy fire. It was the turn of Henri's battalion. They made it to
the top, held on until German tanks appeared to support the
Italian infantry. Forced to withdraw. Henri and some of his
platoon found cover in a crater.

A runner appeared with orders for a general retreat back
across the plain. With him also came terrible news. Dimitri
Amilakvari was dead, killed while organizing the withdrawal,
having taken a shell fragment in the head. Henri gasped,
thinking he would probably have survived if he was wearing a

helmet rather than the black kepi he insisted on. This Russian prince from Georgia, so adored by his legionnaires, his loss would be impossible to bear.

A decision to take. He could follow the order and hope to extract his men, to fight another day. Or have them stand firm while he tried to establish the extent of the German armoured back-up to the Italian machine gun emplacements. In the twilight of dawn. Henri made up his mind, to go forward with Corporal Morel and find out what they could.

Together they advanced some distance, then suddenly the challenge. 'Hands up, don't move' in sharp English and then in French, the command freezing them to the spot. Nothing to do but comply. The Folgore camouflage was so effective, it allowed the two of them to walk right into a trap.

'Drop your weapons,' the Italian voice said. Figures in the dark, carrying submachine guns, came forward and frisked them, removing the revolvers and grenades from their webbing. The two were passed back behind the line and eventually arrived at what appeared to be a command post. They were led to an HQ tent where two officers, one wearing Italian and the other German paratrooper smocks. Both sat behind a trestle table and waved them over to stand before them. From their insignia, the Italian seemed to be a major, the German a captain. The Italian major addressed them in reasonably good French.

'You've probably realized that your Legion attack has proved a disaster. Clearly you have inadequate intelligence on the strength and layout of our defensive positions.'

Henri didn't react, he was looking at the German, the *Fallschirmjäger* captain. For a moment it was just a curious look. Then the German spoke in English.

'It's de Rochefort, isn't it.'

Henri looked at him more closely in the poor light. In disbelief, he said 'Leo Beckendorf.'

If the Italian officer, the more senior of the two, was surprised by this exchange, he chose not to comment. He turned to Henri.

'You've been fêted for your defence of Bir Hakeim. But I doubt that 8th Army and Montgomery are going to be very impressed by your performance here.'

Silence from Henri. The major of the Folgore continued.

'You and the other Allied formations in this sector are going to find it very hard going, and the rest of 7th Armoured Division behind you will be in trouble with the deep minefields. Some of those minefields are yours and some are ours, but the mapping on your side seems to have been lousy. We know your sappers are now equipped with the new Polish mine detectors but it's going to be tough for your armour, very tough.' He paused, then addressed each of them individually.

'Corporal, I'm sending you back to the POW cage in the rear. Lieutenant, I'm going to ask the Hauptmann here to take you to Ramcke Brigade HQ, the German parachute headquarters north of here. Hauptmann Beckendorf is an intelligence officer. He will decide with his friends what value you might be under interrogation, although I doubt you will tell us any more than we know already.'

They left the tent. Henri turned to his Spanish Republican comrade who had fought with him all through since Narvik, and grasped his hand.

'I'll not forget you, Corporal Morel. Keep your spirits up. We'll come together again another day.'

With that they parted. Henri walked with Leo Beckendorf over to a VW Kübelwagen parked alongside the HQ tent. It was now dawn. Once they were out of earshot, Leo turned to him.

'Well, Henri, I never thought I'd see you out here.'

'Leo, what on earth are you doing, dressed in a paratrooper's smock? In our last term at school, you said you were going to fly with the Luftwaffe.'

'The *Fallschirmjäger* are part of the Luftwaffe. I was found to have the wrong eyes. So they switched me to Goering's parachute troops. I was in the Rotterdam and Crete landings, and then on Kesselring's staff in Rome. For some reason they thought I was suited to intelligence. Then it was decided to dispatch a brigade of *Fallschirmjäger* here to help out the Afrika Korps and our Italian friends.'

'Who is Ramcke?' said Henri, noting that as they drove over the soft sand, the relatively light Kübelwagen coped with it better than the American jeeps which had recently arrived on the Allied side.

'He was one of the top commanders during our invasion of Crete, a 1914 War veteran who did his parachute troop training at the age of fifty. It was decided after Crete to form a specialist *Fallschirmjäger* brigade for a mission I can't discuss with you. That operation was scrapped. After our victory at Gazala, it became clear Rommel had the opportunity to push the Allies back to the Suez Canal.'

'Yes. It was touch and go for us. Gazala was a close thing,' Henri interjected.

'We were sent here with the Italian Folgore parachute formation, which we'd helped train. You won't know but apparently Rommel has been in a sanatorium in Germany. General Stumme, who was put in temporary command, dropped dead of a heart attack earlier today. General von Thoma has replaced him. Knowing Rommel, he'll be back as fast as he can get here.'

'He'll have to work miracles. You must know that the United States has been pouring tanks and other equipment into Montgomery's forces. And unlike 8th Army, you have the serious problem of supply lines which stretch back hundreds of kilometres. Fuel and water must be critical for you.'

Leo snapped back. 'Hang on a moment. This war in the desert isn't just about numbers of tanks. Not even numbers of troops. It's about tactics and generalship. And...' He paused for a moment. 'And intelligence.'

There was a short silence, before Henri said 'Oh, you mean Afrika Korps's signals intelligence, or are you implying you have spies lurking in our HQs?'

Leo grimaced. 'I'm supposed to be an intelligence officer. But the decision to transfer the Ramcke Brigade to the desert probably saved me. I'd made a mistake. Can't give you any details. Ramcke's need for experienced officers out here saved my bacon, as we used to say at school.'

Henri wasn't taking the conversation seriously up to that point. Yet, suddenly, he sensed Leo was giving away something.

There was silence. Then Leo turned towards Henri.

'Look, Henri, I think Britain and America should come to some accommodation with Germany. It's ridiculous that we are here slugging it out against one another while Germany is in an epic struggle to prevent Bolshevism consuming Europe.'

Henri thought for only a moment. 'No chance. Neither Churchill nor Hitler would even think of it. Do you have any idea what your country is perpetrating in the East, behind the lines? What about the persecution of minorities, particularly the Jews, not to mention Catholic priests even in Germany?'

'Oh,' said Leo. 'Who told you that?'

'You remember what Rooky said on last our night at St Gregory's, about suspension of the moral law in times of war? 'Read this sometime.' Henri pulled out from his tunic some pages of the London *Daily Telegraph*, printed on thin rice paper. 'It shows that, in America and Britain, the public know

what the Nazis are doing to these peoples. They're extermi-
nating them not only by slave labour, but by gas. The Allies are
only going to be satisfied with unconditional surrender. The
first step towards that may well be right here in the next few
days. Shortly to be followed by Stalingrad if latest reports are
correct.'

Leo waited, and then changed the subject.

'Henri, how's your sister Françoise?'

'I honestly haven't heard anything for two years. I assume
she's in France, with my parents. Of course, Bordeaux is in the
Occupied Zone. Incidentally, you'll never guess who I ran into
before the Bir Hakeim battle.' He paused for effect. 'Rooky.
He's right here, a chaplain in 7th Armoured Division.'

'That's extraordinary. I always liked him. He was in the last
war, wasn't he?'

'Yes, a captain in the Irish Guards. In the same battalion as
the new Allied Commander-in-Chief out here, Alexander.'

They were arriving at what Henri presumed was Ramcke
Brigade HQ, from the look of the tents and *Fallschirmjäger* dug
in around them.

'Not much with wheels on round here,' remarked Henri,
noting only machine guns and light anti-tank guns, no artillery, no trucks.

'That's how parachute units get around, lightweight. Which
means on foot, unless someone else's vehicles give us a lift. The
minus is that if the front breaks, you get left behind.'

'Good opportunity to fight to the last,' quipped Henri.

Leo didn't answer. A very young-looking sergeant in shorts
and parachute smock approached Leo and saluted smartly.

'Herr Hauptmann, General Ramcke wishes to meet this
officer who is your prisoner. He will see you both in the
command tent in five minutes.'

'Very good,' replied Leo, as they switched direction and headed across the sand towards a bunker type position covered in camouflaged netting. They entered down some steps and stood on the edge of what was presumably the General's conference area.

Leo stood at attention in front of two officers sitting behind a table, addressing the more senior.

'Sir, may I introduce you to Lieutenant de Rochefort.'

General Ramcke regarded Henri with a withering stare. 'I'm in command of this Brigade and', he turned to the other officer, 'this is Major von der Heydte who commands the Fallschirmjäger-Lehrbataillon.' He asked Henri and Leo to sit in canvas chairs opposite the portable desk in front of him.

'We're not going to subject you to a long interrogation. There's a battle going on, and I doubt you'd be able to tell us anything new of importance. However, I'm interested in how you and your Free French colleagues regard the Armée d'Afrique, the Vichy French army in Algeria and Morocco.'

Henri thought for a moment. 'In the first place, General, they are unique in that nearly half the men are of French origin, the remainder being natives of the hill tribes in those two countries. Not like the British Indian Army where only the officers are British. Secondly, they've not been defeated, like the French Metropolitan Army has. Thirdly, it's only a matter of time until they change sides.'

Ramcke stared at Henri. There was a stony silence, broken only by background gunfire.

'I'm going to keep you with us for the moment. You may come in useful in the days ahead. Hauptmann Beckendorf, look after the Captain, give him the same rations as you are entitled to, or whatever remains of them. But if he tries to go back over the line to his friends, shoot him.' With that he made clear that the audience was over.

Henri was assigned a tent of his own, surrounded by wire and with a single sentry watching over him. Water and food were delivered at regular intervals, meagre rations, but he accepted that his captors had no better.

After a couple of days, Leo came to see him in an agitated state. 'We're pulling out. Get ready for a fight, and a long march.' He explained that the Ramcke Brigade was almost cut off. Further north towards El Alamein, with the Allied armour following up the initial infantry penetration, the Axis defences were beginning to break up. The Brigade didn't have its own transport and Rommel, back in command of Axis forces, seemed to have given them up for lost.

Even to Henri, the next few hours were hair-raising, as he watched these superb German paratroopers fighting their way out.

They marched west, mainly at night, the *Fallschirmjäger* constantly on the look-out for abandoned supplies. The second evening of the retreat, Leo was sitting close to a small group of NCOs who'd just come together. It was impossible not to feel the sudden excitement. 'We've just made a wireless intercept,' exclaimed one of them. 'A British supply column probably on its way to their tank units, is heading towards us.' From everyone's reaction, this was clearly electrifying news. 'It's obvious, if the convoy of trucks can be halted and the vehicles looted, our situation would improve enormously.'

Fascinated, Henri watched an ambush being prepared. It was almost dark when the leading vehicles approached, with little or no protection. The drivers leapt out of their cabs in astonishment as suddenly dozens of *Fallschirmjäger* with submachine guns appeared in front of and alongside the column of vehicles.

No contest, no shot fired, a fast changeover. The crews of the trucks found themselves on the march back in the opposite direction. The hijacked convoy resumed its journey west, loaded with everything from fuel to cigarettes. While all this was going on, little attention was paid to Henri. He saw his moment and, in the darkness, mingled into the mass of disconsolate drivers as they made off back towards the Allied base areas.

The next morning, Ramcke, von der Heydte and six hundred *Fallschirmjäger* passed through Rommel's temporary defence line up on the coastal road towards Fuka.

⇥⊶⊷⇤

Leo felt uneasy about Henri's disappearance. Ramcke and von der Heydte would have heard about it, but so far weren't calling him in for questioning. The Adjutant asked for a report of the circumstances, but it seemed that was more for the records. It wasn't deliberate of Leo that Henri got away, after all. Maybe careless, and Leo knew in his innermost that he was pleased Henri wasn't on the way to a POW camp.

Then there was what Henri said after his capture, about the camps and the Jews. If there was truth in the *Daily Telegraph* article, the Nazis were committing the most terrible crimes against humanity. The control that Goebbels exercised over the newspapers and radio meant that the German people didn't hear of such things. Any information on what the SS were doing to the Jews behind the lines on the Eastern Front, would have to come via regular Wehrmacht troops on leave, those who saw some of the mass killings. He'd heard things occasionally whispered among the few fellow officers and men who were witnesses to the slaughtering of civilians.

He knew in himself, that Germany was acting outside of the basic rules of morality. The reprisals in Crete, and what Henri was now saying. He couldn't help thinking back to that last night at school, in Rooky's study with Henri and Bill. The discussion the four of them had on the suspension of the moral law in time of war. One part of him was asking whether he was on the right side in this conflict. Another part of him was resisting, arguing that his duty was to his country and its people, and that included his family.

—◦◦◦—

Henri rejoined his unit, 13 DBLE with the Free French Division, after his temporary confinement with Leo and the *Fallschirmjäger*. Montgomery didn't seem to have further use for the Free French in his pursuit of the Axis forces. They spent their time in winter quarters close to the much fought-over port of Tobruk, now liberated by the Allies. The following March, they were suddenly ordered to cover the two thousand kilometres to Tunisia at top speed in order to join up with the other Free French force of General Leclerc.

Henri knew something of Leclerc's epic story. Now that the Free French Division was able to welcome Leclerc's officers into its midst, the details of their trek across the Sahara became clear. Henri remembered how 13 DBLE met Leclerc in Cameroon in the dark days of 1940. Afterwards, Leclerc marched with colonial troops loyal to de Gaulle, to the Chad–Libyan frontier. There he took the Italian outpost at the oasis of Kufra, meeting up with the British Long Range Desert Group. The French government in Vichy stripped him of his nationality and condemned him to death. Leclerc then marched his force, now nearly five thousand men, for several months across thousands of kilometres of desert to Tunisia, presenting himself and his troops to the Allies.

Henri recognized this moment as a new chapter opening for the Free French forces. What would it mean for him? In the meantime, what was happening to Rooky? And where would Leo and his paratroopers end up?

23

The two monsignors sat facing one another across the table in an otherwise empty room in Vatican City, nothing on the walls except a single crucifix. They liked to escape now and then from the routine of day-to-day management of the Pontiff's office, particularly when there was something of real substance to discuss.

The older man leant forward and put his coffee on the table.

'Drama and challenge. If I had to compress today's events into three words, that's how I'd do it.'

'Indeed,' said the younger man.

The older one regarded the other in the friendly pose of a parent. 'Now German forces are occupying the mainland, following Italy signing an armistice, some major issues face the Church. The Vatican's neutrality is at risk. It wouldn't surprise me if the Nazis marched in here as well, and ended our independence as a separate state.'

'I woke up this morning with the same thoughts in my mind,' said the other.

'We need to exercise our influence through diplomatic channels, with the new German ambassador here in particular.'

'I agree,' said the younger monsignor, pausing as though thinking deeply. 'I've been wondering about how the Vatican's perceived in the free world, now and when this conflict ends. We must be seen to have acted with the moral responsibility expected of us.'

'Interesting subject, perhaps you could elaborate, dear friend,' said the older man.

'Well, we all know the moral law is suspended arbitrarily in times of war. An obvious issue is the plight of Jews in Germany and its occupied territories, which now includes Italy. The Nazis have moved from depriving Jews of their role in society, bad enough in itself, to incarcerating them in camps and work places of enormous hardship and where many perish.' He paused. 'Now we've heard of outright extermination on an industrial scale.'

The older monsignor looked up at the other. 'Yes. No one wants to talk about it, but everyone is thinking about it. So where do we go from here?'

'I'm mindful of the Concordat entered into by the Church and the German state, following Hitler's appointment as Chancellor. As you know, this was the work of His Holiness. As Eugenio Pacelli, when he was Vatican Secretary of State. We all hoped Hitler would rectify the anti-religious steps already taken by the National Socialist Party, and protect religious freedom, faith schools and chaplains in the armed forces. That's not happened.'

'I think we're conscious of the enormity of the issue,' said the older man.

'Shortly before becoming Pius XII, Cardinal Pacelli edited the papal encyclical written in German, "mit brennender Sorge", with burning anxiety, criticizing Nazism and implicitly condemning anti-Semitism. The last Pope had it distributed in secret and read out from the pulpit of every Catholic church in Germany, decrying the paganism of the Nazis. That was some achievement, under the circumstances. However, our policy in that regard has been somewhat opaque since then.'

'I suppose that's the case. Hard to know how one gets the message through when we're surrounded by pagan invaders.'

'I think we need a stated strategy to follow from now until the war ends, placed on record for posterity,' said the younger of the two. 'Unless we protect and promote our independence, the Church risks being associated in people's minds as collaborative in the rise of fascism and the horrors it's led to. After all, we're meant to be guardians of the moral law.'

'Exactly. So, do you have a plan?'

The younger monsignor looked hard at his older colleague. 'There's a British Army chaplain just arrived here in the Vatican, a Benedictine, Dom Brendan Rooker. He's one of the POWs from British 8th Army, transferred by the Germans to camps in Italy. He was let free with other Allied prisoners a few days ago, between the Italian surrender and the German takeover.'

'And what's special about him?'

'He knows well the Supreme Commander of Allied forces, General Alexander. Apparently they fought together in France during the last war. He and I have talked at some length about how the Church is perceived after four years of this war. He thinks the general view in the free world is that there's been more collaboration with the Axis countries, Germany and Italy, than should have been the case.'

'And so?'

'Father Rooker believes that punishment and retribution will be high on everyone's agenda when Germany is defeated, now the likely outcome. The suffering and annihilation of millions of Jews will become manifest to all when the camps are discovered. Questions may well be asked about the steps the Vatican took when it became aware of Nazi policies as the war progressed.'

The older monsignor developed a look of part scepticism, part curiosity. 'This Benedictine seems to be a deep thinker.'

'He is, and he's come up with a somewhat outlandish proposal. He's suggested that the Vatican prepares a statement of what the Church has so far done for the oppressed races, and what it intends to do. He would then have this "protocol", let's call it, laid before the likes of Roosevelt, Churchill and de Gaulle. It could also serve as a policy statement for Church leaders in the free countries, for example Cardinal Godfrey of Westminster and Joseph Spellman in New York. After the defeat of Nazi Germany, it would be filtered out to the world's press.'

'With the aim of proving the Church was active in fighting Nazism and fascism, rather than complicit in their development.'

'Precisely.'

'How do we know this Benedictine can deliver?'

The younger monsignor went on. 'He's compelling in his explanation of how such a plan can be achieved. He proposes that the protocol setting down the Church's position and its strategy going forward is delivered to the Allies in a Vatican diplomatic bag. He asked whether we'd received a package from Cairo, or more specifically the Abbot of St Catherine's Monastery in Sinai. It was on-board a London-bound merchant ship which was torpedoed and boarded, and the German crew of the submarine recovered the package. It was addressed to the Vatican just in case of such an eventuality. Well, we do have it, it's right here in the custody of the Head Librarian.'

'How did Dom Rooker know about the package, what's in it?'

'It was originally given to Rooker when he visited St Catherine's Monastery in Sinai and includes the remaining folios of the ancient bible, Codex Sinaiticus. Rooker was asked by the Abbot to arrange for their transfer to the British Museum where a large part of the original folios of that Codex rest. He's now proposing that anything by way of a protocol we want to send to London, be inserted in the folios of the Codex Sinaiticus.'

'Good Lord. We'll need some sort of guarantee that the British will do their stuff,' commented the older man.

'Yes. Rooker says he can obtain a *laissez-passer* for the package from General Alexander. For the Codex, that is. And that the protocol master document can be secreted inside the Codex folios. As an extra precaution, he's even proposing that we translate the protocol into Greek and write it down in the Alexandrian text of the original Codex manuscript.' The young Monsignor was grinning. 'Even if the Nazis get their hands on it, it would be some time before a scholar in Germany, if there are any left, sorted out the meaning of the contents.'

The two of them sat for a moment in silence.

'Well, let's see what His Holiness thinks,' said the older monsignor.

A bell rang and they rose to say their Office.

—◦◦—

Three days later, they were seated in the same room, together with Rooky. The older monsignor smiled encouragingly at the Benedictine.

'I do hope you're comfortable enough here in the Holy City. You'll have noticed that we're looking after a fair number of refugees, and I suspect the number will go on increasing.'

Rooky smiled back, but said nothing.

The older man leant back in his chair. 'We've reviewed the practicalities of what you've proposed, in terms of a protocol explaining the Holy See's position on the Nazi treatment of

Jews in the occupied territories, and of how to get such a document to the intended recipients. There have been discussions at the highest level. We've been instructed to request you to facilitate the transfer of a Vatican diplomatic bag containing the Codex and the protocol document inserted in it, to General Alexander.'

The younger man added 'You would accompany the bag, across the front line and through to the General.'

Rooky looked at both the monsignors. 'I'm humbled that you show this degree of confidence in me. I've been thinking about how I could best find my way through the lines. My proposal is that I attach myself to the Benedictine Abbey of Monte Cassino, as just another monk, until the Germans withdraw from the so-called Gustav Line and the Allies take over.'

The older monsignor said 'It so happens that the Abbot of the Cassino monastery is here at present. I know him and will see if I can make arrangements. I'll tell him only that you've rendered special service to us and that we want to accede to your request to get back to your pastoral work with the British forces.'

With that, the meeting ended. Rooky was introduced to Abbot Diamare who was only too pleased to help, and offered to take Rooky back to Cassino with him. The monsignors entrusted him with the Codex package, complete with the protocol, in a Vatican sealed bag.

In a short space of time, Rooky was casting his eyes for the first time upon the astonishing edifice of the monastery and abbey church as he drove with the Abbot in his old Lancia car past the town of Cassino and up Monastery Hill.

❖❖❖

Later that autumn, Rooky having settled into his life with the monastic community, the talk among the monks was that General Mark Clark's American 5th Army was on the move up the western side of Italy and about to take Naples, only 50 miles to the south. It was likely they would attempt to enter the valley of the Liri river by Christmas. Monte Cassino was standing in their path.

24

The Abbey of Monte Cassino, December 1943

Leo breathed in the chilled air, a faint smell of incense taking him back to another abbey he'd become so familiar with during his schooldays. Kneeling on a pew in the nave of the famous monastery, he wondered at the change of events that led him there. His posting from Ramcke Brigade in Tunis to Italy, to re-join his old formation as intelligence officer, 1st Parachute Infantry Division as it was now known.

He was aware of the sensitivity of any battle to hold Monte Cassino and its abbey. Indicative of that was Lt. Col. Julius Schlegel removing, in consultation with the Abbot, the treasures of the monastery in a fleet of trucks to the Vatican. The intervention of the SS, accusing Schlegel of organizing a massive art theft. How people in high places, close to God as well as to Kesselring, forced the SS to desist.

What about the refugees who kept arriving at the monastery and were camping there? Convinced it was the one safe place to be, thought Leo. German troops already at Cassino were under direct orders from Kesselring to stay clear of the monastery and abbey church. Their engineers, and labourers of the Todt organization, were busy upgrading the defensive fortifications on the slopes beneath, around the town below, and in the surrounding hills. He thought how fortunate he was to be granted special permission to visit the abbey church, now he was already based in the town of Cassino.

His mind was soon back to Theresa. A miracle that she was with the Luftwaffe nurses at the base hospital a few kilometres away. That's where *Fallschirmjäger* casualties would be sent. How they'd managed to spend a weekend together. That friendly and understanding Italian family, up in the Abruzzi. So far south, and yet snow like in the Bavarian Alps. Trying out the skis that were produced for them.

Then suddenly, Metting's message to him about the information picked up by the Lauf station. The Colonel wanted Leo to know they'd intercepted an American signal that a shipload of poison gas was released by the bombing of vessels unloading at Bari. What was it doing there? Urgent efforts being made by the Americans to cover up the secret cargo of their vessel, the *John Harvey*. More than a hundred Ju 88s the Allies didn't know the Luftwaffe had in Italy just devastated the port the British 8th Army depended on. He was to let Metting know if any information on the cause and consequences of the raid reached him.

25

Wehrmacht hospital, Rome, December 1943

Theresa sat at the table. Opposite her were the senior military doctor and a smart uniformed nurse, the Matron perhaps. Why was she suddenly called to the most important Wehrmacht hospital in southern Italy? She'd only just said goodbye to Leo after their wonderful stay in the Abruzzi.

'Nurse Krüger,' said the doctor. 'We've called you here because your service records indicate your original training in Paris included the treatment of patients suffering from chemical warfare agents.'

Theresa thought quickly. In her interviews to join the Luftwaffe, she'd told them about her training at the American Hospital in Paris. She'd given them the report from the Director at Neuilly, which he'd agreed to have amended to her new name. That report covered treating and caring for military casualties from poison gases. What they wouldn't know was that at the same time her father was working in Paris on developing chemical agents as weapons. And that he'd subsequently been doing this for the United States government.

'We're aware of Italian dockyard personnel who have been contaminated with an agent during the recent bombing by the Luftwaffe of the port of Bari. There are many suffering from the poisoning, hundreds in Bari itself, and some are finding their way through the lines to our side. We want to be sure that the disease or whatever it is isn't contagious. We'd like your help.'

Theresa recognized she was not under suspicion at this stage. The danger was that her father's involvement would become known. If they connected her with the missing professor now in America, that would be the end. She must be on guard. 'I'll do what I can,' she said. 'Where can I examine these victims?'

'There are two in this hospital,' said the Matron.

<hr />

She recognized the symptons in both cases. Severe blistering to the eyes and skin, difficulty with breathing, ulcers on the body. They could suffer an agonizing death if not treated correctly. Questioned by her about the circumstances, the patients said they felt nothing until some hours after the explosion of a merchant vessel during the raid on the dock area of Bari. First sign was an irritant to the skin. From then on, gradual deterioration. There was evidence of some burns.

'I can confirm that what they've come into contact with is mustard gas,' explained Theresa to the Colonel and the Matron. 'As long as they're treated correctly, they will not die. The longer those affected remain in their old clothing, the worse the case will become.'

The other two looked at one another. Theresa knew what they were thinking. Either the Luftwaffe was dropping chemical weapons, unthinkable, or the bombs were being shipped to Italy by American or British vessels. Apparently the port of Bari was packed with supply ships when the raid took place. She suddenly realized. If it was the Allies, it would give the Führer the opportunity to retaliate with chemical weapons.

26

'So, how was the Eternal City, my darling?' Theresa noticed Leo checking they were out of the way of other Wehrmacht officers at the rear of the hotel lobby, before he drew her close to him.

'Oh, not much time to see the sights,' replied Theresa. She'd got a message to him that she was to be driven up to the hospital there urgently for some unexplained reason. She knew he'd be curious about why.

'You are a mystery girl. Sending you up there with driver and ambulance, there must be a good reason.'

She hesitated. She loved him so much, she wanted to tell him everything. Not just why she'd been called up to Rome, because of her training in the effects of chemical warfare, but the truth about herself. She knew Leo's unit was there to defend Monte Cassino, that it could be a fight to the death. Yet, when she disclosed her Jewish background, the reason for her change of identity, what would his reaction be? So far, he always sounded ambivalent whenever the Jews entered into their conversation. He was very human as a person, certainly no Nazi. But she worried that he might just drop her, either because of her Jewishness, or because she'd hidden it from him. She held back. Instead she decided to tell him what happened in Rome, and went through the purpose of the trip and what she'd discovered at the hospital there.

Leo was quiet for a moment. 'I'll tell you what I think happened in Bari. Being an intelligence officer, I get to hear these things. Indications from our intercepts are that it was an American supply ship which blew up in the raid. That's where the gas came from. It could be a case of one side taking precautions in case the other decided to use gas as a weapon. The Americans are sending one of their chemical warfare experts over to investigate. We intercepted the signal advising of his arrival.'

Theresa was silent, taking this in. At first, it was just interesting background information. She was thinking more about Leo than what he was saying. Then her mind came alive. They're sending one of their chemical warfare experts over to investigate. He can't mean, it couldn't be. No, impossible. Yet, it just might be. 'Leo, tell me, do you know the name of the expert they're bringing in?'

Leo hesitated. 'I think, yes, it was Steiner.'

A sharp intake of breath from Theresa. Her body flinched.

'What's the matter?' he said.

'Oh, it's nothing. I'm just so tired after that long drive. Let's go up.'

'Okay, here's the key. You go ahead. I'll get some sandwiches and beer and bring them up. No room service in wartime,' he said, laughing.

She let herself into the room. Not bad. A large bed, a desk and table with two soft chairs. And their own bathroom. Luxury, she thought, remembering that weekend in the Abruzzi together. It was the first time they made love. Wonderful, but she was hesitant. She knew him well, but not like that. They felt their way. Now was different. She was going to make it something very special for him. She loved him and she wanted him to remember this night together, whatever happened to them afterwards.

The door knock, just a tap. It opened and he was there. He came forward, placed the food and drink on the table and turned towards her. She let him pull her into his arms, and sank against his uniform and the body underneath.

'Darling, I love you,' he said after a long deep kiss.

'You can't love me as much as I love you,' said Theresa. 'And I'll show you how much. Stand still. Don't move. I'm going to undress you.'

With that, she started to unbutton his tunic, laying the garment over the chair beside them. Then she undid his tie and opened his shirt, moving her lips over the hair on his chest as she slid her hand down and unbuttoned the front of his trousers. She felt him stir.

'Gentle now, stay still.' She bent down, unlaced his shoes and, with his help, took them off and then the socks. She rose up again. He was now trying to pull her towards him, but she pushed him back. 'Easy, you're not undressed yet,' she said. 'Come over here, and she led him to the bed. Before he could react, she pulled off his vest. They looked at one another, neither moving. Then she went down on one knee and placed her hands down inside his pants, and eased them off him.

'What's going to happen next?' he asked in a rather hoarse voice.

'Just wait,' she said, and she eased his body onto the bed so he was lying face up, entirely naked. 'Stay like that. Now, just watch me,' she said, and slowly she took off her blouse.

She knew her breasts aroused him, that they were larger than those of most of the girls, and were firm. She removed her bra, watching his eyes. She might be a little taller than Leo, particularly in the legs, but she knew he loved her body and now she was going to give it all to him. Completely naked, she turned the main lights off so that the only light came from a lamp close to the bed, throwing a dim light over them.

Gently, she lay down on her back and placed her hands behind her head, stretching upwards to show him the spread of her breasts and the flatness of her tummy.

'You're incredible, Theresa, so beautiful, all of you.' He started to raise himself towards her.

'Wait, darling.' She lifted herself, looking down at him. 'I want you to remember this. Forget the war tonight, and its terrors. Just think of me.'

Her lovemaking was open and passionate, as they explored the most sensitive parts of their bodies, showing their intense love for one another.

⊷⊶⊷

Later, Theresa knew this was the moment. She'd been warned never to disclose the truth about herself. But their lives were both one and the same, and in deadly danger. 'Darling, there's something I have to tell you.'

He took the words in slowly, the realization this might be something he didn't want to hear, ought not to hear. 'Are you going to tell me you're married after all?'

'Oh Lord, no. But you might think it's worse than that.'

'You're joking,' he said, raising himself up on one arm, seeing how serious she was.

'Hold me close for a moment.' It may be the last time, she thought. They embraced closely, his hard body against hers. After a moment, she pushed him away gently. 'Leo, I'm not who you think I am.'

'What do you mean?'

'Something happened back in Munich, before I joined the Luftwaffe nursing service.'

'What happened?'

'I changed my name. I mean, I changed my whole identity.'

'What on earth did you do that for?'

There was a long pause, as she brought herself to say it.

'Because I'm a Jew.'

Leo was silent, didn't move. The moment was charged with emotion.

'My father and mother came from Jewish families, originally from Odessa, although I was brought up a Christian, a Catholic.' She felt him tense up in surprise, shock even.

There was a long silence. He got up, went over to the table and poured himself a glass of beer, and lit a cigarette. She was watching him, terrified at what his reaction would be. Finally he said 'Let's take it step by step. Tell me the whole story.'

She told him about the ending of her university days in Munich. 'My father was a professor in medical sciences, working before the war at the Pasteur Institute in Paris. That's why I trained as a nurse at the American Hospital in Neuilly. He was a friend of the director there.

My father was working in Paris on vaccines, and other things. I once overheard a conversation. He was involved in chemical weapons development. That must be why the Americans wanted him. Our family name is ...' She hesitated. 'My father's name is Steiner.'

Leo froze. 'Steiner. You don't mean he's the one.' He paused. 'The Professor Steiner on his way to Bari?'

'He must be,' she murmured. 'When the collapse of France was imminent, both Mother and Father escaped to America before the Wehrmacht arrived.'

'And you?'

'I already returned to Munich when war broke out. I felt I belonged there. I wanted to help my people, my country. Then some of my Jewish friends began to disappear. I was a Catholic but I came from a Jewish family. Friends warned me what to expect. At best, I would be confined to a ghetto, more likely to forced labour in the camps, even death.'

He went over to the table and brought her back a drink.

'I met this priest,' she said. 'I got to know him well. We used to go on hikes together, with other friends. I decided to confide in him, how I could escape. I told him I wanted to become another person, leave my past behind me for good. It was he who came up with the idea, a way for me to take on the identity of a dying woman of about my age. I won't go into the details.'

'Theresa Krüger.'

'Yes. Theresa Krüger.'

Leo leant across and took Theresa in his arms. 'I understand, darling.'

She was so relieved she started to cry. 'I don't want anything to happen to you in this place. People are talking about a gigantic struggle to hold Cassino.'

He was quiet for a moment, before saying 'Face up to the fact, we're going to lose this war. The resources of America are unlimited. The Russians are on the offensive, millions of fresh troops from the East.'

'Why doesn't Germany negotiate an armistice?' she said.

'The Führer will never surrender. He'll take the German people down with him.'

'Surely, something can be done to halt the slaughter?'

'It's too late. The SS now has a stranglehold over everything key to perpetuating the war. They're an army within the Wehrmacht. They operate their own factories, making the wonder weapons Hitler is promising. Even if we asked for an armistice, the Allies wouldn't talk to us. They've already said it's unconditional surrender or nothing.'

There was a heavy silence, she could feel the despair in his voice.

'Where does that leave you and me?' she murmured.

'Our families, the civilian population, the children, are dependent on the Wehrmacht for protection as the enemy closes in on all sides. You and I, darling, are part of that protection. We have to fight on.'

27

Theresa's mind kept returning to it. Somehow she must reach her father. It might only be for a fleeting conversation, but she had to try. There might never be another opportunity. No one could predict what would happen to Germans like her when the fighting ended. Leo was despondent. No chance of victory he'd said. That meant defeat.

She couldn't involve him in any plan to reach her father. Crossing the lines was desertion at best, more likely treason. Everyone knew the penalty for that. He could be implicated if she was caught. But if she could find a way to get to her father, she was going to try. He would be in Bari, on his mission for the American government. How could she get there? By sea was possible in theory. By land meant finding a way through the lines to the other side, attaching herself to someone who did so officially. Was there anyone? Wounded prisoners of war were sometimes exchanged. Neutrals moved with some degree of freedom, for example Swedes and Swiss. In theory, the Vatican was neutral. Whoever it was, they would be questioned, and a female was the least likely to be let through. It was said that many walked out of prison camps between the day Italy changed sides and the day the Germans took control. They were hiding on farms and in the hills, trying to find a way south.

Then there was the Red Cross. In the hospital, the talk was about the gas poisoning in Bari. The word was out that she was trained for such cases. That was a slight exaggeration, but it might serve her purpose. At least it might get her closer to Bari, if not into the port which was under British control. An ambulance convoy was being sent there to collect some cases, mainly Italians whose families were in Fascist-controlled territory. The Red Cross were involved including Swiss personnel.

Theresa reasoned that a French-speaking Swiss Red Cross official might break through. Finding her father when the British were obsessed with keeping the poison gas affair under wraps, was another matter. How should she approach the Red Cross, what sort of proposition? She could hardly tell them Professor Steiner was her father. They'd probably not been advised by the Americans of his arrival and mission to investigate.

It was a Swiss doctor she'd met several times at the hospital, working with the Red Cross in southern Italy, who offered the chance one day. She and André were in conversation about the gas disaster. She was showing off, talking about the difference between chemical and biological weapons. That chemical agents used chemicals to harm the enemy, whereas biological weapons use organisms which cause disease. And about the different gases such as phosgene and mustard gas.

'Geneva is taking a very keen interest in what happened in Bari, not just the immediate consequences but what it could lead to,' said the Doctor. 'You'll have heard about the ambulance convoy going there to bring out casualties whose families are this side of the lines.'

'Yes, I can imagine why the Red Cross is concerned,' replied Theresa. 'In theory, Germany could use the shipload the Americans brought in as a pretext for launching into poison gas raids on specific targets. Our problem though would be how to deliver the stuff.'

'You mean the shortage of aircraft.'

'Exactly. The Luftwaffe apparently pulled together a hundred Ju 88s for the raid, from all over Italy. Von Richtofen was in charge, cousin of the fighter ace in the last war. Goering would need a lot more aircraft than that.'

'You're well informed, Theresa.' He smiled, and went on. 'I'm going to Bari with the convoy because I want to meet officials who were there when the mustard gas, or whatever it was, hit the port. Geneva wants me to report back. I need someone with me who has knowledge about the gas and its effects. You speak excellent French. If I could arrange something, would you come? There is risk involved, it won't be a weekend by the seaside.'

Theresa grinned, but her heart was racing. This was the opportunity she'd been craving for. Now it was there to take, she held back. The danger flashed through her. Should either side capture her, it would be the end. On the other hand, this was just the chance she needed. She made up her mind.

'Yes, I'll do it,' she said, almost surprising herself.

Her Swiss doctor friend gave her an admiring look. 'Nurse Theresa, thank you.'

<hr />

'This is the plan,' he said as they sat together in the canteen the next day. 'We have to report to a Red Cross liaison unit at Foggia. That's where Mussolini built major airfields in the thirties, now in British hands. But first we must cross the lines. A route through the hills is being worked on. The German Corps commander, von Senger, has agreed in principle.'

He went on to outline the route, and the crossing point where Red Cross officials from the Allied side would meet them.

'What about me?' she said. 'You were going to provide a Red Cross *laissez-passer*, but I'm dead scared they will see through the sham.'

He touched her arm. 'I'll be with you all the time. As we agreed, you are based at Red Cross HQ in Geneva. Sure, you have a German passport, but you worked in Paris before the German occupation, when you transferred to us in Switzerland. You and I will always speak in French. If there's a problem at the crossing, you'll be sent back to the hospital here. The Red Cross accreditation I'm having prepared will protect you. Then, when we are in British-controlled Italy, you stick with me all the time and I'll create hell if they try to grab you. So will Geneva. You may think you're more vulnerable as a woman, but the opposite is true. No one believes either side will use women in a front line role.'

Theresa didn't argue. She just doubted what he'd said. What were his real motives? Did he really have to bring her because of her perceived knowledge of gas warfare, or did he have other designs on her? Time would tell, but she must be on her guard. Her tallish and very slim figure attracted men trapped in war zones, starved of female company. She'd learnt how to defend herself, and having Leo in her life helped her resist the advances of others. Like some of her nursing friends, she carried with her chloroform pads which would knock out unwanted Casanovas in no time.

The ambulance they were riding in lurched around on the poor road as the convoy wound its way through the high country. Soon they were approaching the Gustav Line, across which the opposing armies confronted one another as the worst of winter approached. In consultation with Corps HQ, they had chosen to cross at a point where there was no fighting, and both sides were expecting the convoy. The Allied fighter bombers also knew about them and held off.

On arrival at the designated British checkpoint, they were waved down and asked to leave their ambulance and go into the tent which served as a guard room. A middle-aged officer examined their papers and asked a few questions. Theresa replied in French, and the Red Cross man translated. The vehicles were searched thoroughly. Additional jerrycans of fuel were loaded up as a contribution from 8th Army, and they were away. Theresa was astonished at how smoothly it all went. Yet she knew how ugly things could turn in a flash, should an Allied unit take a disliking to them. Opel ambulances, with or without large hospital crosses on the fabric roofs, were not likely to be popular.

       ⇥✦⇤

The Red Cross liaison point on the edge of Foggia turned out to be a fine villa. They were to spend a night there before proceeding to Bari.

'We should have a good meal tonight,' said André as they carried their bags through the rather grand entrance and into the hall, where they were greeted by a member of the family living temporarily in the servants' quarters. 'Someone said they still have their chef from before the war.'

The meal was served in an imposing salon, and was indeed delicious, especially after Wehrmacht canteen cooking. They all sat around a long dining table presided over by the grandfather. He and the other family members of course professed to detest Mussolini, who was free again after Hitler ordered his rescue by special *Fallschirmjäger* unit from where he was being held on the Gran Sasso.

Bari, January 1944

Theresa was expecting horrible sights among the casualties when she and André arrived at the Policlinic, a Mussolini creation. Now a large British base hospital, it was receiving the victims of the mustard gas poisoning. She learnt that many were brought in just after the bombing raid, with their bodies eighty per cent covered with blisters and ulcers.

She and André received a briefing from the senior MO and the Matron. She was staggered with what they were told about the medication being used. She knew about penicillin as a discovery, but there was no application so far in the Wehrmacht. Apparently, the growing of the cultures and conversion to full-scale production was a long and laborious process. Suddenly, here in Bari, she found that the Allies were using it to treat the burns of the wretched casualties from the gas poisoning. Penicillin dressings were being used for the first time, and with remarkable success. The effect on burns treatment by application of dressings of penicillin gauze was astonishing, as was the very fast recovery of those patients. Theresa took notes of what she saw in the wards, and what she and André learnt from interviewing the patients. Adding her own limited knowledge to describe the original condition of the casualties shortly after the attack, she followed through the process of treatment and recovery.

She was writing up her notes in the quiet of the library, in an area reserved for medical reference books for staff use, when a man came in. Older than those she was used to seeing in and around the Policlinic, she didn't pay much attention to him. He glanced at her, and then sat down and started to go through a pile of medical reference books. Almost at once he stopped. His body was as though frozen to the spot, no movement at all. Then he slowly raised his head. She felt his movement and gaze, rather than saw it. She looked up, and their eyes met. She was speechless, then said the first thing that came into her mind, 'Shalom, Daddy.'

He kept staring at her, his face still frozen. Then gradually he began to smile. 'Shalom, Elisabeth,' he said, ever so quietly. Theresa moved slowly over to him as he stood up. He took her in his arms. They held on to one another. She felt the gap, how long it was since they last saw one another in Paris. Then, fear stepped between them. She was suddenly fearful someone might enter and see them.

'Daddy, we have to be careful,' she said, gently pushing him away. 'I'm not meant to be here. I'm from the other side. I came to try and find you. Is there somewhere we can talk privately?'

He stared at her, a look of love and incredulity. 'Why, yes. Follow me to my room. If you have to hang back, it's room number twenty on the second floor of the staff quarters.' With that, he got up and walked out.

⇢⟩⟨⇠

That was easy. Her room and André's were also in the staff quarters. The Professor's door wasn't shut and she walked in. Suddenly she felt awkward. She'd left him and her mother and sister in Paris just before war broke out. They tried to persuade her not to go. Although they were Jews and there was no way they would return to their old home in Munich, she felt rebellious at the time. She wanted to continue her studies, to become a doctor, and her university degree was from Munich. Her nationality was German, as were her friends. Certainly her nursing training in Paris fitted in well with her father's job as a professor at the Pasteur Institute. But if there was to be a war, her duty was to the German side. She was too pig-headed to realize the danger a person of Jewish origin like her would face under the Nazis.

'Daddy, I owe you an apology. First of all, I should have taken your advice and stayed in Paris, then gone with the family to America when France was invaded. Secondly, I'm potentially compromising you by being here.'

The Professor came over to her, put his arm around her shoulders. 'You mustn't think that way. I don't know what you've been up to in the past four years, but you are a brave and loving girl, my daughter Elisabeth.'

She held back the tears that were about to burst forth like a breach in the Hoover Dam.

'Daddy, I don't know how to explain this, but my name is Theresa. I had to change my identity. I'm now Theresa Krüger.'

There was a long silence, or that's how it seemed to her. She then told him the story. The advice she received from her friend the priest, and from the nuns at the convent in Garmisch. The death of the terminally ill nun, originally from Hamburg. How she took her name, Theresa Krüger. The new Theresa's recruitment into the Luftwaffe nursing service, and transfer to North Africa.

Her father listened without interrupting. When she finally broke into heavy sobbing, he held her to him, stroking her hair.

'There's one more thing I have to tell you, Daddy. There's a German Parachute Captain whom I met in Libya. He's now on the Gustav Line, based near Cassino. I love him terribly. I share everything with him. His name is Leo.'

'I presume from your Red Cross armband that you're part of the mission which just arrived here.'

'Yes.' She wiped her face with a khaki handkerchief. 'I work with a Swiss doctor in the Red Cross. I spun him a line about my experience with treating casualties from poisonous gas weapons. When we were in Paris, I learnt that your work on vaccines was not the only thing you were researching. And I realized why you wanted me to include the treatment of chemical weapons cases in my training.'

The Professor let that pass.

Theresa continued. 'From Leo, who's an intelligence officer, I discovered the American government was sending an expert over to find out exactly what happened at Bari. As soon as I heard the name Steiner, I knew it must be you.'

'Yes. Naturally, we were worried that the accident might encourage the Nazis to let fly with chemical weapons. And of course, I wanted to examine the casualties, as I think you and your Red Cross doctor friend have been doing.'

'That's right,' she replied.

'Then you will have noted something else. This is the first time that penicillin has been used on such a large scale, and it's a real breakthrough in medicine.'

They talked freely together, first about how he and her mother and sister established themselves in Baltimore where he took up his new professorship. Then she recounted her experiences in North Africa. They knew this was the one and only private time they would have together.

'So, Theresa. I'll have to get used to the name.' The Professor laughed. He then became serious. 'I have to return in a couple of days to Algiers to make my report, and in due course go back to Baltimore. What's going to happen to you?'

Theresa thought how best to answer this, realizing there was no obvious future for her. Would she see anything of Leo after she arrived back at the base hospital. He wouldn't be far away. Yet, there was a massive battle expected at Cassino, and he'd be in the thick of it. Afterwards, if his predictions were correct, they would be pushed up Italy by the Allied armies until, until what? Until the end of the war. No one knew how they would be treated after that, and maybe he wouldn't even be alive.

'Daddy, Leo says we will lose this war. That there's no way Germany can now halt the Allies in the West and the Russians in the East. He says he must fight on, do his duty, that the civilian population depends on the Wehrmacht for protection. I'm going to do the same.'

'My darling. Your mother and I, and your sister, will have you in our hearts all the time. When this conflict is finished, there will be a home for you in America. Maybe, you can even study to become a doctor. You obviously love Leo. To me, he represents the enemy. When the time comes, I will give him a fair chance. In the meantime, only you can decide your future.'

'I knew you'd understand, Daddy.'

She shed some more tears, as he consoled her. Then they parted.

--❦--

Theresa thought a lot of her family that evening, and of Leo. She and André were due to re-join the convoy the next day, to transfer the recovering casualties back to their homes in Fascist Italy. Later, she reflected on the consequences of the arrival of penicillin. Her father told her that by the nature of its production process, it would remain in short supply for a long time. Only the Americans and British possessed it. She'd seen how transformational it could be in treating infections, whether from war wounds or just in everyday life. Countless German lives would be lost without access to it. Then suddenly it struck her that the value of this wonder drug would be enormous on the black market. Could that just be the real motive for André organizing their mission to Bari?

Foggia, January 1944

Theresa was half expecting it would happen. They were on the return trip, staying overnight in the villa just outside Foggia. The next day they would cross the lines back into German-occupied territory.

She was prepared, just in case. Having slept a few hours, she found herself awake and with time to think. Her mind was full of Leo. What would their future be? He was everything to her. They faced only danger, their duties overwhelming the options they would enjoy if it was peacetime.

Then there was André. He'd made his intentions clear several times in Bari. First, there was the financial incentive. He was persuasive. Central Europe needed penicillin. They would be helping those whose wounds would kill them unless they could be treated with the new drug. Children injured in the bombing, a whole life before them if their infections could be cured. War should not prevent the humane distribution of new medications across frontiers and battle lines. Why should American and British doctors be able to save lives, but not those of Germany and her allies. The Red Cross existed to reach out to the suffering of all nations.

Those willing to take the risk of facilitating the supply to those who didn't have penicillin, should be justly rewarded. It was simply a matter of carrying the dosages in one's clothing and baggage. They wouldn't be searched. Even if they were, most people wouldn't know one medicine from another. He was a doctor, she was a nurse, and they would be expected to carry medicines.

Then there was the other side of him. He made obvious his interest in her. It was in the looks he gave her, in the subtlety of what he said to her. When she failed to react, he didn't give up. It became relentless, he seemed so sure he was going to succeed. She felt he was going to pounce on her any time now, and wouldn't take no for an answer.

Her nursing friends in the desert talked amongst themselves about this sort of problem. Men starved of women for months, even years, would sometimes become desperate. A small number could do desperate, brutal things. You must be prepared. Chloroform would knock them out, if you could hold the pad long enough over the face. Attracting attention would frighten any man off, the penalty in the Wehrmacht for rape was too great to contemplate.

It was gentle, just a tap on the door. Her body went rigid with fear. How should she react? She'd already told him she was in love with someone else. That didn't deter him. Reasoning with him about the fruitlessness of his attempts was about all that was left to her, unless ...

Now a louder knock. If she didn't let him in, he would force his way in. She stood on the floor in her nightdress, grabbed her nurse's tunic and put that on. Slowly she opened the door. It was André.

'Theresa, please let me in. I just want to talk to you, be with you. Don't worry, it's just that I can't sleep. I must have your company for an hour or so.'

She felt his pressure on the door. He would come in whether she tried to stop him or not. She relented.

'Will you have a drink?' she said.

'Just some whisky if you have some.'

She poured a modest portion into a glass for him, and added some water.

He came straight to the point. 'Theresa, you know how I feel about you. I want you as my partner on this return trip and back at the base hospital. Together we're going to make money.

I just need your help to carry some of the penicillin I have with me, through the lines. By doing so, we'll be saving lives.'

'André, I've told you I already have a fiancé. And I don't buy into your humanitarian and financial arguments. We can talk for a bit and then you must go back to your room.' She felt herself shaking.

'Theresa, I just want to be with you. I want to make love to you.'

So this was it. The worst case. She knew he was going to have her one way or the other.

He moved suddenly, almost frantically, as he forced her onto the bed.

She knew what she must do. One hand went down between her legs, to protect herself. The other stretched over towards the bedside table, as he took off his coat and, now naked, climbed over her.

'No,' she screamed.

He covered her face, silencing her.

The hand over the table grabbed the ampoule she'd put there earlier and, in the same motion, she wrapped her arm around the back of his neck.

'Stop, André,' she shouted in a muffled voice.

'He removed his hand from her face, replacing it with his own face and mouth.

She thrust the ampoule into the back of his neck. They continued to struggle for a few seconds, and then he went limp, the weight of his body pressing down on her.

Theresa was not prepared for what to do next. She pushed his body on the floor, and put on her clothes, then looked outside into the corridor. No one was around, it was still the early hours of the morning.

Knowing his room was down the floor from hers, and remembering the number, she went to make sure it wasn't locked. Returning, she dragged the body down the corridor and into his room.

Back in her bed, the emotion of the traumatic experience suddenly overwhelmed her, and she burst into tears.

Eventually, she recovered sufficiently to reason it out. They would find him in the morning. It'd be obvious he was contaminated when in Bari, with the spores of mustard gas infection. With the right care, he would recover, but the blistering of the eyes, ulcers and burns on the body, would be dreadfully painful. As a Swiss official of the Red Cross, no doubt his employer would repatriate him to his home country. There would be no trace of the anesthetic she'd inserted into the contents of the ampoule.

28

The Abbey of Monte Cassino, January 1944

The Feast of Epiphany, twelve days after Christmas, Leo was there again, sitting back in one of the pews towards the rear of the nave. His thoughts and prayers moved from his family and home to Theresa. The monks in their stalls were singing Vespers. He listened to this famous Benedictine community, only a few of them left. No doubt a good number moved away to serve in parishes across that part of Italy as war took hold. The magnificent Gregorian chant filled the church. They filed out in couples at the end of the Office of Vespers. He found himself staring at one of them. There was something familiar there, but with the monk's cowl pulled down, it was impossible to see the face.

Suddenly he realized he wasn't alone. Something told him to be on guard. Someone a few pews behind him. After he rose to walk back down the nave, this other person did the same. He recognized General der Panzertruppen Fridolin von Senger und Etterlin, Commander of XIV Panzer Corps, covering that part of the Gustav Line which included Cassino. He'd met Frido von Senger before, at Kesselring's HQ, when the General commanded Axis forces in Sicily. As they came out of the abbey church, the General looked hard at Leo, but in a friendly way.

'It's Beckendorf, isn't it? I thought the monastery was out of bounds.'

'Yes, sir,' replied Leo. 'I was given special permission to make a visit, an invitation from one of the monks here who knew of the Benedictine monastery school where I was educated.'

'Ah, I know something about that. You have an English-born mother, and you were educated at St Gregory's abbey school. I'm what is called a "lay Benedictine". I went to Oxford as a Rhodes Scholar. I understand you're an intelligence officer and just transferred from General Kesselring's staff to 1st Parachute Division.'

'Yes, sir. I served with the Division in Crete. I came down to take a look around the Cassino area since the Division is being transferred here from the Adriatic coast.'

Von Senger thought for a moment.

'Yes, they've fought well, particularly in the last few weeks against the Canadians at Ortona. Kesselring's right in choosing the *Fallschirmjäger*. They have particular qualities, even when they're not dropping from the sky. Trained to fight in small groups, isolated from support units and, should they have to, without officers.'

'Hopefully, it won't get to that,' said Leo, now feeling more at ease with the Corps Commander.

'We expect the Allies to give all they've got to take the town of Cassino and Monastery Hill. The Panzer Grenadiers have fought well here so far and will continue to do so alongside you. It's going to be tough.'

Leo nodded, and von Senger continued.

'Captain, I'm going to rely on you for precise intelligence as the battle unfolds, and for as long as it lasts, which may be months. We have to hold Cassino. By forcing the Allies to maintain their current twenty divisions in Italy, we can reduce the effectiveness of their eventual landing in France.'

Leo took in the General's words, surprised how he was taking him into his confidence.

'My Corps HQ is being moved to Castelmassimo, thirty kilometres north of here. I'll want to know the designation of enemy units which arrive and are replaced in and around Cassino, so we can assess relative strengths. In particular, watch out for the French. They understand this type of mountainous country, and will be much more mobile than the Americans and British. Alphonse Juin, their Corps Commander, is probably the best general the Allies have in Italy.'

'That's interesting,' said Leo, recalling his friend Henri's comments to Ramcke during the Alamein battle, about the French Armée d'Afrique.

'Both sides could suffer heavy losses. We have the topography on our side, our hill defences are well placed, and the *Fallschirmjäger* will give in to nothing. The biggest single problem is the Allied air superiority, and God knows what their bombers might do to this place. Our great advantage is that we command the high ground, and the hill-top positions can give each other supporting fire in repelling any attack.'

They discussed the command aspects of the defences, and how intelligence would be fed to von Senger's HQ. The General added, 'In the heat of battle, information at platoon and battalion level is often not passed further up the chain. It's essential that Division and Corps are kept informed constantly. I hope the *Fallschirmjäger* will remember this, you're an independent lot.'

'We will, sir,' said Henri.

'You know, in an emergency we could even speak to each other in English, and if we did it cleverly the enemy would assume we were their own people communicating. How about a private password between us, perhaps the word "Vespers" would do,' he said.

Leo was unsure whether von Senger was serious or joking, making a proposal like that to a lowly parachute captain.

'Of course, Herr General, but let's hope an eventuality of such seriousness will never arise.'

The General stared at him.

'You know, Captain Beckendorf, it's to the top of this hill early in the sixth century that St Benedict came, to contemplate. It's here that he wrote his Rule. You and I have to some extent lived by this Rule, as have Benedictine monasteries through the ages. What would St Benedict think of us now? We and the Allies each have chaplains who celebrate the same religious services with their fellow soldiers. And together, we are blowing ourselves to pieces.'

With that, they saluted and parted company.

29

'Take a look at this, Captain Beckendorf.'

The junior signals officer passed Leo a copy of the message from the Panzer Grenadiers' forward HQ. It confirmed the extraordinary advance by the French, and the serious threat posed. Leo was at the HQ of 1st Parachute Division. The *Fallschirmjäger* just took over its defensive positions at Cassino. He knew of the rapid consultation between von Senger and Kesselring's HQ north of Rome, Kesselring rushing down reserves in the form of two Panzer Grenadier divisions.

Von Senger was just in time, Leo thought, remembering his encounter with the General at the monastery four weeks earlier. He walked over to the wall map on the other side of the bunker where von Senger was talking with General Heydrich, newly arrived commander of the *Fallschirmjäger*. They were expecting him.

'Captain Beckendorf,' said Heydrich. 'Come and join us. As intelligence officer, you'll know what this map is showing. The French are north of Cassino, at the foot of the hills leading to the Abbey. We have to be wary of the quality of General Juin's force. The skill and tenacity of its leadership at junior as well as senior officer level is remarkable.'

'That's not all, sir,' said Leo. 'We just intercepted a signal indicating that the US 34th Infantry Division has joined up with the French. They're within a mile of the abbey. A small

American group has come within four hundred yards of the abbey walls, but the defensive fire of 2nd Parachute Regiment has stopped them.

Von Senger reflected for a moment, then said, 'The ample time we've had for preparing our defences has been put to the test. The 34th must have suffered enormous casualties.'

'Casualties are estimated at over three-quarters of their fighting strength, General. It seems they're being replaced.'

'By what formations?' said von Senger.

'We believe the 2nd New Zealand and 4th Indian divisions are taking over, sir, transferred from the British 8th Army on the Adriatic coast. General Freyberg has taken command.'

'Freyberg,' muttered Heydrich. 'He was in command at Crete nearly three years ago when New Zealand and British forces slaughtered our parachute and mountain troops. Yet in the end they evacuated the island. To a New Zealander or a *Fallschirmjäger*, you could call this a return match.'

Von Senger moved his stare to Heydrich. 'It's my view, now the Americans and British have landed at Anzio, that they'll attempt to cut through the Alban Hills to Rome before Kesselring can counterattack. They'll also try to cut off any withdrawal of German forces from here on the Gustav Line. It will be touch and go on both counts.'

⊷⊨◉⊨⊷

Leo was again at Division HQ, a couple of kilometres from Monastery Hill, two days later. The unmistakable drone of a mass of incoming aircraft turned into a roar. At the same time came the thunder and tremor of exploding bombs, rising to a crescendo. General Heydrich turned to his staff in the HQ bunker. 'Is it Cassino town or, God forbid, the monastery?' Nobody spoke. A few minutes later, a motorcycle dispatch rider hurried into the bunker, saluted the General, and handed him a message. Heydrich scanned the form, then lifted his head. 'They're bombing the monastery. The smoke is blocking any view of the structure but there are hundreds of aircraft, it'll be destroyed, even after we told them our troops would not occupy it.'

He and the others knew that the 2nd Regiment of *Fallschirmjäger* would be well dug into their bunkers on the hillside below the monastery. Formidable defences, the newly completed bunkers and fortifications, carefully sited sniper positions and supply dumps. They'd studied in great detail the particular challenges of the terrain, working out what options were open to the attacker and the points of maximum exposure to attacking forces. Their armament was the best the Reich could offer, essentially machine guns, mortars and some anti-tank weapons, sited to greatest effect, including their own artillery units.

⋆⟫⊜⟪⋆

Leo was sent to the forward HQ of 2nd Regiment, immediately following the bombing. He carried the written order. The *Fallschirmjäger* were now ordered to occupy the ruins of the monastery, which would immediately improve the scope of their defences.

At the Regimental HQ, the rain was lashing down, the temperature close to freezing. He found there'd been almost no German casualties from the bombing attack on the monastery and surrounding area. But there was carnage among the refugees occupying the monastery and abbey church. It was the turn of the civilians, a hundred casualties in this case.

General Heydrich came through on the signals land-line. 'We have to go in with our medical teams and do what we can for them, now the Allied artillery has let up somewhat. See how we can best get the wounded out.'

Leo was selected to lead the relief party. Stretcher teams formed up. As they entered the abbey he saw for himself. The few monks still in residence were administering to the wounded, laid out on rugs or whatever came to hand. Leo brought two army doctors with him and they went to work, as did the field medical orderlies. The monks came and went with supplies of water, food and whatever else. Then Leo saw him. He'd thought there was something familiar about one of the community when they filed out after Vespers that evening several weeks ago, before his conversation with General von Senger. Now Leo could see his face. It was Rooky, Dom Brendan Rooker, whom he remembered so well from his school days.

Rooky looked up at that moment, saw Leo, hesitated, and then went on with administering the last rites to a dying refugee. A few minutes later, Leo was closing down the wireless transmitter after reporting back to Regimental HQ, when he heard that familiar deep voice from the past.

'Beckendorf, don't give away the show. I just happen to be here. You've my assurance that I'm in a totally non-military role. I'm here because the Vatican sent me. Just let me continue as one of the monks and forget we met.'

Leo thought for a moment. How could Rooky have found his way behind enemy lines? Why Monte Cassino, the monastery? He had to believe him. No military role, he'd said.

'Of course, Father. But should you need me at any time, I can be contacted through 1st Parachute Division HQ, a few kilometres from Cassino. Just ask for Captain Beckendorf.'

Rooky nodded. 'May God look after you, my friend,' said the padre, making the sign of the cross as a blessing.

With that they both got on with it, the monks and the medical team doing what they could for the living, and in due course the injured were taken down the steep path by mule. Leo was shocked by the experience, not least the sudden appearance of Rooky.

⇥⊙⊡⇤

Intense fighting the night after the bombing of the monastery. The *Fallschirmjäger* knew they were up against the superb 4th Indian Division, and that this included the Sussex Regiment which attacked first. They were ready for them and it was a slaughter. Intelligence later told them the Sussex lost more than three-quarters of its officers and over half its men. The following night, it was the 9th Gurkhas and Rajputana Rifles sent to attack a specific defensive point. And the 2nd Gurkhas crossing valleys and ravines to capture the ruins of the monastery itself. Another disaster for Freyburg, the attacking force suffering very heavy casualties.

Leo operated between Division HQ and the regiments on the hill, and in the town. Then suddenly a pause, turning into a lull of four weeks as appalling weather conditions set in.

⇥⊙⊡⇤

Leo was at the HQ of the 3rd Regiment, commanded by Colonel Heilmann, just as a second massive air raid took place, a month later after the monastery bombing. This time it was the town.

Entering the bunker after making a preliminary recce of the damage and casualties, he saw General Heydrich there with Heilmann, clearly awaiting him. As he saluted the two commanding officers, there was a commotion behind him. Into the bunker walked Frido von Senger.

Looking tired and worn, von Senger regarded the scene, 'I made my own way from Corps HQ. I was alone on foot for the last part.' He paused, looking at Heydrich and Heilmann. 'I felt you would need my support.'

They all knew the Corps Commander was following fundamental practice in the German Army that when a senior commander wanted to know what his subordinate commanders were faced with, he went himself to find out.

There was silence.

Von Senger added, 'The terrain I passed over reminded me of the Somme.'

Again, no one said anything.

Turning to the Divisional Commander, he said 'Tell me first, General, what's your estimate of our losses, and what tactics are the survivors employing?'

'The Battalion occupying the town of Cassino was right underneath this latest bombing and the shelling which followed. Observers say nearly five hundred aircraft pulverized the place. I'm surprised Freyberg thought that a town rendered to such a state could be penetrated against defenders who will use the rubble for cover. Captain Beckendorf here has just been in there. There's no way of saying how many have survived, possibly half of them since they'll have taken cover in basements and caves in the cliff side under the castle.' He looked at Leo, and nodded to him to report his findings.

'I couldn't get far,' said Leo. 'The situation is extraordinary. You can't even make out how the streets ran. The place has been obliterated. We'd watched the heavy bombers, B17s and Liberators, go in and they were not accurate. I should think many bombs fell on Allied units. But the two-engine aircraft which followed were spot on. Attacking infantry are going to find it very hard to penetrate the rubble.

He didn't have to say that those of his comrades who survived, would continue the fight when they recovered from the trauma of the raid. They all knew their training as paratroopers meant they were able to fight in small dispersed groups when the normal command structure broke down.

'The Battalion HQ was in the basement of the Continental Hotel, and right behind it are caves in which they'll have taken shelter. Another defensive point was at the Hotel Rose.' He paused at that name. Theresa flashed through his mind. He wanted to think of his time at the hotel with her, but he must finish his report. 'There's no building left standing, wreckage and rubble everywhere. Combined with the heavy rains, it's impossible for vehicles of any sort other than bulldozers, to navigate through.'

Heydrich turned to von Senger.

'A platoon has gone in to make contact with those two points. We'll start taking out the wounded and sending in reinforcements as soon as we can.'

Von Senger was looking at a large-scale map. 'Probably Mark Clark was shaken up by the German attack on the Anzio perimeter, and ordered the raid to distract us.'

Heydrich went on. 'We know there's a New Zealand armoured unit to back up their infantry, but it seems no tank will get over the rubble without bulldozers going in first. The opening of the dams on the Rapido river has turned the ground around the town into marshland.'

⊷⊷⊷

Eight days after the bombing of the town, it became evident to Leo and his comrades that Freyberg was calling off the battle. Prisoners indicated that the New Zealanders and Indians were near to breaking point. As Heydrich put it at his divisional

command conference, 'The *Fallschirmjäger* may have been trau-
matized by the bombing, but they have made a fast recovery and
although exhausted, have won the first two battles of Cassino.'

For Leo, there was something else he would keep to himself.
The day after the bombing of the town, a medical orderly sent
a message from the field hospital close to town, reporting that
one of the monks, critically wounded, was asking for him. Leo
knew what this meant. He went straight there and, directed to
a line of beds, came face to face with a doctor. He asked for his
prognosis on Dom Brendan Rooker.

'Nothing can be done. His chest was crushed by falling
masonry and his lungs are punctured. It seems that he moved
from the abbey after it was bombed, to help in the town. He can
just speak, but he hasn't got long.'

Leo went forward to the figure on the bed, bandaged almost
all over.

'Beckendorf,' a hoarse voice exclaimed. 'I wanted you to find
me, so good of you to come.' It was clearly a massive effort to
talk. 'You're my last link with those I taught and loved. Come,
sit by me over here.'

Sitting down on an ammunition box next to the bed, he
placed a hand over Rooky's, which were clasped in front of
him.

The Padre spoke breathlessly, obviously in great pain. 'You
know, Leo, my life really began when I was ordained and
started to teach. So many fine boys, all different they were, that
was the challenge, we were a Benedictine family. You and your
friends Henri and Bill, what you have achieved, the people you
turned into, these are my rewards. Thank you.'

The monk paused, gasping. 'Now I'm at the end of my
mission. Please, I ask you to do two things for me. First, take
the package from under the bed. It contains part of a Codex and

a Vatican document. You're on the wrong side, but somehow you must get it through the lines to the Allied C-in-C, General Alexander, for forwarding to Cardinal Godfrey in London. Alex knows me, we served together in the last war.' He stopped, probably searching for the strength to continue. 'If you can't reach him, hang on to it until you can give the package to someone able to pass it safely to the Cardinal. It's not military material. But it will help people to understand what the Church has been doing in this terrible war.'

Leo couldn't prevent himself thinking of the consequences. Found with such a document, he'd need a watertight explanation or he might be in big trouble.

Rooky went on. 'Secondly, give me Communion and the last rites. Take the pyx from around my neck and put one of the consecrated hosts on my tongue, then give the remaining hosts to one of your padres. Just follow the prayers and actions which I'll dictate. The wooden box here by the bed contains the holy oils for anointing, and there are a couple a candles to light.'

Having helped with administering the two sacraments, Leo held Rooky's hand. The dying monk looked at him with love in his eyes. 'I was with your schoolfriend Henri, in the Libyan desert. I helped out at Bir Hakeim.'

'I know. He told me. He was my prisoner for a while, at Alamein, and then escaped.'

With a big effort, Rooky said finally 'We went together to the Monastery of St Catherine in Sinai. He seemed disturbed by his experiences in the war. I told him to find silence in the desert, for contemplation, to feel the love God has for us, to get closer to Him.' He closed his eyes.

Afterwards, Leo clasped the Vatican package. He knew that to accept it from a British officer and agree to its delivery, would mean he no longer believed in what he was fighting for.

He would continue to do his duty for his country, but inside himself he realized that everything had changed. Maybe this had been coming about for some time, but seeing Rooky on the point of death, suddenly crystallized everything for him.

⊷┠══◉══┨⊷

Sitting on his own, a dejected figure, Leo felt a touch on his shoulder. A female nurse. It was Theresa.

'I was watching you,' she said. 'I know who he was. You don't have to tell me anything.'

30

Bill Lomberg couldn't stand it much longer. The interior of the freight car was unbearable. Over a hundred human bodies inside for three days. Jolting to a stop for an unknown reason. Trundling forward again to an unknown destination. Just buckets for their excrement. Straw sodden with piss slopping about the floor. The sliding door unlocked from the outside morning and evening so that water could be replenished. No food at all. Just the stink, dominating everything. Any sleep was taken standing up.

He tried to focus on how he'd ended up there. At least the raid was indelibly clear in his mind. They'd wanted him because of his low flying experience. It was to be an ultra-low-level raid. Mosquitoes were to be the aircraft, led by Pickard. He knew him from Tempsford when they were both on the moon flights, landing agents in France. "Pick" as they all called him, a group captain at twenty-eight, with three DSOs. Everything was urgent. The target couldn't wait. They called the mission Jericho. To rescue *résistants* awaiting death at the hands of the Gestapo. Now he was in the same state as those they'd been rescuing.

Jericho was his most hazardous mission. Weather terrible at the briefing the evening before. Still terrible at five the next morning. Better visibility as they hit the Belgian coastline. Spitfires either side of the Mosquitoes, that was reassuring. Decoy route to deceive the enemy, north over Belgium, then east, and a double-back to west as the Spits left them. There were the rail tracks to Amiens. He and his navigator were in the second wave. Should see the smoke from bombs already dropped. Right down on the deck. There was the smoke. Where was the outer wall? There, great, now it was all about accuracy. Fifty feet above ground, in they came. Bombs gone. People were running from the central prison building towards the breach made in the outer wall. *Résistants* condemned to death, now was their chance.

Must get the hell away from it all, gain some altitude before they hit a power line. Then, that sudden crack and the airframe juddered, must have been hit by flak. Fire, they had to get out. Was it high enough to bail out? Must take the chance. Jettisoned canopy. Last thumbs up to the navigator alongside, as he rolled the machine over.

Bill was stuck in a tree. Cut himself clear with the knife in his boot. Once safe on the ground, looked for the navigator. He was already looking for Bill. That was real luck. Their decision was to head for Amiens, before the searchers and dogs arrived. Long slog, diving into ditches when anyone was spotted. Found the house of Pierre's parents with whom he'd stayed in 1940. From there on, it was into the escape line and hopefully home via Spain. That was the plan, but it didn't work out that way. The escape ended in a shoot-out at a farmhouse. Taken by the Milice, who handed them over to the Gestapo. *Terrorflieger,* that's what they called them, treating RAF prisoners as terrorists. Lumped them in with *résistants,* some were even those they'd released from the prison.

A shuddering halt and clattering of couplings brought him back to reality. Cries from outside as the doors were slid open.

Aussteigen! Everyone out. In their filth, starving. Uniformed SS guards stood along the platform. Had to help those who could no longer stand. Then they were being marched away towards God knows where. Someone said Buchenwald. Two hundred RAF personnel who should have been in the custody of the Luftwaffe. They saw the high wire fences and machine gun towers. Into the compound, and over to one corner of the roll call square. Kapos marshalled them into line, ordered them to take off their clothes. Hoses trained on them by other Kapos, to wash off the filth. No fresh clothing provided, the old carted away. The SS stood by, submachine guns at the ready in case someone made a run for it.

It was late evening, almost dark. Bill realized this was their initiation, the breaking in. Violence began on arrival, the signal to them that they were nothing, at the mercy of the guards. They stood naked, stripped of their dignity. If they moved, even to scratch, they were screamed at, the whip was administered. It was July, but not warm. He fell into a sort of coma, in between consciousness and oblivion. Hours later, just after dawn, the siren sounded for morning roll call. Several of his RAF mates were on the ground unconscious, left where they fell. Every name taken and recorded before the Kapos marched them to a tented area. The SS visible again, in the background but in absolute control. The daily routine explained. Warnings and rules, crimes and punishments, all read out. How long would they be there, wondered Bill. Would news of their status and treatment reach the Red Cross? No one here would admit to the Geneva Convention. Would news filter back to Britain?

⋯⊷⊶⋯

When did it happen? Must have been ten days since their arrival. Although the RAF were in a separate tented compound, meals were taken in one of the camp canteens. Bill caught sight of Justine among the helpers, one of the very few females. Although a wreck compared with when he last saw her, it was unmistakably her. He remembered the night his Lysander picked her up from that field in France, with Françoise. Now she had no hair, her long back stooped as she and others carried the buckets of slop. He gazed at her. She put down the food, and suddenly looked up. Why? He didn't know. Her eyes fell on him for an instant. No reaction. He kept looking as she moved back to collect another supply of soup. Again, Justine looked up. Their eyes locked on to one another this time. Was it recognition, or just curiosity? He risked a signal, a smile and a shallow nod. She raised her arm towards her mouth, then moved away, as if saying do nothing. His heart was pounding, he had to get to her, ask where they could meet. Or was that impossible?

Then, the extraordinary happened. Air raid sirens screamed their wail. Before dark, how was that possible? He remembered the Americans flew during the day, to see the target in daylight. Maybe one of them was in trouble? Bill made his way towards the end of the canteen, where the empty plates passed. No sign of her. He prepared to leave. Then, suddenly, a hand pushed at his waist above the hip. He looked sideways.

'Bill,' she said. 'Don't look at me, just listen. When everyone's finished, wait ten minutes and then go to the far side of Hut 7 in this same compound. The hut's wired off, it's the *Lagerbordell*, the camp brothel. Use the coupons you've been given for camp spending. Ask for Josephine, when you see the Madame. I've done a swap with another girl.'

'How did you know?' he said.

'Go now, say nothing. Meet me in the cubicle.'

⊷⧫⊶

There she was. 'I couldn't believe my eyes when you came into our food hut,' said Bill to Justine after he'd closed the door of the small room. Just a bed in there, nothing else.

She touched his arm. 'I saw your name on a list sent by the Luftwaffe. Be careful. I'm told they look into the cubicles. We have to act the part.' She turned away from him, raising her arms above her head. 'Lift off my clothing. The regular girls have been sterilized, but I haven't, so be careful.'

An unbelievably thin body. 'What's that?' Bill gasped as he saw the marks on her long concave back. The signs of deep wounds. He couldn't take it in. Then he felt a vicious anger spread through him. 'Who would have done that?'

'That can come later,' she said. 'We haven't much time. About fifteen minutes. If you want to get out of Buchenwald, we must concentrate on that.'

'I must tell you something first. Your sister Claudia's safe in England.'

Justine turned round and held him closely, joy on her face. 'Oh God, that's wonderful, Bill. How?'

'She got out of Berlin. Escaped to Malta, where I collected her and flew her to London. It just happened to be me, because I'd trained on the new Mosquito.'

Justine gasped. 'I know about the Berlin operation. I helped her. When we got to Italy, I was caught. She was heading for Malta. That's wonderful, she made it.'

He felt her break down in his arms, sobbing. He said 'I'm going to protect you. If we can somehow get out of here, I'll get you home. Tell me what happened.'

'No details, I'm afraid,' she said haltingly. 'I was taken by the Gestapo. We'd been on a secret mission. They tried to beat it out of me. I had my L-pill, but I couldn't use it. I wanted to fight. To kill every Nazi I could. That's how I keep myself going, the hate burns inside me.'

He pushed her gently away from him, still holding her around the waist. 'Justine, how do we get out of here?'

'I work for Ilse Koch, the wife of the former Camp Commandant. German is my native tongue, and she wanted someone for clerical work. She's in charge of the female prisoners. The *Häftlinge*, the inmates, call her the Witch. She knows I'm classified as Jewish, two of my grandparents were. I'm here because I helped Claudia escape deportation from Germany. We were involved in an espionage operation for the British, which I can't go into, but the people running Buchenwald don't know that. After my arrest and interrogation, I was sent here. I'm registered as a French *résistante*.

'So they accepted you went to Berlin to help your sister escape, avoid deportation?'

'Yes. Now listen carefully. I have access to Ilse Koch's office, and see the movements in and out of the camp, including that your RAF group was expected.

'Interesting,' said Bill.

'It seems the Luftwaffe regard you as theirs and are trying to get you out. You belong in one of their POW camps. That's why your food has improved recently.'

'I hadn't noticed,' said Bill. 'So, how do you get out of this place?'

'I've been thinking about it. We may be able to escape together, if we can use your Luftwaffe transfer when it happens. I'll work on that. We must fix our next meeting. Let's try the same tomorrow. I'll signal to you in the canteen again. I'm going to fix things with the Madame,' she said, pulling on her garment.

'Have you worked anything out?' he whispered. He was on his back on the bed.'

'Careful now,' she said, lowering herself on him.

Bill felt a surge of emotion, he was beginning to want her.

Suddenly she asked, 'Any news of Françoise? I know you two were serious about one another.'

Bill froze for a moment. He knew this was coming. He loved Françoise. But he was human. He must play it straight, if he could. 'She had to pull out of Vichy after your escape with Claudia to Italy. Some Gestapo man in Berlin checked with her in Vichy. She backed up your cover story.'

'Oh my God, she could've been dead by now. How did she evade arrest, execution?'

'She walked out of the office, was pulled in by a French Milice officer, and then shot him dead in his car. She was on the run a long time. The last I heard was that she was in hiding on a farm somewhere in the middle of France.'

'I can't believe it. First she rescued me from the round-up of Jews in Paris. Then she saves me from arrest at the railway station in Berlin. Now she's still holed up in enemy territory.'

'So, you think you can link our escape to the Luftwaffe transfer of us RAF,' said Bill. 'But what happens then? As I understand it, Buchenwald is in the middle of Germany. Presumably we should aim for somewhere close to the advancing Allies. I heard the break-out from Normandy has begun. People say they should be at the Rhine in no time, given that most of the Wehrmacht reserves are concentrated on holding back the Russians.'

'There's something I must tell you, Bill. Something that makes it doubly important we reach the British or Americans as soon as we can.'

'Oh, what's that?'

'Ilse Koch has a friend, a senior SS officer from Berlin. He's on the Waffen SS planning staff, and drives down here often to see the Witch. He has a driver and unlimited fuel, it seems. One night, I was working late at the villa, and saw his briefcase lying in the hall. They had already gone upstairs.'

'And so you had a look inside?'

'Exactly. I positioned myself so I would know immediately if one of them decided to come downstairs. I was supposed to be finishing a manifest of female prisoners and their provenance. In fact, I read much of what was in the briefcase. My fluent German made that easy, although there were some military terms which didn't mean much to me. Anyway, the long and the short was that there's a plan to form a secret panzer army capable of cutting off the Allied armies as they advance across northern France and Belgium.'

'You must have a good memory,' said Bill.

Justine smiled. 'More than that, I had access to the latest copying machine the Witch was supplied with. I copied fifty or so pages of what looked the most interesting. Essentially, the plan is to create new armoured divisions with the latest tanks, and Panzer Grenadier divisions. Plus a new division of the *Fallschirmjäger*, parachute troops. Nobody's to know anything about these units. Training is to be in secret and starts shortly. There's to be total radio silence. The Führer is in direct control.'

'Fascinating,' remarked Bill. I wonder where they'll find their air cover. The Luftwaffe is a busted flush. The latest aircraft are fighter jets, as I understand, dedicated towards preventing our bombers wiping out what remains of German industry.'

'Even that's been considered,' said Justine. The timetable envisages the attack towards the end of this year, and it will take place in bad weather conditions when flying is impossible.'

'So, where will the force strike?

'That depends where the American and British forces have got to by then. But Belgium is regarded as the most likely. If that's the case, the aim would be to slice through the Allied lines and secure the port of Antwerp.'

'My God,' exclaimed Bill. 'So we have to get these plans out of here and back to Eisenhower and his staff. Tell me how?'

Justine was silent for a moment. 'According to the latest schedule of camp movements, there's to be a convoy of trucks the Luftwaffe intends to send in for you lot. I'm working on how to join you.'

'What about papers?' asked Bill. 'We'll need papers and a cover story, presumably.'

'I have a contact in Berlin, who helped me and my sister Claudia two years ago. We must hope he still exists.'

Bill nodded. 'So, the big challenge is how you join me on the convoy, Justine. All sounds horrendously risky. Wouldn't it be safer for you to stay here and let me smuggle out the plan for the counteroffensive?'

'If I stay here, my chances of surviving to the bitter end are not great. More likely, I'll starve to death or be shot.' She paused. 'Let's meet again one more time here in the brothel. I'll get a signal to you.'

--•-|=●=|=●=|-•--

Bill was on the look-out for the next few days, until Justine re-appeared in the canteen and passed him a note. He was to meet her afterwards in the camp brothel.

He listened to her plan as she lay on her back with her arms about him. She would accompany him and his RAF friends when the Luftwaffe came for them, equipped with an auxiliary worker pass issued by the Luftwaffe. She'd seen on the Witch's desk a summary of camp movements indicating the Luftwaffe had persuaded the SS to give the RAF group up and transfer them to Stalag Luft III in Sagan. It would happen soon. She'd be ready and would attach herself to the party.

'How on earth are you going to manage that?' asked Bill.

'I went to Ilse Koch and said I had some nursing experience, and that I was willing to help in the camp hospital. That was untrue, but worth the risk.'

'My God,' said Bill. 'Some risk, I would say.'

'Ilse Koch emphasized the doctors were doing wonderful work for the Reich, in very difficult conditions. Doctor Hoven was in charge. The research they were undertaking would be of enormous benefit to mankind as well as to the war effort. When I was with them, I had to show absolute obedience. It wasn't for me to decide whether a particular test or experiment was appropriate. I shouldn't forget I was a prisoner without rights, because of my terrorist activities against the Reich.'

He sat up in amazement. 'And she fixed it?'

'I knew they were short of staff. So many nurses in Germany were being transferred to the front, to the base hospitals, even the field dressing stations. I presented myself to the SS Doctor Hoven at his office in the hospital block. He'd been briefed by Frau Koch. He made clear to me that what they did was secret. That I should be aware of the consequences of any breach of that strict rule.'

'You would be shot immediately, I suppose,' said Bill.

'Yes. I told him I understood. Doctor Hoven said he was going to see how I performed. One of their main research projects was the study of typhus so that vaccines could be developed and tested. Success would enable them to take appropriate measures to eradicate the disease in the occupied territories. I was to assist in the injection of Russian prisoners with typhus bacillus. Some would die, but that was necessary if we were to achieve our aim.'

'My God,' Bill exclaimed. He felt total revulsion, how could such a regime operate?

She took him close to her. 'I know. I was horrified to hear the way he put it. I wondered about the man. Educated, professional, skilled, yet leading a team practising systematic genocide. How could I be part of this? I knew the Nazi regime described the Russians as sub-human, but how could professionals like Hoven believe in that propaganda?'

Bill thought for a moment. 'I suppose they're subsumed into the culture of supremacy and hate which pervades Nazi Germany.'

Justine went on. 'You know, when I first arrived in the camp, others who'd been here for some time told me very large numbers of Russian POWs were brought to a separate compound at Buchenwald after the German forces swept across the Ukraine, cutting off whole divisions of Russian troops. These Russians were brought to work in industrial projects nearby. Few were in a fit state for anything. They hadn't been fed during the long journeys from the Eastern Front. With no facilities prepared here, apparently they were put in tents. Still they weren't fed, hundreds dying each week. And now it's the wretched Russians whom Hoven and his team are experimenting on.'

'That's genocidal, as well as plain stupid,' said Bill.

'Anyway, Doctor Hoven ended the interview and called for a medical orderly who took me to the hospital wards.'

Justine explained that she and Bill would have to move quickly when the date of the Luftwaffe transfer of RAF prisoners became known. She was performing her role as nursing assistant diligently. She assumed Ilse Koch was keeping an eye on her. She was still required to work in the Witch's villa at certain times. This gave her sight of prisoner movements, since copies were delivered to Koch's desk of all movement lists. She would know when the Luftwaffe was coming to extract the airmen and transfer them to one of their own POW camps.

Several of the airmen were in the camp hospital. She'd told the male nurse in charge of them, that she was ready to help when any unusual workload called for assistance. SS staff were in very short supply because of the demands of the Eastern Front, and her offer was accepted and no attempt to stop her came from Frau Koch, nor Doctor Hoven. The male nurse warned her a Luftwaffe advance party just arrived to agree arrangements for the transfer of the airmen, and the sick ones at the hospital were to go as well and would have to be looked after during the trip to their new camp. A Luftwaffe doctor came and asked about the cases. Justine saw her chance, telling him she was ready to help and accompany them on the first part of the trip, to Berlin.

She went on to explain that the airmen she'd been looking after were pushing for her to stay with them for the journey, and the Luftwaffe doctor agreed to speak to Frau Koch to determine whether Justine could go on temporary release for the purpose. On the face of it, there was no reason why Frau Koch should agree. But Justine knew there was a special factor in play. One of the Communist leaders in the camp told her the powers that be were closing in on the Witch. Ilse Koch couldn't hide her worries about the way the investigation into her activities was going. Her husband had been found guilty not only of the corruption charges, but the murder of prisoners for their personal possessions, and was imprisoned awaiting sentence.

'So, how did you convince Koch to let you out?' asked Bill.

'I was back in the house for a cleaning session. I just went for it. I told her she'd been understanding and good to me. I would like to return her generosity, if there was some way I could. The Witch looked suspicious but also curious.'

Bill was staggered. 'I can't believe your boldness.'

'I told her I had family in Switzerland, which is true, who could arrange a crossing of the border and safe haven in that country should she ever wish to take a rest there. That my aunt in Freiburg was a senior official in the German Red Cross, the DRK, and her work with Swiss colleagues involved visits to Switzerland. Also true. Frau Koch said she'd make some inquiries. I assumed she would be speaking with the DRK to check out the truth of what I told her.'

'And, what then happened?'

'I was with her again next morning, and she said she'd take me up on my offer. Also, that she'd heard the Luftwaffe medical team would like me to accompany the sick airmen as far as Berlin. My status here would be advised by teleprinter to the Commandant of Gatow air base with instructions that I was to be back in Buchenwald within three days. I would travel on a special letter of authorization from SS Doctor Hoven, and my ID papers would remain here at Buchenwald.'

Bill gasped. 'So we're on, you're coming with me. What if something goes wrong?'

'Don't worry, leave it to me,' Justine said. 'If I fail, I'll be shot, and you mustn't let that deter you from getting out. Otherwise, behave normally. When we're on the move, I'll tell you when I think we should make a run for it. Trust me. Remember, I've been trained for this sort of thing.'

With that she was up on her feet, her emaciated but still beautiful body erect in front of him. For a moment, he felt a surge of excitement, but that was fast extinguished when he heard the Madame strike the door. 'Raus, raus, aussteigen!' she shouted, ordering them to get out.

Bill and his RAF friends were marched to the Luftwaffe trucks lined up beside the camp compound. He was worried about Justine. Could this extraordinary woman really engineer an exit for herself when he was transferred out? She would have the copies of the secret plan with her. Could they expect to travel across Germany together without being re-captured, and escape through the lines to join the Allies? The information on the German counteroffensive must be delivered at all costs.

He looked out of the back of the truck at a damp and grey September day, the convoy rolling towards the gates of the concentration camp. Two blue-grey Opel ambulance trucks in the middle of the line of vehicles. No sign of Justine, but he wasn't expecting her to show herself. A note from her the day before bore two words only, 'With you.' She would have to be inside one of the ambulances. Through the main control gate, clear of the wire, the convoy heading for the Luftwaffe base where the first night was to be spent. There were cheers and jibes from everyone, such was the stupendous relief to be out of Buchenwald.

31

It was almost dark when the convoy pulled into Luftwaffe Gatow air base, on the edge of the city. Bill knew Justine was with them. He'd looked across at the ambulances when the convoy halted for a break earlier in the day, and spotted her. She was climbing down from one of them, wearing a blue-grey uniform coat with red crosses on the shoulders. What a change, he'd thought, from the drab garb of concentration camp inmate. He knew he was in with a chance, once sure she was in the convoy. Alone, without papers and money, he'd be picked up in no time.

A hot meal was ready for them on base, and a not unfriendly reception. Bill watched fascinated as Justine chatted up the base doctor, who didn't act as though he knew she was a prisoner on remand. The sound of air raid sirens came from the direction of the city. Afterwards, she told him they'd discussed the bombing and the impact on the civilian population, and she'd asked him whether in Berlin the public wanted revenge. The reply was that on the whole, the airmen shot down were handed over to them without trouble. The doctor was surprised the RAF party were taken by the Gestapo.

'I told him I'd never seen Berlin,' said Justine, 'and asked whether I could go into the centre to look around. His response was that the Berlin they all knew didn't exist any more. Most of the buildings around the centre having been so heavily damaged by the bombing. Many civilians evacuated to the countryside, government workers to the suburbs. But he said I could go in on the S-Bahn from Gatow station.'

'Wow.' Bill was again surprised by Justine's style, her amazing boldness. 'Is this our way out?' he asked.

'Yes, I aim to have a Luftwaffe travel pass for you tomorrow. Don't ask me how I'm going to get it. And we must have papers for you before we leave Berlin. I've thought a lot about the best place to head for, and Freiburg seems the right choice.'

'Why Freiburg?'

'Two reasons, it's not far from the French and Swiss borders. And I've the address of a safe house, given me by a priest in the camp, where we can try and make contact with the Allies.'

'How're we going to get there, without being caught I mean?'

'I met someone when I was last here. When the family moved from Berlin to Bordeaux, my sister Claudia stayed behind. I told you I met up with her here two years ago and helped her escape. I made contact with someone who, if he's still around, might be able to help us. In the meantime, we can camp either in Claudia's apartment in the Schöneberg district, or with someone else.

'Sounds dodgy,' said Bill.

'Don't worry, I'll fix it. And by tomorrow, I intend to get my hands on a Luftwaffe uniform, for you.'

※

Although the RAF POWs were being held in a separate compound, the base hospital was close by and Justine's doctor friend had the sick POWs in there until they left for Silesia. Bill was able to watch Justine passing between compounds, going to a laundry vehicle parked nearby. She calmly looked inside, unhooked something, and just walked away with it.

'I have the uniform,' she said to him a few minutes later, in a matter-of-fact voice. 'You'll be a Hauptmann, equivalent to Flight Lieutenant in your world, I think. We need to time our exit carefully, and you must be wearing the uniform and cap when we walk out. I'll still have my uniform coat on and Luftwaffe pin in the lapel.'

'What about the guards?' said Bill.

'The guards are much more concerned with people entering the base than those going out. If we choose a moment when they're occupied with a vehicle, we should have a fair chance. If we're stopped, I'll use my German. We should travel in the rush hour and there'll be less worry about being checked. Let's aim to leave the camp at eight tomorrow morning.'

⋅→∘∘←⋅

They found one another early the next day. No problem walking out of the camp entrance, Bill dressed as a young Luftwaffe officer complete with field cap. In no time they were clattering along on the S-Bahn, heading towards central Berlin. Looking out across the city, they were amazed by the destruction on all sides.

After changing trains and coming out of Schöneberg station, they made their way to Claudia's old address. Evidently, the district had suffered terribly. The building on one side was badly hit, but the apartment seemed intact, although there was no glass in the windows which were covered with boards. When they arrived at the third floor, it became clear the apartment had been lived in by someone else, usual when the previous owner had been Jewish. Now it was empty. The electric power wasn't on, but Justine found some candles for use later.

'Now for your papers, Bill,' said Justine. 'I'm going to try my original contact. Just praying that the Gestapo haven't taken him. I'll try the same dead letter drop as before. It's probably too much to hope it's still in use, but we might be lucky.'

'Who is the old contact?' asked Bill.

'A Czech businessman, he called himself Claus' was all she would say about him.

Bill waited in the apartment while Justine went out to the place of the old drop and left her message. She returned with some civilian clothes for Bill. The message was returned by Claus the next day. They were to meet him at St Matthias's Church after morning Mass. They were there the next morning, but no sign of him. The second day, Bill felt a nudge from Justine. Claus was there but without showing any apparent recognition. After the service, however, he walked a hundred metres behind as they returned to the apartment. He followed them indoors and, as soon as the door was shut, exclaimed his delight at seeing Justine again.

Claus hugged her warmly. 'I was told they'd caught you somewhere in Italy, and assumed that was the end of you, although London sent me later the "mission successful" signal.'

'Well, it's a long and painful story.' She told him briefly of her capture, interrogation and eventual dispatch to Buchenwald. She continued to keep her silence with him and Bill as to the true nature of the mission two years before.

Bill broke in to explain his background and how he and Justine met up in the camp.

'Fascinating,' Claus said. 'So you're after some papers, I presume?'

'Yes, and we need your advice on whether I can continue to dress up as a Luftwaffe Hauptmann,' said Bill.'

'That depends partly on where you're going,' said Claus.

'Freiburg.'

'Well, I'm not sure what Luftwaffe bases there are near Freiburg, and there's the danger that you'll run into a real

Luftwaffe officer on the train or wherever. And the owner of the uniform you took from Gatow will be after it, particularly as one of the POWs is missing.

'That's true,' said Bill.

Claus continued. 'Better surely, Bill, that you should be someone who can explain his poor German and has a motive for travelling which can't be easily checked up on. Justine, what's your reason for travelling when you're asked?'

'When in the camp, I met a priest from Freiburg who ended up in Buchenwald in the late thirties for giving sermons critical of Nazi policies. He gave me the address of a safe house there, and an introduction to the Medical Centre hospital at Freiburg University, where I could use my nursing experience. I don't have much, but can tell you a lot about typhus.'

Claus gave her an odd look.

'Remember that my real nationality is German. When I was in Berlin last time, travelling with a false French identity, I hid my German passport in my sister's apartment here. I could travel on it. Here, have a look,' she said, handing it to him.

'Thanks,' said Claus, 'I'll have it checked.'

Claus thought for a moment.

'Bill, as I understand it, you were educated in England but came originally from South Africa, still your parents' home. Does that mean you speak Afrikaans?'

'Yes,' said Bill.

'Well then, I think we should turn you into a Dutch electrical engineer from Philips at Eindhoven. You're on secret work concerning aircraft instrumentation. You have been in Berlin visiting AEG, and are now to spend some weeks at Freiburg University to assist with special studies on instrumentation in high speed aircraft, in the aeronautics engineering faculty.'

'You're a genius, Claus,' exclaimed Bill.

'If you're questioned, you can explain this in a mixture of German and Afrikaans and they should accept that you are Dutch, unless you are subjected to full interrogation. I'll provide you with appropriate correspondence between Philips AEG and Freiburg University, to back up your story.'

Justine interjected, 'Claus, how long do you think it'll take to have the papers ready?'

'Hard to say exactly. Shouldn't be more than ten days.'

'We're enormously grateful to you, Claus,' she said. 'Tell me, could you get a message through to London that I'm out of Buchenwald, on the way back with an RAF officer whose name is Lomberg?'

Claus thought for a moment. 'We've no wireless contact any more. Our links are very indirect, via Prague and then on to the Czech government in exile in London. I'll see what I can do.'

After pocketing Justine's passport for updating, it just remained for Claus to take passport photographs of both of them, and then he was off.

Claus was round at the apartment again only five days later. He'd worked miracles with his counterfeit ID friends. There was a pack of documents for Bill, including a Dutch passport for a Willem Rovekamp, engineer at Philips, and the letter of introduction to Freiburg University engineering faculty. And for Justine, who would be travelling on her German passport which had been brought up to date with a new photo and the addition of some recent stamps, there was also a Freiburg University Medical Centre offer of employment. This was of course fake, but adequate for controls during the trip there.

'You'll be getting your train at the Anhalter Bahnhof, and will have to change at Frankfurt-am-Main for Freiburg. The first train is tomorrow morning, leaving in theory at eight-thirty, depending on air raids.' Claus paused, and then smiled at Bill. 'Give me your Luftwaffe uniform, it may come in handy some time. And, for one of you, I brought this.' He pulled out a Luger automatic pistol, and some clips of ammunition. 'There's always the possibility of a thorough search, but it's worth taking the risk. Probably better that Bill has the gun since if it were found in a woman's baggage, it would be impossible to explain.'

Bill took the weapon, and they parted company, Claus bowing and putting his worker's cap back on his head. Then he was gone.

'A brave man,' said Bill to Justine. 'He deserves to survive.'

⇥⊙⊙⇤

It was Doctor Hoven, Head of the camp hospital, who raised the alarm. Justine Castillon was missing. It was now four days since she left with the Luftwaffe convoy, looking after the sick RAF prisoners. Ilse Koch was also worried, although keeping her head down, as the SS started their investigation with a thoroughness most police forces would have envied.

Within forty-eight hours they identified the connection between Justine and the unaccounted for fifty copies made on the copy machine in Koch's villa. Alarm bells started to ring. It was unclear what the copies were of, the briefcase and its owner having long left for Berlin. Nevertheless, the SS weren't going to take any chances. They knew Justine was either in Berlin or on her way somewhere by train. One of the RAF POWs was also missing. Bill Lomberg. They scrutinized every rail transport manifest for trains leaving Berlin for the west in the known timeframe. The profile they had of Justine and Bill, including photo IDs from Buchenwald, led to evidence they were travelling to Frankfurt-am-Main, and then on to Freiburg.

32

Looking out of the rectangular window in the corrugated fuselage of the old Ju 52 transport aircraft, Leo caught his breath
for a few seconds. The scene below was utter desolation. Where
was the medieval city of Cologne? He remembered back to the
devastating raid two years before, a thousand bombers in one
night they said, no one in the Luftwaffe thought the RAF could
manage that. There seemed to be nothing standing except the
great Gothic edifice of the cathedral with its twin spires, the
hallmark of the city.

The destruction below took him back to the death of Rooky,
pulled out from under the rubble of Cassino. His hand went
to the kitbag beside him and felt the package the monk and
school master turned padre entrusted him with. Just afterwards, the epic fight for Monastery Hill temporarily ended as
the flooding rivers, snow and ice forced General Freyberg to
call off the Allied assault. Leo remained in place with his fellow
paratroopers until, nearly two months later, it was the turn of
the Polish Corps to die in their thousands before the murderous
defensive fire of the *Fallschirmjäger*. Leo thought of Cassino
as the defining moment of his life, ending with orders to the
surviving paratroopers to withdraw down the last escape route
to the valley below.

He was jolted back to reality as the wheels of the aircraft
bumped onto the concrete. They turned off the runway, and

taxied in no time into a bomb-proof hanger. A Kübelwagen was waiting for him, and he was driven in brilliant warm sunshine from the Luftwaffe base of Köln-Wahn to the headquarters of 2nd Parachute Division.

'Come in Major, I was so pleased to hear of your promotion,' said the long thin-faced aristocratic-looking German officer who advanced across the map room into which Leo was shown.

Leo knew him so well. Friedrich August Freiherr von der Heydte, a Bavarian baron and strong Roman Catholic. Leo's Battalion Commander in Crete. And one of Ramcke's senior officers on the Alamein line.

The Colonel smiled. 'Our paths cross again, Herr Major, first in Crete, then at Alamein, and now here in this devastated city. However, the good news is that the beer and pork are as good as ever as long as you know where to find them.'

'It's an honour to be asked to serve under you again, Herr Oberst.'

The Colonel poured Leo a schnapps. They clinked glasses. You'll have heard that the 6th Regiment based here was only formed a few months ago. One way or another I've been able to bring together some veteran *Fallschirmjäger*. You'll know many of them.' He paused, a glint in his eye, steel or humour? 'Incidentally, I'd be interested to know what happened to that ex-schoolfriend of yours, the one who was our prisoner as we pulled back from behind the advancing British at Alamein. You held on to him until we hijacked that convoy of Allied trucks.'

Leo froze to the spot. He opened his mouth, but nothing came out. Van der Heydte didn't miss a trick. Henri de Rochefort escaped because Leo turned a blind eye.'

'Don't look so embarrassed, Herr Major. I realize that General Ramcke ordered you to shoot him if he attempted to escape, but in the fog of war.' The Colonel stopped, smiled, and then looked more seriously at Leo. 'Your mother was from England, and mine was from France. We both went to Benedictine schools. I've had my problems too. I happen to be a cousin of Count von Stauffenberg. After he left the bomb under the Führer's conference table, anyone remotely close to him fell under the scrutiny of the SD. But I've survived so far. You, on the other hand, were busy with the 1st Division at Cassino. Let me just say "Well done". I hope you've enjoyed your leave, you certainly earned it.'

'Yes, thank you, Herr Oberst. I've been staying with my parents near Berlin. My father's in the Foreign Ministry, and because of the bombing his department was evacuated from the Wilhelmstrasse.'

Von der Heydte moved across to a wall map showing the southern part of the German frontier with France.

'Herr Major, as you know, the new formations of *Fallschirmjäger* in training here are no longer parachute troops. The average age is under eighteen. Nevertheless, they preserve the spirit and much of the training excellence of our original regiments, helped by the veterans among them. Importantly, they retain the famous name. They're to be employed solely as infantry, but still fall under the overall command of General Student in the Luftwaffe.'

'I'm looking forward to this opportunity, Herr Oberst. I'll do my best to pass on my experience to these very young men.'

'I'd intended to employ you initially in a training and staff officer role. However, an urgent problem has arisen in Lorraine, in eastern France.' Von der Heydte ran his hand over the mountainous country of the Vosges, just west of the Rhine. 'After break-out from Normandy, Patton's 3rd Army has not wasted time. He stormed across France but paused outside

Metz after having outrun his supply lines. When he re-starts the advance, only the Vosges will bar the way to Strasbourg and the Rhine. General Student has been asked to transfer experienced *Fallschirmjäger* into the Vosges to reinforce German forces already resisting attacks by the Free French.'

'Sounds like the right place to hold up the Allies through the coming winter,' said Leo.

Von der Heydte continued. 'I understand the French forces include the same Foreign Legion unit of your ex-schoolmate whom we captured at Alamein. Maybe you'll have a second chance to bring him in,' said the General with a grin. 'Units of the 17th SS-Panzergrenadier Division form the core of the German force. However, an ad hoc *Fallschirmjäger* force is being assembled to deal in particular with the infiltration of British commando units behind our lines. You will report immediately to Freiburg where the HQ of the special force has just been established.'

Leo kept his thoughts to himself.

Von der Heydte laughed, and then said 'Now, could I suggest you go to your quarters for a rest, and my driver will collect you at seven. We can dine together where the best of Cologne cooking is still to be found.'

⋙⋘

'Reports are coming in that a substantial British SAS force has dropped into the Vosges. They're equipped with heavily armed jeeps and no doubt plan to link up with Resistance groups, the Maquis as they call themselves.' The Adjutant was briefing Leo soon after he arrived at the Divisional HQ close to Freiburg. Shortly afterwards, Leo was handed a message saying he'd been chosen to assemble a *Fallschirmjäger* strike force of motorized infantry in order to penetrate the area from where these reports were coming. He and his fellow commanders had no idea of the make-up of the Allied units operating behind the German lines. The widespread and frequent ambushes and raids suggested they were operating in strength.

All the time, Leo was conscious he was carrying the Vatican package which Rooky gave him just before he died. Meantime, it became obvious that the Americans and French were likely to capture Strasbourg. He started to think again about how he could offload the package on someone able to arrange delivery to England. He accepted Rooky's assurance that the contents were of a non-military character. After all, it was addressed to Cardinal Godfrey of Westminster.

He'd been thinking he might get the package somehow to the British Embassy in Switzerland. But the border into that country was now intensively guarded on both sides of the frontier, given the expected exodus of Nazi officials on the run. Then, with General Leclerc on the point of taking Strasbourg, Leo made his decision. He would enter the city as the German garrison was withdrawing and find a way of handing over the package to an officer in the Allied forces. He thought of Henri, knowing that his unit was with the French forces. How could he get a message to him?

33

Freiburg, September 1944

Leaning against the windscreen of the Kübelwagen parked right opposite the exit from the trains to the station yard, Leo admired the lovely medieval buildings and cathedral of the old university town around him, no evidence yet of Allied bombing. There were troops everywhere, and he thought about the build-up of Wehrmacht strength there as the Americans and French approached the Rhine, only a few kilometres away.

Leo watched as the train pulled into the station, the black-uniformed SS lined up along the platform. Passengers climbed down from carriages and walked towards the control point and exit. A tall thin emaciated woman came out, crossing the station forecourt. But it was the man in civilian clothes accompanying her, who attracted his attention. Tall, broad-shouldered, a second row forward thought Leo with surprise and shock. He looked at him just as the man's gaze moved across to his. Their eyes locked together. The man stopped suddenly, as if frozen to the spot.

Leo moved forward. The woman, realizing something unexpected was happening, looked around her as though thinking she might make a run for it. How could this be happening? No doubt who he was. He decided to speak in English. 'I think you and your friend better come with me,' he said, gesturing towards the vehicle and driver. Turning to the woman, he said quietly in German, 'Do what I say. I know your friend.'

They climbed into the Kübelwagen, the one suitcase between them. It was only a short ride before they arrived at a building on the edge of town. No one said anything. Up the steps to the entrance. At the desk in the hall, a paratrooper jumped smartly to attention and saluted. It wasn't the Nazi salute. A few words were exchanged and Leo led them to a room on the first floor, sparsely furnished with a trestle table and chairs. He told the paratrooper to remain outside. When the three of them were alone, he gestured to Justine and Bill to sit down at the table. He remained standing, pacing up and down the floor as he spoke.

'Bill Lomberg, what are you doing in Germany? Shot down, I suppose.'

'Yes,' muttered Bill, at the mercy of his old schoolfriend. 'Six years since our last term together. There's no point in pretending I didn't recognize you at the station.'

Justine jerked around towards Leo, amazement written all over her face. She opened her mouth as though going to say something, but there was only silence.

Leo's face was stern, just nodding before he said, 'I'm not sure who your friend is, although I've a feeling I might have met her somewhere before. Tell me your story.'

'I was one of two hundred RAF aircrew taken by the Gestapo to Buchenwald,' said Bill. 'In case you haven't heard, it's a concentration camp near Weimar. Thanks to the Luftwaffe, I was transferred out of the place, which was when we escaped. In the camp, I met Justine who lived in Bordeaux and was a close friend of Henri de Rochefort's sister, Françoise.'

'Henri was my prisoner at Alamein,' said Leo. 'He later escaped during our retreat back towards Tripoli. I'm in the Luftwaffe myself since the *Fallschirmjäger*, our paratroops, come under Goering. I didn't know about the Buchenwald episode. It's just as well you got out.'

There was no comment from Justine. Leo turned to her.

'Mademoiselle, how did you get to Buchenwald and meet Bill.'

Justine explained she was caught while acting as a courier in the French Resistance.

Leo knew there was little option but to hand them over. He looked at both in turn. His memory flashed back to their school days, to the rugby field where the South African excelled. To Henri and Françoise, and his visit to their home in Bordeaux during one of the holidays. Suddenly, he remembered he'd met Justine on that trip, at the de Rocheforts.

He put his hand on Bill's shoulder. 'Do you have somewhere to go to in Freiburg?'

'Yes,' said Justine, 'We know of a safe house.'

Leo knew this was the moment. Either he did the obvious, his duty. Or he attempted to help them in some way. Was it possible, and should he take such a chance?

Suddenly, noise of a scuffle outside in the hall, shouting. The door burst open. 'SS, on your feet, hands above the head,' said an officer in black uniform.

Leo's hand went to the Luger on his webbing. 'What's your authority. I'm your senior. What do you mean by this outrage?'

'I've orders from Berlin, direct from Prinz-Albrecht-Strasse. These two are terrorists.'

'He's an RAF officer. The Luftwaffe has custody of all air force prisoners. You've no right to intervene. If you have a problem, try Reichsmarschall Goering.'

The SS man hesitated. 'Take the girl,' he said to the NCO beside him.' With that, they dragged Justine across the room. Bill moved to block their way, but Leo stopped him.

When they'd gone, he said to Bill 'Nothing you can do. Go out through the back door and find your way there on your own. I'll meet you tomorrow morning at nine, in the back of the Münster. Say nothing to anyone about our encounter. If you do, you'll probably be shot. Remember, this town is full of SS.'

Back in the room, Leo sat down, alone. He was thinking about the opportunity presented by his decision to help Bill. Should he use this to give Bill the package he'd been entrusted with by Rooky before he died? He was going to put Bill in touch with someone he'd met through the help he was giving the priests at the Münster. She was a nun who, he knew, was in touch with the other side. Yet, just how certain was it that Bill would ever get through? More likely, he would somehow be re-captured and sent to a POW camp, at best. Better that he held on to Rooky's package until a safer solution presented itself. He did have an idea.

Out in the street, Bill headed for the safe house, suitcase in one hand and a city map Leo had given him, in the other. The house turned out to be next door to the presbytery where the priests of the cathedral stayed. No questions were asked. He was just treated as a lodger, and given a room and a hot meal in the evening.

Now on his own, safe in the small bedroom, he opened the case and checked the counteroffensive plan was still there. There was no way he could mention to Leo that he had the copies taken by Justine in Ilse Koch's villa, however fine were his schoolfriend's motives in helping him to escape. Now was the moment to read through the plan. The papers might be lost in his efforts to cross the lines. Two nights of study should give him a fair appreciation of the scale and tactics, and put them to memory.

The words 'Wacht am Rhein', Watch on the Rhine, were the first he read, on the cover. Starting to read through the sheets, the scale of what was planned became quickly apparent. Eight panzer divisions and sixteen infantry divisions involved just didn't seem possible. But even half that number would overrun the Americans unless they were warned and had the time to re-inforce their front line units on the Belgian border.

What was it Justine said? If anything happened to her, he must not only get the sheets to the Allied High Command, a copy should go to her sister, Claudia, in England. She was a cryptologist and could hear and read things most generals could not. This seemed very odd to Bill, but he'd taken her word for it. He would have to find Claudia. Justine gave him the name of her London contact, someone called Archie Weatherspoon, in the Secret Service.

⇢⊷⊷⊷⊶⊶⊷

The following morning, Leo was already there in the Münster when Bill arrived and knelt down beside him.

Leo looked up, saying 'It's safe to talk here. Tell me, what's your objective, Bill?'

'I must rescue Justine, then get out of Germany fast, either through the lines or across the border into Switzerland,' said Bill.

'Justine's lost,' Leo snapped back. 'No way the SS will let her go. She'll be on her way to Berlin for interrogation if they think she's involved in more than just the escape. God help the poor thing.' He paused. 'Switzerland's out, the frontier's now completely sealed off.'

There was a long silence.

Leo continued. 'If I can get you to Strasbourg, then either there'll be a guide who can take you to a Maquis and through the lines, or you'll have to wait until the city is taken by the Allies.'

Bill exclaimed, 'Why are you doing this, Leo, taking such a risk?'

'This war's lost to us Germans. It should end now, before millions more die. Yet neither your leaders nor ours want an armistice. Yours will only accept unconditional surrender. Ours, at least Hitler, want to fight to the end. If I can save you, whom I know and respect, then this is my chance. Be here tomorrow. A nun will find you. Do what she says.' With that, Leo rose and was gone.

Bill felt shattered by this exchange. How could he forget Justine? He desperately wanted to find her. Yet Leo, his ex-schoolfriend, was adamant he should get out, and was risking so much in helping him.

<hr>

The nun, who looked in her sixties, presented herself in the same part of the Münster the following morning. Bill took her back to the nearby safe house and up to his room. He perched on the edge of the bed and motioned to the nun to take the only chair. She smiled in a sympathetic manner, and came straight to the point. 'I'm Sister Hilda. I've been told that you have to visit the battle zone, which at present means crossing to the other side of the Rhine and into the Vosges mountains where the fighting is.'

'Yes,' said Bill. 'I badly need your help.'

The nun continued. I've been in touch with the other side. The British have mobile commando units operating behind the German lines. They seem to think that with the right wireless equipment, it would be possible for you to make a rendezvous with them. First of all we'd have to get you to the Vosges and a

Maquis unit in touch with the British.' Sister Hilda felt the large crucifix on the front of her habit, then went on. 'The French Resistance in the Vosges is cooperating with the British Special Air Service. The plan is for you to travel to Strasbourg, which of course is still in German hands, and then join up with a guide who will take you to a Maquis camp in the hills. That's where contact can be made with the SAS who should get you over the front line, and to your intelligence friends.'

Bill travelled the short distance to Strasbourg in a wheezing charcoal gas bus, accompanied by Sister Hilda, who then introduced him to the guide. After a night's sleep of a sort, in a draughty workshop building, he said goodbye to the nun and made his way up into the Vosges.

34

The Vosges, October 1944

Bill was given a bicycle but much of the climb was to be on foot, toiling up the hills using minor roads. Eventually, in some dense woodland, he came upon the Maquis, or rather the Maquis came upon him. The guide disappeared, and Bill was suddenly confronted by what looked like three desperadoes, dishevelled, and sporting Sten guns. Bill followed them back to the camp of the Maquisards, and after a preliminary exchange with the group in French, a young man came forward and introduced himself. His uniform was British battledress, and he spoke to Bill in English. He wore the insignia of a sergeant in the SAS.

'I'm based with this Maquis, and was briefed to expect you. We'll do our best to get you over to the other side, but there aren't many of us left. Our mission here didn't work out as planned, and the decision was taken to close it down. Most of the party made their way out in small groups but thirty-five or so officers and troopers have disappeared. A few of us are remaining behind to support and train the Maquis. We're supplied with arms and fuel from the air.'

'Sounds like you've been having a rough time of it,' said Bill.

The SAS Sergeant continued. 'There are two of our remaining chaps going on a recce in a couple of days' time, and there's a spare jeep you can have. I suggest you take your luck and follow them, and they'll point you the way through the lines.'

It was early on a foggy November morning when Bill pulled out, after saying his adieus to the Maquisards. Tanked up to the gunnels with fuel, he'd been driving for about an hour at a respectable distance behind the other jeep which was armed with a Vickers machine gun, when without warning there was a powerful explosion. He was lucky to escape the flying dirt and rock. The jeep in front had been flung off the track and was a wreck.

They'd hit a mine he assumed, as he dived into the woodland scrub alongside the track. After a few minutes it became obvious there wasn't any ambush. He examined the two bodies ahead of him, and confirmed both were dead. The wireless equipment was clearly useless. Having heaved the two into the back of his jeep, Bill collected what personal possessions were strewn around, and headed back to the Maquis. There was no way now he could be sure of connecting with the main American and French forces. He needed to play safe with Justine's copy of the counteroffensive plan.

A couple of hours later, he drove back into the Maquis camp. The leader of the group, known to all as "Brutus", heard his story.

'That's not the first time the Boche have laid mines at random on the secondary routes which they think the British commandos use. Don't worry, we'll get you out. In the meantime, stay with us and you can watch how we work. There's a major sabotage operation pending, which will really hit the Boche where it hurts.'

35

The floor of the hut was littered with discarded decrypts, always an affront to Claudia Müller's orderly eye. This time her mind was on something else as she prepared to head back to her digs. The buses were lining up close by the security fence. That day her team was involved in translating signals intelligence decrypts of SS messages. A large-scale transfer of concentration camp inmates was developing as the Russian armies advanced on the Eastern Front. Transports were being directed towards the camps in central and west Germany, in particular Bergen-Belsen and Dachau. But it was a camp the SS administered in France that Claudia was suddenly drawn to. Struthof was up in the Vosges mountains above Strasbourg, close to the village of Natzweiler, a ski resort before the war.

It was a single message. A British Commando unit was in the hands of the SS, following an ambush by regular Wehrmacht troops in the Vosges mountains. The 'Kommandobefehl', Hitler's so-called Commando Order, was to be applied, meaning they were to be summarily executed without trial. Struthof was equipped with a gas chamber and ovens. Claudia went straight to her supervisor. The urgency was such that in her presence he picked up one of the two red telephones on his desk. 'I'm going to speak directly to C,' he said.

The next morning, she was dismayed when he dropped by her desk and said there was nothing that could be done. An exchange of POWs was sure to be vetoed by the SS. A bomb attack by Mosquitoes was ruled out. It would kill the French *résistants* held in the confined space of what was a small camp.

That evening, as she opened the door into the farmhouse where her digs were, the wife of the farmer was in the hall holding the phone. 'Ah, Claudia, just the right moment, it's for you,' said the farmer's wife.

She reached for the phone. 'Claudia Müller here.' She recognized the voice at the other end, clipped and with an Oxford accent, as they called it.

'Claudia, it's Archie Weatherspoon. Sorry to call at this hour.'

'No problem, Archie.' She remembered him well. Nearly two years ago, it was Archie who did the first debriefing on her arrival in England after her Berlin escape. His boss was C, Head of the British Secret Service and responsible also for Station X.

'It's this Struthof place, Claudia. Sorry about the SAS troop. Nothing we could do. You can be sure their comrades will seek out and destroy the killers when this war's over. But something else just happened. You remember Françoise de Rochefort?'

'Of course, the great friend of Justine, my sister.'

'That's the point,' said Archie. We're in close touch with Françoise, she's behind the lines in France, close to Strasbourg.'

'Oh,' gasped Claudia. She knew there was something nasty coming.

'She's trying to rescue your sister. The SS grabbed Justine after she escaped from Buchenwald, and they're holding her at Struthof.'

'Oh my God,' exclaimed Claudia. 'They'll murder her as well.'

'Believe it or not,' said Archie, 'Françoise has an agent on the other side, who may have it in his power to get her out.' I just wanted you to know at this stage. Stand by to come up to London if we need you.'

Claudia looked out of the bus window at the filthy weather outside, early in the morning. It was a week after that call from London, and Justine was very much on her mind. They swung in through the gates, past the armed sentries, the odd-looking country mansion in sight. Beyond it, the lines of huts and recently finished brick buildings stretched everywhere.

Walking from where the bus dropped her, she stepped into her hut, grabbed a cup of strong tea from the pot lying in wait just beyond where the coats were hung up. As she went over to her desk, the phone nearby rang, and one of the team called across to her.

Claudia took the receiver. It was Archie again.

'We've got her,' he said. 'She's safe, with our people, close to Strasbourg. Can't say more over the phone.'

Her breath was gone. She only managed to gasp 'Thanks be to God.'

'Claudia, are you okay?' Weatherspoon sounded anxious.

'Yes, I'm okay.'

'There's an RAF officer who's just turned up from France. He wants to speak to you urgently. Looks important. Can you get a train up right away?'

'Of course,' she said. 'Will be with you by teatime.'

She was to go to the address opposite St James's Park underground station. That's where Françoise sent her after they met in London the year before. Where Claudia voiced her concern to Archie about information leaked from Station X to the Russians.

On the train to Euston, she realized she'd have the opportunity to tell Archie of the frustration she and her colleagues felt about something happening behind enemy lines in north-west Europe. The latest decrypts from Tunny, the most secret source of all, were throwing up communications between OKW, the German High Command, and Field Marshal Model, Commander of Army Group B. After decryption, translations into English were being summarized and passed through to the few British and American generals given access to Ultra, as the output from Station X was called. Yet, there appeared to be no response from the Allied Command to the enormous build-up in the strength of enemy forces just behind the Rhine, facing Belgium. She would tell Archie, one of the few allowed into Ultra. But before that, there was this RAF man, who was he?

36

It was not just another cathedral. Henri could see its Gothic magnificence towering above the city with the Rhine snaking its way through Alsace, as he sat beside Legionnaire Corporal Morel in the jeep. They talked about their respective escapes back to the Allied lines after both were taken prisoner at Alamein. How they and their Free French compatriots ended up first in Tunisia and then on the Adriatic front in Italy. Now at long last, they were fighting to liberate *la belle France.*

The wireless receiver crackled. It was the confirmation they were waiting for, the liberation of Strasbourg by General Leclerc's Armoured Division. An announcement on public radio from Paris described how the General just ordered the hoisting of the French tricolour over the great cathedral. He was fulfilling the pledge he'd made three years before at Kufra, to his small army of followers in the Sahara, 'Jurez de ne déposer les armes que lorsque nos couleurs, nos belles couleurs, flotteront sur la cathédrale de Strasbourg.' repeated in English on Radio Paris, 'Swear not to put down your weapons until our colours, our beautiful colours, will be floating above the Cathedral of Strasbourg.'

His thoughts were racing. Entering Strasbourg meant so much to the Free French, after the frustrations and battles of the past four years. He'd heard from Bordeaux that his parents were all right. What about his sister Françoise, was she okay?

What about his schoolfriends, did Leo survive after Alamein, what became of Rooky, and Bill for that matter?

Henri thought through the strange request from British intelligence for him to head for Strasbourg and collect a secret package from the Vatican. He was to rendezvous with an enemy officer in disguise, what was that all about?

He told Corporal Morel to head directly for the cathedral and wait for him outside.

The nave was immense. A further message from British intelligence told him he could expect to meet the disguised German officer close to the steps down to the crypt. The password was to be 'Benedict still lives'. The package to be transferred was to contain folios of an ancient copy of the Bible or Codex. He knew he'd been chosen to collect it because of his involvement in the original transfer of the Codex from St Catherine's Monastery in Sinai. But in the intervening two years, much must have happened to those secret papers. All he was told was that it was to be delivered to a cardinal in London. Why was it so important to the Vatican, was there more to it than the folios of the Codex Sinaiticus?

⇥▬◉▬⇤

Henri waited on one side of the nave of the cathedral, close to the steps down to the crypt. Where was this clandestine German officer? There was hardly anyone around. Mass was about to start in the side chapel close to where Henri stood. The celebrant arrived clutching to his chest the chalice covered with white silk cloth with flat card on top, his vestments flowing, black three-pointed biretta on his head.

He addressed Henri. 'Bonjour, Monsieur le Capitaine, est-ce que vous voulez assister à la Messe? J'ai besoin de quelqu'un de servir sur l'autel.' Henri understood the priest wanted him to serve on the altar.

Their eyes met, and suddenly Henri knew. The priest took off his biretta, bowed towards the cross with Henri beside him, and the two of them stepped up to the altar. It was a long time since Henri served Mass. In the field, it was usually one of the legionnaires who served on a makeshift altar. But it came back to him from his school days, as second nature.

When they reached the offertory, the celebrant turned and appraised the congregation in the small side chapel. There were very few, a couple of old people and a nun.

'There will be no Communion today,' said the priest. With that, he came down the two steps from the altar, took a flat package from under his vestment and gave it to Henri, muttering 'Benedict still lives', the password Henri was waiting for. There was friendship in his eyes. He paid no attention to the nun who was bowed, deep in prayer. Then slowly he made his way out into the nave, and disappeared.

The nun looked up, smiled at Henri and whispered, 'He's a fine man, and a brave one. Please deliver the package he gave you, personally if you can.'

Later, Henri opened the outer packaging of the flat parcel Leo Beckendorf had given him. It was addressed to Cardinal Godfrey in London. Inside was a bundle of ancient folios, and a letter from the Vatican to the Cardinal. Attached to the letter was a white card. It read:

Requiescat in Pace
Dom Brendan Rooker OSB
Irish Guards 1915–1919, Royal Army Chaplains'
Department 1939–1944
Killed in action, March 15 1944, Italy

He rests amongst his friends in the grounds of the Monastery of Monte Cassino.

So, thought Henri, they'd lost Rooky. In so many ways, he'd been the glue that helped him, Leo and Bill share friendship and respect for one another, even in time of war.

37

Claudia hardly knew London. She thought back to the inter-rogations and debriefings when she arrived from Berlin. The British reached out to her, trying to accept this woman from inside Germany, to believe in her. She was alien, from the heart of the enemy. It can't have been easy for them. Her work in Berlin was secret, they knew that. Just a tiny number knew why she'd been persuaded to come over. They wanted her to help them understand the Geheimschreiber and read the signals which could make the difference between victory and defeat. Now as the cabby drove through the streets from Euston to St James's, she stared again at the bomb damage, the destruc-tion, the suffering people. Berlin was getting that way when she escaped with Justine two years before. Now, she was sure, it must be a lot worse.

There was the familiar building, opposite the underground station. She paid the cabby, and the front door was opened for her from the inside as she approached. The same meeting room, more like a comfortable lounge area, where many of those hours of interrogation took place. Archie came towards her, immaculate in blue pinstripe suit.

'Claudia, I'm so pleased to see you, thanks for responding so promptly.'

'Good to meet again, Archie. Wonderful news about Justine's escape.' Claudia was conscious as always of her German accent.

At least the others in the hut at Station X were finally used to it. Used to having a German, someone from the other side, in their midst.

They sat down at the polished table in the centre of the room. Archie seemed pleased with himself. Not arrogant, but smart and upper crust as the English say. That's how she always remembered him.

'Yes, Claudia, your sister's someone for whom we have enormous respect. Like we do for Françoise who arranged the operation. He paused. 'Now, the RAF officer, Bill Lomberg. You'll remember Bill who flew you here from Malta.'

Her mind flashed back to the Flight Lieutenant and his Mosquito. The secret new aircraft on that bombed-out airfield called Luqa. 'I'll never forget, the most uncomfortable journey of my life, by a long way. It nearly killed me.'

'Well, Bill's here. He's had a tough time. Shot down in France, and badly treated. Fell into the hands of the Gestapo. He eventually escaped, and has quite a story to tell. I'm going to ask him in here, in a moment. But first of all, I need to remind you ...'

Claudia interrupted him. 'I know, you're going to say he's not in the know regarding the Tunny decrypts and the Geheimschreiber machines that originate the data.'

'Correct. He does have other things to say and discuss. I'll leave that to him to explain.'

With that, Archie got up, went across the room and opened another door, on the far side of which Bill was evidently waiting. 'Come on in, Bill,' he said.

In came the tall, broad-shouldered South African. The same person she'd met in Malta, but desperately thin and not much hair on his head.

'Claudia,' he said as he embraced her with a bear-like hug. They laughed and looked one another up and down. 'I often think of you and that flight. Crazy. Locked up in the bomb bay of the Mosquito. How you survived those hours confined in that space, I'll never know.'

'You were wonderful, Bill. And that navigator of yours. When we stopped for those couple of hours in Gibraltar, I didn't think I could go on.'

'Well, we all made it. And now you're a British subject, I hear. Congratulations.'

Archie helped with the hot drinks the tea lady brought in.

'Bill, go ahead and tell Claudia what all this is about,' said Archie.

There was short silence, before Bill started to speak.

'Claudia, first things first. Archie tells me you already know about your sister Justine. I was in a camp with her. A terrible place.' His face was now deathly white. 'We escaped. But afterwards she was grabbed by the SS. It was when we reached Freiburg and got off the train. We walked out into the station yard, and I ran into a friend from my schooldays in England. He sheltered us, if I can put it that way. He was an officer in the German parachute troops. Leo Beckendorf, his name was. When interrogating us, the SS burst in and took Justine away.'

'Oh, my God,' said Claudia. 'But I was told she was now safe.'

'Yes, her friend Françoise de Rochefort was in France, behind the lines with the FFI. She tracked her down to a concentration camp close to Strasbourg and, by some miracle, got her out.'

'I remember Françoise, an amazing woman. So where's Justine now?'

'On the way to Switzerland. So is Françoise.'

Claudia was overcome with emotion. In past years, she and her sister Justine weren't always on best terms. She knew Justine was critical of how Claudia stayed in Berlin when war broke out, whereas the rest of the family were already in Bordeaux after fleeing Germany because of the Jewish connection. They met in Berlin when Justine came at great risk to bring Claudia out, to escape deportation. From then on, and particularly when she escaped to Malta and Justine was captured, she felt really close to her sister for the first time.

'Now,' said Archie. 'Bill brought with him something extraordinary. Tell her, Bill.'

Bill sat back in his chair, his broad frame dominating the table.

'Justine worked at Buchenwald for the wife of the former Commandant, and got access to the briefcase of the woman's senior officer friend who was staying overnight. While they were up in the bedroom, Justine was able to copy part of the plan for a massive counterattack against the Allies in north-west Europe.'

Claudia looked as though she wanted to say something, but didn't open her mouth.

Bill went on. 'Justine asked me to carry the copy of the plan when we were on the run. Maybe it was a premonition that they'd get her. I came out of Germany and through the lines in the Vosges. I saw Justine at a Maquis camp there, emaciated but her spirit was as strong as ever. Françoise was there also. We escaped a German Army attack, and they made for Switzerland. I got back here with the counteroffensive plan, codenamed Wacht am Rhein.'

There was silence until Claudia said 'Bill, you've been marvellous. I don't know how to repay you. Wonderful that you came through all that, and Justine also. Let's meet again, soon.' She paused, then adding 'In the meantime, Archie and I clearly have something to discuss.'

She held back until the door closed behind Bill.

'Archie, that's amazing.'

He waved her back to the table, and called for more tea. With a lovely smile of reassurance, he opened his hands, sat back, and waited for her. She had the impression he knew what she was going to say.

'Archie, there's something that's been niggling me and my colleagues at Station X. After what Bill said, I realize it's in fact vitally important. What Bill's brought back from Germany, and what I know from decrypting Tunny, startles me.'

His expression was now dead serious. 'And what's that?' he exclaimed.

'In my book too it's called Wacht am Rhein, which means something like Watch on the Rhine.'

Archie was visibly shaken, clearly he'd heard of the same code name from the documents Bill and Justine brought out of Buchenwald.'

'Go on,' he said.

'For some time now we've been decrypting OKW messages to Von Rundstedt and Model, about a secret army that's being assembled behind the Rhine. The scale is unbelievable, given the fact that most of known German forces are trying to hold back the Russian tide pressing in from the East. The information's only coming through from Tunny. Otherwise, there's total radio silence, no other signals intelligence. No wireless interceptions, no Enigma messages. Wireless communication appears to be solely by the Geheimschreiber encoding machines from Hitler and OKW to the commanding generals.'

There was silence. Archie stared at the ceiling, then back at Claudia. 'So, that corroborates the codename Wacht am Rhein in Justine's copies of the counteroffensive plan.'

'Yes.' She paused for effect. 'My concern, and my colleagues share this, is that nothing seems to be happening on our side.'

'What do you mean by that?' interjected Archie.

'Well, although we've been sending summaries, prepared and translated from the German decrypts in the usual way, to the privileged recipients of Ultra, there's no evidence that steps are being taken to meet the threat.'

'I see,' he said. 'So, it's almost as though the Allied Commanders don't want to believe you.'

⟶⟫●⟪⟵

She was surprised when Archie asked if she would stay and have a light lunch with him and his boss. Settling down with copies of the *Illustrated London News* and *National Geographic* magazine, she wondered whether something would now be done about Wacht am Rhein and its threat to Allied forces in north-west Europe. If so, would it be too late to bring up reserves, and for Patton's 3rd Army to turn on its axis and march north?

A waiter came to collect her, and they walked up a floor and into a room overlooking St James's Park underground station. A polished dining table was laid for three. Asked if she would like something to drink, she asked for a tomato juice with Worcester sauce, popular among Station X staff when vodka was added. A moment later the door opened and in walked a dark-haired man of medium height, in immaculate double-breasted suit. Just out of *Tailor & Cutter*, she thought, remembering the magazine she flipped through that morning in reception. Archie followed him in.

'Claudia, if I may call you by your first name' said the man shaking hands with her. 'My name is Stewart Menzies. I've met your sister Justine.'

Claudia could see he was watching her intently, which was not surprising. A German woman in her early thirties, formerly working in Berlin on top-secret encoding machines, now part of his empire which included the Secret Intelligence Service and Station X. 'I'm very pleased to have the chance of meeting you, sir. Interesting that you know my sister.'

'Call me C,' said Menzies, smiling as was Archie. 'Justine was here a couple of years ago, before her trip to Berlin. Mind if I smoke?' he said, pulling a silver cigarette case from inside his jacket, and offering her one.

Claudia took the cigarette, and a light from him, as she commented 'I hear she's been rescued from the SS, which is a miracle. Her Bordeaux friend Françoise de Rochefort organized the escape.'

'Yes, I also met Françoise when she was here with Justine,' said C as he waved her and Archie to the table. While the food was being served, he looked intently at her. 'Claudia, I took a great interest in your escape to England, and your joining Station X. Archie has kept me informed on how you cooperated with the debriefing which followed your arrival, and with your induction into the work of Hut 6. We're enormously indebted to you. You are not only a first-class mathematician, but a brave woman also.'

Archie nodded his agreement.

Claudia simply said 'Thank you, C.'

He went on. 'Now to business. This Wacht am Rhein secret was certainly well kept, limited to Hitler and a handful of others. The radio silence during the assembling of the new army was total. I know your hut at Station X has been intercepting the

Tunny messages and feeding the decrypted summaries through. Yet the Allied Army Commanders clearly don't want to believe it. They can't conceive of Hitler creating all these divisions as he looks defeat in the face. Bradley, Hodges, Montgomery, they're in denial.'

Claudia didn't respond. This was the man she and Justine risked all for two years ago. The trauma of photographing the drawings of the Geheimschreiber machine where she worked in Berlin, and the escape to Italy with Justine, was still buried inside her.

C continued. 'I just called Ike's Chief of Staff at Supreme Headquarters in Versailles. He listened to me, taking time to respond to what I was reporting from Station X. I presumed the decrypts were brought to his attention and Eisenhower's. I gained the impression that Ike relied on Bradley, Hodges and Monty, and that their judgement was the threat was not great and could be contained until reinforcements were brought in.'

Claudia looked up, and said 'Our latest information is that the attack will be massive and will come through the forests of the Ardennes.'

'Yes, and that's what is now worrying Ike. The American defences in that area are their weakest. I've a feeling that Ike's first call after he'd heard about mine was to Patton. His Chief of Staff did tell me they were putting 101st Airborne on stand-by.'

'H hour as they call it, is soon. They're going to launch while there's heavy fog, and our air forces are grounded,' said Claudia.

'Yes,' said C. 'I'm on the case, and will ensure that Ike's Chief of Staff is also.' He looked at her with cool steady eyes. 'Claudia, since you agreed to leave Berlin, your contribution to the Allied effort has been immense.'

38

Arriving at Padeborn airfield from where they were due to take off, Leo was only too aware that with him were junior officers with no battle experience. And that most of the troops were between sixteen and eighteen years old. He marvelled at their enthusiasm, proud to wear the smock of the *Fallschirmjäger.* For some this would be their first jump. But they were well trained infantrymen. He and his veteran NCOs were determined to stand by them in the freezing conditions they would drop into.

In the wait before take-off, his mind was on Theresa. Always part of his life. Reading her note again, saying she was at the base hospital close to Cologne, he took comfort that she wasn't far away. Somehow they must both survive to the end of this conflict. The struggle which should have ended months ago when even a fool could see that all was lost, was being relentlessly pursued by their Nazi leaders. The useless loss of hundreds of thousands more lives lay before them, from teenage soldiers to refugees overrun by Russia's rampant armies.

Battle Group Heydte was to drop on the first day of the Wacht am Rhein offensive. In his intelligence officer role, Leo was one of the twelve hundred *Fallschirmjäger* selected. Still total radio silence. They were only permitted to open their sealed orders the day before the attack. Most of the men thought they were going on an exercise. He knew it was madness. The wind strength over the drop zone was well above permissible levels. That maniac Sepp Dietrich, over-promoted to Army Commander, was focused on two things only, keeping to the timetable and reaching Antwerp. He paid no attention to their warnings.

As Leo expected, the drop was a disaster. Many pilots of the transport planes lacked experience of dropping paratroops, and at three in the morning the harsh winds blew the *Fallschirmjäger* way off target, landing them over a wide area. Their task was to cause confusion among the Americans, and block reinforcements being brought in from the American-held city of Aachen.

Leo saw horror and chaos everywhere. He and the other veterans struggled to bring together as many of the young paratroopers as they could. Rations began to run out. The terrible cold, snow and ice persisted. What idiocy brought him into this? His Commander, von der Heydte, couldn't have his heart behind the counterattack, stupendous but surely doomed. Only a few days before, the sight of the latest panzers pouring along the forest trails, shrouded in fog, must have been an inspiring sight. The observer would have looked at the crews, many just boys, backed only by a sprinkling of veterans. It would end in death and destruction.

The radio silence, complied with rigidly for weeks beforehand, was maintained. It was paying off. The unreadiness of the Americans was evidence enough that nothing like this was expected. Surprise and panic were etched on their faces as the Panzer Grenadiers and motorized infantry carved through disintegrating defences. But Leo realized Battle Group Heydte was having little meaningful effect. Word came that the panzer formations, now out of the Ardennes forests and in open Belgian countryside, were heading for the Meuse. The prayer was for the bad weather to continue, preventing enemy air strikes. The dreaded Thunderbolt and Typhoon fighter bombers were still grounded. Snow and ice was everywhere. For the first time in the West, conditions were like those his comrades faced in Russia.

⇒▸▶◆◀◂⇐

Battle Group Heydte Headquarters now established, they were receiving reports that the Americans were suddenly holding their ground. In particular, at the town called Bastogne, the intersection of several routes along which the panzer divisions were to advance. The vital timetable was slipping. What was at the core of the American defence of this town? Unclear, until an intercepted message provided an explanation. 101st Airborne just arrived to join the garrison. Hardened paratroopers, victorious after their drops on Normandy and Nijmegen.

Leo and von der Heydte knew the capacity of the Allies to bring up reserves was overwhelming, were they given the time to do so. Above all, there was Patton. His 3rd Army was down south, re-building its supplies after sweeping across central France. With it was the Free French Division. Leo knew his old friend Henri was likely to be with them. Aerial reconnaissance indicated some of Patton's units were already turning north.

Then the worst happened. The weather was improving. American and RAF ground attack aircraft appeared in great numbers. Holding up above like taxis in their cab ranks, they swooped down one by one as ground units called them in. Terrifying for the boys lacking battle experience, as they saw their comrades blown to pieces. With the Luftwaffe conspicuous by its absence, the long columns of German armour, caught in frequent traffic jams on the narrow roads, presented easy targets. Casualties on both sides mounted. And in Bastogne, where there was a *Fallschirmjäger* unit in the attacking force, paratrooper fought paratrooper.

⊷▸◦◦◦◦◦◦◦◦◦◦◦◦◦◦◦◦◦◦◦◦◦

'This can't go on much longer,' von der Heydte said to his intelligence officer.

'Just heard that Patton's spearhead has broken through to relieve Bastogne,' said Leo.

Both knew the relentless pressure from fresh Allied reserves and blanket air cover were grinding down the Wehrmacht. At the same time, the panzer army was running out of fuel.

Together, they both entered a building, seeking food and cover.

Von der Heydte was in bad shape, and Leo insisted he rest. About an hour passed. Suddenly there was a commotion outside, shouts in American and the noise of half-tracks. They froze to the spot. After so much, four years of fighting and sacrifice, the end game was over. An American voice shouted to them to come out, hands in the air.

Aftermath

Henri de Rochefort walked up Ashley Gardens, just off Victoria Street, the towering red brick cathedral on his right. He was holding a bulky package. At the sign marked 'Archbishop's Residence', he pulled the bell chain. The door opened and an aged, stooping woman greeted him, regarding his French Foreign Legion uniform with some suspicion. Henri gave his name, and was shown into a comfortably furnished waiting room. Almost at once, the Cardinal entered the room. He held out his right hand, and Henri went down on one knee and kissed the ring on the Cardinal's finger. Rising again, he handed over the package, saying, 'Your Grace, I was instructed to give you these folios from the Codex Sinaiticus, by the Abbot of St Catherine's Monastery in Sinai. There is also a sealed envelope from the Vatican, addressed to you and Cardinal Spellman in New York, given by Monsignor Roncalli to Dom Brendan Rooker. Father Rooker was killed shortly afterwards, during the battle of Monte Cassino. Before dying, he gave the envelope and folios to a German officer, who just recently passed them to me.'

'I heard that tragic news,' said Cardinal Godfrey. I understand that Dom Rooker taught you and the German officer at the same school. Thank you for bringing the package to us. There must be a story to tell one day about how it found its way across war-torn Europe to London, from the silence in the desert.'

While he was speaking, the Cardinal picked up a paper knife from a table in the corner of the room, slit open the envelope, and started to read the contents.

Henri waited. He was summoning up the courage to ask something. When the Cardinal looked up, he decided it was the right moment.

'Your Grace, please forgive me for making an inquiry about the contents of the envelope. I must be honest and say that it has intrigued me since Leo Beckendorf passed it to me with the folios, in Strasbourg Cathedral. If you can see your way to indicating to me its purpose, then I might understand better why Dom Brendan Rooker and my German friend took such risks to ensure it reached you.'

'Well, Captain de Rochefort, I can't of course go into the detail of what is a private communiqué from the Vatican to me and Cardinal Spellman. What I can say is that its purpose is to help an understanding of the path the Church has been following during this terrible conflict, to combat the treatment the Nazis have directed against oppressed races and minorities. For example, the Church in Rome has had to balance its moral obligation to stand up for the Jewish race, against retaliation Hitler could have taken against the Catholic population of Germany and the occupied countries.'

Stuttgart, June 1945

Leo Beckendorf stood to attention in front of the young French recruiting officer. 'So, you were a major in the *Fallschirmjäger*,' said the Frenchman, looking down at the POW file on the table. I understand you have applied to join the French Foreign Legion, now that Germany has finally surrendered. I'm surprised that someone of your background should want to do so.'

'All I know is soldiering,' said Leo. 'I'm only half German by birth, and was educated in England. Both my parents were killed right at the end of the war, in an air raid on the town to where they'd been evacuated from Berlin.' In himself, he fought his decision not to seek out Theresa. There was no future for him in a defeated Germany, and she must be free to make her own future.

'It's true,' said the Frenchman, 'that we've started to consider applications to join the Foreign Legion, in particular for units to be sent shortly to Tonkin and Vietnam. One of these is a new parachute battalion. But you must understand that all recruits have to begin as legionnaire. In due course, you might rise to corporal, and then sergeant. The officers are almost exclusively French, from Saint-Cyr military college.'

'I accept that,' said Leo.

A Foreign Legion colonel entered the room while they were talking. He now spoke. 'I know who you are, Major. General von der Heydte mentioned you to me. Your application is accepted. You will report first to Marseille to be kitted out, and then transfer to Sidi Bel Abbès in Algeria for induction into the Legion. The fortunes of war are cruel, Herr Beckendorf. You and I have fought in what were two of the most effective formations of any army in this war. Now you start at the bottom again, while your colleague from schooldays, Henri de Rochefort, retains his rank and fine reputation. At least you will have a good friend to keep an eye on you. I wish you luck, Legionnaire Beckendorf.'

Paris, July 1945

Theresa sat at a table on the Avenue de Neuilly, close by the American Hospital, a coffee and *Le Figaro* in front of her. In her hand was a letter from her father. How wonderful he'd been, extricating her from Germany after the surrender, and using his influence in Paris to find her a role at her old hospital. The Gestapo had murdered the American Director, her father's old friend, for his Resistance work.

She knew that Leo was taken prisoner in the Ardennes, but there was no news of where he now was. She loved Paris, but without him a part of her was missing. Scanning the back of the newspaper, and passing over advertisements from those searching for relations lost in the camps, her eyes came to rest on an announcement from the Légion étrangère, the French Foreign Legion. Nurses experienced in working overseas were being sought to join the Legion in Tonkin and Vietnam. Alongside was a quotation.

'France made me what I am. I will be grateful for ever. The people of Paris have given me everything. They have given me their hearts, and I have given them mine. I am ready to give them my life.' Josephine Baker, 1940.

END

Historical note

The flying accident referred to at the start of this novel is based closely on an event that occurred at Downside School on 15 May 1943, when a Sea Hurricane on a training mission crashed into a crowd of boys and other spectators during a cricket match at the school. Nine boys and also the student pilot were killed, and a further ten boys seriously injured.

All characters referred to as relating to this accident, the hearing in the House of Lords, and the subsequent court martial are entirely fictitious, as are the events that followed the accident.

Acknowledgements

The second novel should require less help than the first. But without the first, there wouldn't be a second. So, I start by expressing my thanks again to those who gave their all to help me pass first base.

This second novel would not be what it is without Christopher Blount's expertise on naval law and the Fleet Air Arm, and Simon Mounsey making me aware for the first time of Catapult Aircraft Merchantmen or CAM ships. I thank them both. And my sincere thanks to Sir Martin Smith for his encouragement and tenacity in reviewing manuscripts.

On a professional footing, the team at The Literary Consultancy, and Imogen Robertson in particular, added a dimension without which I would be just an also-ran. Kim McSweeney at Mach 3 Solutions Ltd and Graham Frankland handled typesetting and proof editing respectively, with their accustomed expertise. Thank you all.

Then to my wife Anna, my heartfelt gratitude not only for her patience, but for the invaluable help she gave where my ambition overran good style.

DL
Malmesbury, England,
October 2017

About the Author

David Longridge's life and work experience across Europe complements the historical emphasis of his writing, as does his special interest in how young people from these countries interrelated during the Second World War. His first novel *In Youth, in Fear, in War* illustrated the great but largely over-looked role played by young women in the secret underworld of that conflict.

David's second novel *Silence in the Desert* focuses on events often overlooked in the popular history of the war, with an underlying theme of signals intelligence. New characters join some of those from the first book, both as allies and on opposing sides. Together, they face the war-induced suspension of the morality of their upbringing as new allegiances conflict with friendships of the past.